ACKNOWLEDGEMENTS

First, I'd like to thank my Heavenly Father for blessing me with the gift of writing. Without You, none of this would be possible. I'd also like to thank the special man in my life. I'll keep your name on the hush hush (smile). Thanks for all your input and arguing with me when I made the Hardy character weak. To my mother, Roxie, thanks for your unconditional love, never-ending support and late-night talks. To all my crazy cousins (way too many to name), thanks for keeping me laughing when I wanted to cry. Oh, and thanks for introducing me to Moscato. I'm so happy I finally finished this book I just might have a glass right now. Love you, Aunt Vaughn and my BFF, Nycole!

Special thanks to all the professionals who have worked diligently on my project; Kellie your graphics are awesome. Thank you for all that you do. Leslie, I can't tell you how much I appreciate you and what you've done for me. You're a beast when it comes to these books. Keep doing your thang. To my publisher, Azarel, thank you for taking a chance on me once again. You're definitely a woman whom I admire.

On a personal note, Keisha G,. I can't thank you enough for all your support. Most will think some of this book is about my life one hundred percent. I'm so thankful for my test readers; Shannon, Cheryl, Ashaundria, Virginia, and last but not least, Tonya Ridley. Tonya, I never knew what a ride or die chick was until I met you. LOL. To the rest of the LCB Crew…Jackie Davis (Married to a Balla) Danette Majette (Bitter) Miss KP (Dirty Divorce Series) J Tremble (Bedroom Gangsta) VegasClarke (Snitch), Carla Pennington (The Available Wife), C.J. Hudson (Chedda Boyz) Tiphani (Millionaire Mistress Series), Capone (Marked), and Mike Warren (Sweet Swagger). I know for sure I'm on the best team in the industry. Let's keep putting out hits!

Thanks to all the black book store distributors who pushed my first book, Rich Girls and continue to support me; Black and Noble in Philadelphia, Afrikan World in Baltimore and JMC Trading. Thank you so much!

As always, I like to hear what people have to say about my work. Hit me up @ facebook.com/authorkendallb.

Peace,

Kendall Banks

The One Night Stand Specialist!

PROLOGUE

Thanksgiving Day

I stared, watching him closely from the other side of the glass door, praying he'd let me in. While I shivered, crossing my forearms across my tits, I purposely pretended to be a victim. Chills draped my body thinking about how I would torture him, and all the things that would bring me revenge. Suddenly, he unlocked the door, smiled and let me in. Little did he know, I was far from the victim, but the villain, instead. He was just like the typical male; green for a female's smile and potential pussy.

Pow! He was hit with the butt of my gun.

"Nooooo," he attempted to scream and flee, until I cupped his mouth with my free hand. With the other, I gripped the handle of the .32 caliber, now pointed at his temple. Not wasting any time, I told him he'd have to go with me. Dreadfully quiet, he wiggled to escape my grip.

Out of the blue, his savior appeared and attempted to punk me, thinking I would be afraid of his body type and size. Oh, so two against one? I had already accepted the challenge. My chest heaved up and down while my breathing nearly stopped. Things were now getting crazy, and not going according to plan. The escape should've been easy with a quick in and

1

out. Now someone would have to die. "What's the fuckin' procedure when you got a gun to your head?" I asked the buffed
man who stood three feet away from me, ready to attack.

"You don't have to do this! I give in. Game over," he
pleaded.

"Game over?" I questioned through hurt eyes. "The
game is just beginning. I knew I seemed demented. Hell, I was.

I'd been hurt.

Stumped on.

Betrayed.

And now all I wanted was revenge.

Quickly, I pointed the gun back to my hostage's temple
and thought, *somebody's gonna die. And it wouldn't be me.*

1 ··· *Zaria*

October
(Rewind...One Month Earlier)

The sight of Brent's new, shiny, black Camaro annoyed me to the core. It was parked curbside, downstairs when I first pulled up to my building. I waltzed inside like a mad-woman and tried to demolish the up button positioned next to the elevator. Of all evenings for Milan to bring that nigga up in here, why tonight? Usually there wasn't enough money on the planet to keep her home on a Friday night. Pleaseeeeeeeee let them be on their way out the door when I get off this elevator and turn my key, I told myself heatedly.

I never understood what Milan saw in that deadbeat anyway. She was beautiful and could snatch up any guy she wanted. But, nooooo…she wanted Brent. I could never understand what she saw in all her fly-by-night boyfriends anyway, but him especially. At least the others had jobs. Brent just wanted to lie up under his parents and bleed their fuckin' pockets dry with his lazy, overgrown ass. I huffed just thinking about him. That's so pathetic; twenty-six years old and still expecting your parents to pay your way through life. They needed to kick him out and let that nigga fend for himself ; freeloading mutha-fucka!

I had to admit, when Milan first met him he seemed kind of cute. There had always been a soft spot inside of me for thug types and roughnecks. Brent's dreads, dark skin, hard walk, and hip-hop slang secretly turned me on. But, when I found out he wasn't authentic, the attraction quickly faded. In fact, it turned into hatred. Fake people irk the shit out of me, I shrieked while watching the numbers to each floor light up as the elevator climbed slowly.

Brent, or "Bee", which he prefers to be called wasn't hardly from Queens, Harlem, or Brooklyn, where I was from. He was the son of wealthy parents so he'd grown up in man-sions and penthouses in the ritzy part of Manhattan. He was a rich kid who'd gotten his thuggish swagger and ghetto style of dress from watching too many rap videos, not from growing up in the Queens Bridge Projects, or doing a bid in Rikers. He was nothing more than a fake.

When the sound chimed, I stepped out of the elevator onto the twentieth floor and slowly made my way several doors down to my own. I couldn't believe it was nearly eight o'clock at night. Signing on to help out with that tired ass talent show should've been a no-no. I knew it was gonna throw me behind. Spending most of my weekend grading papers that piled up be-cause I had to devote so much time towards helping get this evening's show together wasn't necessarily my idea of enjoy-ment. But some of my own students were performing so I agreed. Now here I stood at my door having to get a late start because of it. I should've said hell no, from the start.

I found myself rambling through dozens of ungraded pa-pers in the bottom of my tote bag that read, *Everybody Deserves a Good Teacher*. Once again, I couldn't find my keys. "How can I be so damn stupid? All I have to do is put them in my pocket before I leave school every afternoon. How hard is that

to do?" I asked myself angrily. The amount of papers in my bag
seem endless, but my keys are here. I know they are. They have
to be. I fret to myself hoping my neighbors don't catch me talking to myself again.

Then it hit me.

Laughter.

Who the fuck was laughing at me?

With that thought, I realized it was the voice of children.
Perhaps my own students, I questioned. I stopped, turned, and
looked with an expression of disgust. There was no one. But
then the children's laughter grew louder. While feeling like I
was all of a sudden surrounded, I kept searching. Suddenly, I
found them. I snatched the keys from the bag and held them
high, hoping the laughter would stop. I wanted them all to see
what I'd accomplished. But instead, there was no one. Everything had gone silent.

I found myself alone and on my knees with no one to
share my accomplishment with. The loneliness made me drop
my eyes to the tote bag. There inside, among all those papers
was a piece of my past, a reason for my loneliness now and before. But despite how the pain made me feel, letting it go would
never happen. The DVD at the bottom of my bag would always
be part of me. The contents, shameful, and something I could
never cleanse myself of. Such was life and sadly made me who
I am today.

Quickly, I pushed the case that protected my past to the
bottom of the bag, rose to my feet and placed my key in the
door. Going to bed and crying myself to sleep was now the plan
after thinking about the DVD. I burst inside feeling crazy emotions building up in my body. But when I rushed past Milan's
bedroom door, the unexpected sounds of her pleasure-filled
moans caught my attention. The door to her room appeared
slightly open and I found myself drawn to it. Within seconds
my eyes witnessed Brent's moonlit covered muscular frame. He
was ass-naked in Milan's bed with his face buried between her

long, slender legs. His head moved in a slow rhythm with Milan's hand guiding it and keeping it pressed into her pussy, my heart raced. I couldn't help letting my gaze follow their every move. Her eyes were closed and soft, sensual moans escaped her lips repeatedly until Brent picked up the pace.

Suddenly, Milan shouted, "Ohhhhhhh, Brent!!!! Yessssssss. It- f-e-e-l-s s-o-o-o-o-o good!"

The fact that he ate her out like he was eating a sweet slice of watermelon got me horny, and made me remember the last time someone touched my body like that. It had been three months. Seeing Milan getting hers off made the time seem like forever.

Not wanting to get caught, I stepped away from the door and placed my back flat against the wall with a clear view. Brent finally lifted his head from his feast and began to slowly make his way up Milan's body with soft passionate kisses. My heart pounded and my juices flowed. His long dick looked so damn good. There was no way I could control myself.

I dropped my bags and fondled myself a bit. My eyes gawked as Brent entered her, taking long, deep strokes. Within seconds dirty talk escaped his mouth and Milan fucked him back just as hard as he fucked her.

"Fuck this pussy," she shouted.

"Oh, this what you want!" he blasted, turning onto his side and yanking Milan's trim ass onto his dick.

Their backs were now turned to me but even the sweat that poured from their bodies turned me on. Soon, my panties were soaked all the way through. Seconds later, Milan's bedsprings began to squeak. Her moans grew louder, causing me to undo my pants and ram my middle finger inside myself. I wanted to cum so badly but I quickly realized that my finger wasn't enough.

My pussy needed what Milan was getting. And I knew what had to be done. What she thought was her dick would now be mine too. After all, we were roommates, thick as thieves…buddies to the end. My low-budget shirt and twenty dollar jeans were off within seconds. Before I knew it, I was completely naked and creeping into Milan's room ready to join them. My body wanted every piece of him. I just hoped that Milan wouldn't get upset when Brent saw me and wanted me badly.

Two steps from the bed, they were still going at it un-aware that I was near. Gently, I lifted the covers and slid close to Brent's body, ready to place kisses on his back, just beneath where his dreads hung. Suddenly, he turned and looked at me like he'd seen a ghost.

"I know you want this?" I told him conceitedly.

"What the hell?" he asked totally surprised.

"It's okay, Brent. I'm here."

Milan jumped from the bed with her long, wavy hair swinging. Her eyes immediately grew wide like a paper plate. I could tell she was beyond angry, not understanding why her man now wanted me.

"Zaria, what the hell are you doing in here?" she screamed, while quickly wrapping a sheet around her tiny breast.

Brent stood but didn't attempt to hide his erection. He just stared at me strangely. I wanted so badly to tell Milan that I was lonely and tremendously needed to be loved tonight, but I couldn't. Instead, I could only jump out of her bed, run out of her room, and slam the door behind me. With my back pressed against the wall, frozen; just like it had been moments ago, my tears flowed.

"I can't believe she did that," Milan's voice sounded from the other side of the door.

"That bitch is crazy," Brent commented.

My eyes closed tightly and my hand cupped my mouth with embarrassment. I just wanted to be loved tonight. Why can't they understand that? I thought as I listened to them bash me like I was nothing.

7

"I thought you were trying to move out of here?" Brent asked Milan.

"I am, Bee, and I will," Milan assured him angrily.

My eyes opened immediately at that statement. I felt betrayed. I grabbed my clothes and rushed to my own room, now livid. Moving out? Leaving me? That ungrateful bitch. She'll pay, I told myself.

2···$\mathcal{H}$ardy

Being faithful to one woman had always been impossible for me like a leopard tryna change its spots; can't fuck with it. I've always preferred to dabble with them all; White, Black, Latin, Chinese, Japanese …doesn't matter. Pussy is pussy. Shit, the only thing better than pussy is more pussy. Knocking bitches off had never been a problem for me either. They loved my swag, voice, style, and definitely the way I laid that pipe. My biggest problem was my marital status. I had a wife.

Married with children.

Married with restrictions.

Always feeling chained.

My pity party was interrupted when my I-phone rang. It was my most gullible hoe, Yvonne. "I was just thinking about your little, sexy ass," I told her, lying to her as usual when I answered. "I think about you all the time."

"Same here," she replied, real sexy-like.

"So, what's good?"

"You. Gerald, I miss the taste of you in the back of my throat. Where you at?"

"Where you want me to be, baby girl?" Little did she know, I was sitting in my tinted out, black Tahoe in front of my

9

house.

"In this pussy? When you coming by?"

"You know I like it when you talk like that." I made a hissing sound like I was sucking up my own saliva, and couldn't help myself.

Yvonne just laughed.

Now, that's what I like right there; a woman who had absolutely no shame in being a proud, certified headhunter. Although Yvonne was only twenty-one, she gave head better than most bitches I'd come across, twice her age. The crazy thing about it though was that by simply looking at her you'd never be able to tell. You'd swear she was a good girl. Between her glasses, proper voice, and conservative dress, she looked like she could be somebody's wifey. But Yvonne devoured dick like a wild animal. In fact, I called her my little gremlin when she's sucking my dick because she sounds just like one of them little muthafuckas after you've violated the rule about feeding them after midnight. And Lord knows I love to feed her ass after midnight whenever possible. Of course she caught me off guard when I heard her say, "Gerald, do you love me?"

"What? Girl, why would you ask me something like that?"

"Cause, I wanna know."

"Look here, sexy. What I truly love about you is that you're a real woman who knows how to please her man. You're not one of those play with the dick type of women. You suck my dick right." I paused to hear her giggle. "You don't just bob your head up and down or back and forth on the dick. You switch shit up, taking the whole thing down your throat. You not scared, baby. And that's what I love about you."

Yvonne's stupid ass giggled some more and was probably smiling from ear to ear after hearing about her dick sucking report card. But on the real, she did drive me and my dick crazy, making my toes curl like a woman with five inch nails. And the amount of spit she uses blew my mind. I never knew a bitch's mouth could manufacture that much saliva until I met her. So much of it spills from her mouth when she's doing her thing that she usually leaves a huge puddle of it on the bed underneath my balls. Simply put…Yvonne was amazing.

"So, are we going to hook up tonight?" Yvonne asked. Her voice came through loudly from my cell phone as I felt the leather in the seat of my car, hoping I hadn't just bust a nut. Nervously, I looked toward the front door of my house.

"I'm not sure," I told her.

"Why? It's been a week since we've seen each other," she whined.

"I know but I've got to handle something important tonight."

"What? It's Friday night. And I miss you, Gerald Hardy," she said, all of a sudden trying to sound innocent. But of course, I knew better. "I hate when you make me miss you this long."

A smile stretched across my face. I love making this hoe fiend for the dick like a crack head. But I hated the fact that she knew my first and last name. "If I let you see me every day, you'd get bored with a nigga." I told her. "Keeping you missing me is what keeps it interesting."

"I'll never get bored with our relationship," she tried to assure me, her voice purposely expressing her feelings for me. "No man makes me feel like you do."

"So you'll never stop loving me, right?" I asked, already knowing the answer. I just liked to hear her say it.

"You know I'll never stop."

An even bigger smile stretched across my face. Damn, she's a dizzy bitch. Just a few lies and the taste of my dick had this hoe sprung. The phone beeped. My other hoes were calling. "Hold that thought," I told Yvonne and quickly glimpsed at the screen to see an incoming call from Keisha. Immediately, I clicked over. "What's good?" I asked, answering her call.

"You," she said seductively.

"Is that right? What's so special about me?" I asked nonchalantly, already knowing what she loved about me most.

"Everything," she said, "except the fact that you don't spend any time with me."

"Awe, c'mon Keisha, I was just thinking about your little, sexy ass." I said, lying to her using the same words I'd just recited to Yvonne. "I think about you all the time."

"I think about you a lot, too. Can we do something tonight, Hardy?"

My dick moved inside my pants at the sound of Keisha's voice, knowing exactly what she wanted a nigga to do to her body tonight. I closed my eyes for a second and pictured myself pounding away at that juicy, black ass from the back once again. Keisha was my southern broad. I called her that because she's fresh from the ATL and equipped with a body so amazingly thick and an ass so incredibly fat that even females stared at her frame in admiration. From her green eyes down to her always freshly pedicured toes she's poetry in motion for real. Keisha wasn't a joke in the bedroom either. She was a damn beast. She could take my dick in all her holes for hours with no problem at all, making me fight to keep from cumming. But tonight wasn't good.

"I got something I need to handle," I told her, knowing it would break her heart.

"Is it something you can handle tomorrow?"

"Why?" I asked. She was sweating. I loved making her sweat.

"Because, I really want to see you," she said pleadingly. "You know I do."

Quickly, I told her to hold the line, so I could dismiss Yvonne. Within seconds, I was back on the phone laying my mack game down. "So Keisha, if I let you see me, what are you gonna do for me?"

"Anything you want." Her voice grew more seductive.

My hand grabbed the crotch of my True Religion jeans

12

and squeezed. Punishing Keisha's frame sounded tempting. But then my phone beeped again. "Hold on," I announced and looked at the screen to see an incoming call from my Puerto Rican mommy, Angie. "What's good, Mommy?" I asked, clicking over.

"You, Poppi," she sang happily.

Just like the other two jump offs, she was trying to see if I had time for her tonight. I switched the line back and forth, talking to each of them over the next twenty minutes. Finally, I abruptly ended each conversation after seeing the curtains from my bedroom move too many times. I let each hoe know that if I could get out of my plans tonight or finish them early, I'd come through. Chances were slim to none though. I had big plans.

I climbed out of my truck and headed past my well manicured lawn, and up to the house that sat perfectly about five yards from the street. A Tyler Perry movie was showing on the television in the living room as I closed the door and saw my wife, Dana, lying on the couch in a Juicy sweatsuit.

"Daddy!" my nine year old son Terrell screamed excitedly, charging me so hard he nearly knocked me off of my feet.

"What's up, Little Man?" I asked, hugging him tightly.

It never failed to amaze me how exactly like myself Terrell looked. We both had deep, dark, smooth skin, his looking more Moroccan than mine. And sets of matching bronze colored eyeballs that normally drove women, of all ages, wild. Even though I was bald and Terrell had jet black, curly hair, looking into his face was like staring into the mirror at my own reflection. Gratefully, spending time with him always made me feel like a child myself.

"How was school?" I asked.

"It was okay, Dad."

"It was just okay?" I said, picking him up, tossing him over my shoulder, and tickling him thoroughly under his armpits.

Terrell screamed and laughed uncontrollably.

"How was school?" I asked again, continuing to tickle him mercilessly.

"It was fun!" Terrell screamed over his own laughter.

He seemed so light even though he weighed eighty-eight pounds. I kept tossing him back and forth over my shoulder and running my hand through his curly hair. I kept hitting him with question after question. "And what did you learn today?"

He could barely speak for laughing so hard. "N-o-t=t-t-h-i-n-n-g-g-g-g."

"I can't hear you," I lied, still tickling him. Solidifying the importance of education in my son had always been important to me. Seeing my son grow up to believe that graduating was unimportant was something I couldn't let happen. It was the key to a black man's success.

"It was fun! It was fun, Dad! And I learned about the thirteen colonies."

"Are you sure?"

"Yes! Yes, Dad. I'm sure," he continued laughing, now just slightly, and exposing his adorable dimples.

I finally placed him back on the floor and sat on the couch beside my wife, planting a kiss on her cheek. "Hey, baby."

"I made plans for us tonight," Dana announced firmly without even looking at me.

Damn, I hate when she does that; making plans without discussing it with me. "What kind of plans?" I asked.

"We're going bowling with a few friends from my job. Be ready by eight."

"I can't do it," I blurted out then stood and headed for the kitchen to grab a beer.

Dana jumped up quickly and followed me like an angry bull. "Well, why not?" she asked, bucking at me like she didn't weigh one hundred and five pounds.

"I promised my sister that I'd ride down to Jersey this evening and help her move."

"When did you make that promise?" my petite wife asked, now highly annoyed.

"She called me this morning," I told her, stopping in my tracks. I loved my wife's small frame, but hated her big, boisterous mouth. She wasn't the *go with the flow kinda wife* that I needed.

Her voice rose two notches. "Why is it that every time I try to make plans for us, you always have plans for yourself?"

"Dana, I don't want to argue," I said, reaching into the refrigerator and grabbing a Heineken. There were only four left, but I was certain that I'd down the rest before I left.

"I'm not arguing. I just want to know why that is? You keep saying you're going to spend more time with me and Terrell. But every time I try to get you to, you always have a reason why you can't."

I walked past her to the bedroom to begin packing for the trip, expecting her to stop me and ask to smell my balls. I hated when she did that insecure ass shit. Anytime I made plans to be away from her, she swore there was some pussy involved somewhere in the equation.

"Well, how long are you going to be gone?" she asked following me, her bare feet stomping the floor like Bigfoot.

"I'll be back Sunday night," I told her, patting my pocket to be sure that my keys were there, knowing that if she got her hands on them, she was going to hide the keys to my truck.

"It takes a whole weekend to move?" she grunted. "Bullshit."

"Some of the family's gonna be there also for a get together."

"Yeah, right. Who is she, Hardy?" she asked, convicting me with no evidence or jury.

"Dana, I'm not going through this with you," I belted, grabbing my suitcase and tossing it onto the bed.

"Is she the bitch you've been in the driveway on the phone with for the last hour?"

I ignored her, knowing that if I stayed quiet during the storm, it would blow over. Her thunder always faded when un-stirred. Glaring at her, I wondered how we got here. Dana was pretty, intelligent, and sought after by many men. She was a good wife. A good mother. And she was probably all I needed, but I just hadn't made myself into a one-woman, man just yet. I needed time.

"What's her name?" she asked. "Can you at least give me that much, asshole?"

Those reverse psychology games never worked on me. Besides, I was thirty-two now, a seasoned veteran. There was no way in hell I was going to admit to doing wrong so she could say, *I knew you were cheating*. If I admitted it, I'd never hear the end of it.

"Be a man," she continued with her hands on her hips, following me around our bedroom like I'd stolen something from her and she wanted it back. "What's her name? Admit it," she badgered.

"You're paranoid, Dana," I said, shrugging her off.

"Why do I keep putting up with this shit?" she asked herself out loud, grabbing her head and knowing she'd asked that question more times than she could count.

As I packed, my ears tuned Dana out. I answered only occasionally with quick 'yes's and 'no's and volunteering no unnecessary information. Within twenty minutes my ass was back in the driver's seat of my Tahoe, dialing up this weekend's jump off.

"Be there in twenty minutes," I told her, slowly slipping my wedding ring off of my finger and placing it in the glove compartment. "Have my pussy warm."

"I can't wait for you to get here," the sweet voice moaned, exciting me to the core.

Immediately upon hearing my voice she began explain-ing everything she was going to do to me over the weekend; nothing short of super nasty and freaky. With every word my dick grew and throbbed. I drove like a bat out of hell taking the exit for the Triboro Bridge. Suddenly, my phone beeped. I had another call. After only giving a quick glance at the screen and seeing my wife's attempted incoming call, I pressed the ignore button. I didn't have time for arguing this weekend, only pussy. Warm pussy.

3···*Zaria*

"I'm that bitch!" I shouted with my head now raised to my kitchen ceiling, unwilling to look at another bill or ungraded paper spread across the table in front of me. A chuckle made my body tremble with enjoyment as Mary's "Never Hurt Again" played loudly from the stereo in the living room. I went off... "That's my jam!" I shouted.

Mary had so many old hits that I loved like crack, but this one was one of my ultimate favorites. That fact that I had decided to never let another man hurt me again made me feel confident inside. And I vowed not to let anything get me down today.

Quickly, I hopped up and pressed my face against the stainless steel toaster hoping to see myself clearly. I needed to get my own opinion. You know what I need to do today? I need to go down to the place on Livingston and pick up a couple of old movies. I hadn't watched any good ones in a while, I told myself, pushing the toaster aside and sitting back down. My thought was to rent a classic like, Jungle Fever, or Why Do Fools Fall in Love featuring Vivica Fox since she was my favorite actress. I loved movies and knew some lines by heart since they always seemed to settle me. Lines like, "Show me the money," in the movie, *Jerry McGuire*, or like Joe Clark yelling in *Lean On Me*, "code 10, code 10, the enemy is here!"

Yup, nothing's gonna get me down today. And I'm not gonna allow anyone to take that away from me. I started my usual chant to myself. 'Smiley face, Smiley face. Can everyone see my smiley face?' Though that jingle always worked great for my students, at times it didn't work for me. It was something I'd learned years ago from my first psychiatric doctor.

Someone's playahatin eyes were on my back. I could feel them. I wasn't sure why Milan thought it was alright to just stand at the doorway behind me and just stare at a bitch. She thinks I don't know she's there? I felt those sneaky-ass green eyes of hers burning a hole through the back of my skull. Everyone thought her eyes were so pretty and exotic, and she was so perfect. Everyone. Even my damn aunt, the one who always told me I was beautiful.

But I knew the real Milan; the Milan who offered herself like a prostitute to any nigga with money to spend; the Milan who dressed like one of those skanks in rap videos and gave her pussy away to any new nigga that came her way. She told me to my face that she only fucks Brent as if I passed the test to become an elementary school teacher by being a dizzy bitch.

Milan's nothing more than a sneaky skank just like the rest of them light skinned hoes; always plottin' on a muthafucka, always thinking they're better than me because my skin is slightly darker than theirs.

Smiley face, Smiley face. Can everyone see my smiley face? I kept repeating that line to myself over and over again.

Today is my day. I won't let her piss me off today. I'd much rather kill her with kindness. My body twisted and I greeted Milan with my happiest smile, almost like some perky white girl. "Good morning, Milan."

I got no response…just crossed arms and a twisted lip.

See? That's the fuckin' shit I'm stressing right there. I

say good morning to this funky, stuck up, high yellow bitch and she's just standing there with this weird look on her face like I'm the crazy one. I just want to smack the shit outta of this hoe's mouth!

"Be nice, Zaria. Some people can't help being natural born haters," I silently reasoned with myself. "I made breakfast," I told her, still smiling. "It's on the stove."

Still, only silence and an even weirder stare come from Milan. What the fuck? Does she only understand sign language? Did she ride the short bus to school when she was growing up? Did her mother accidentally drop the dumb hoe on her head when she was little? I swear she's a simple bitch. But I'll play nice.

"Why are you staring at me like that?"

Now the bitch shot off a nervous look. What the fuck is wrong with her?

"Are you okay, Zaria?" Milan finally asked me, nervously.

"I'm good. Why?"

Milan stared me down with uncertainty. It almost looked as if she was scared of me. I swear this bitch is looking at me like I'm schizo or something and it's pissing me off, royally. But my composure remained calm.

"Why?" I asked again.

"Because you've been sitting here talking to yourself for the past ten minutes," Milan said with bass in her voice.

See! Didn't I tell you this slut was sneaky? Just because I didn't turn around and show her some damn attention when she thought I should've, now she wants to make up lies about me. That's so fuckin foul. But still my composure will remain calm.

"You just heard me singing with Mary," I said, shrugging off her lie and turning back to the table to sort through the bills again.

"But, Zaria," she continued, quickly walking around the

table to face me. "I turned that cd off a half hour ago. You were playing it so loud I couldn't take it anymore."

The bitch is looking at me weird again. She's really irking the hell out of me.

"Didn't you notice I turned it off?"

"Of course I noticed." That answer seemed like the only one that would get her off my back. "I meant I was just singing one of her songs to myself. That's not a crime, is it?"

"I guess not," she responded hesitantly. "I mean you've just been doing weird shit lately, like last week when you thought you saw rats in the kitchen. Just think, we spent all that money," she reminded me showing that she was still pissed, "and there were no sign of rats."

I kept silent and Milan finally backed off.

"Get you some breakfast before it gets cold," I told her.

"Zaria, I'm not hungry." Milan yanked a chair from underneath the table and sat down. "We need to talk about what happened last night."

"What about last night?" My eyes began going over the October phone bill.

"Zaria, what do you mean, what about last night?"

"Milan, as you can see from all these bills and ungraded papers, I'm a little busy. Can you get to the point?"

"I can't believe you're acting as if climbing into my bed last night with Brent and I was absolutely okay."

Damn... that completely skipped my mind.

"Zaria, I don't get down like that," she continued. "I've never done anything that disrespectful to you. And I can't understand why you would do it to me."

My hands tore into another envelope which I didn't even bother to see who it was addressed to. Little Miss Motor Mouth across the table from me just had me needing to do something besides listen to her whining ass. So what, I was gonna fuck the hell out of her man! She was just scared that he would've loved this good pussy so much that he'd leave her. Besides, I wouldn't have fucked him anyway. Although I was lonely last night and needed some dick, I would've come to my senses before I let that deadbeat ass nigga touch me. I just wanted to show Milan that a honey coated bitch like me could be a threat to her yellow ass.

"Zaria, I really don't appreciate that at all."

Milan completely lost my attention as my eyes finally realized what I was reading...A RESTRAINING ORDER!!! And from of all people, Jamal. He can't be serious.

"He filed a restraining order against me," I told Milan in disbelief, totally interrupting her whining. "I can't believe him!"

"Zaria, I'm serious," Milan continued to rant, ignoring me. "I need you to respect..."

A furious anger and rage filled me as Jamal's lies and broken promises packed my head, drowning out Milan's voice. He was always turning against me and attempting to make others do the same. But this was the final straw.

"Me and Brent were talking last night and..."

My arms felt like bugs were beginning to crawl up and down my skin. I knew they weren't really there but I couldn't resist the overwhelming urge to scratch. It was a part of my mental state.

"Look, Zaria, the new modeling agency will be sending my check for the shoot I did last week. When it gets here, I'm going to begin looking for my own apartment. Hopefully by the end of the month I..."

"If that son of a bitch thinks a restraining order is gonna keep me off of his ass, he's crazy. He knows I'm the best thing he ever had. I just wanted to make him see that."

"Zaria, I hope the two of us will always still be..."

Hearing my name made me realize that this whining ass bitch was still talking to me. Why won't she just shut the fuck up?

"I appreciate everything you've done for me and I promise that after I find my apartment and move out…"

Move out? No this hoe didn't just say she's moving out. I couldn't have heard her right.

"What'd you just say?" I asked. I was sure my face twisted in disbelief.

"I said that I appreciate everything you've done for me so I promise that after I move out…"

"Don't you even fix your mouth to say you appreciate everything I've done for you, Milan!" I hissed with fierce bitterness. "If you did, you wouldn't be moving out!"

"Zaria, I do appreciate…"

"You're a lying bitch!"

Milan got quiet. Then became speechless.

Both my breathing and heart rate intensified. "You just wanna leave me just like Jamal. There's no fucking appreciation," I churned out in a deep rage and with narrow eyes. Milan's fear of me possibly leaping across the table and snatching her little narrow ass was clear to me. I wasn't a big girl but thick enough, a size eight to be exact, to handle her anorexic looking ass. My flared nostrils urged me to lash out.

"You were probably fuckin' Jamal and laughing at me behind my back." My teeth gritted like an angry pit bull with every word released. If she only knew just how badly I wanted to dig my nails deeply into her beautiful face.

"Zaria, what are you talking about?" Milan carried a worried expression. Almost pity in her eyes for me. "I would never do that to you. We're like sisters. Besides, the both of you broke up two months ago."

"You can never treat him better than I did." I began to cry and each word rambled so quickly they were nearly stumbled over. "I did what a real woman was supposed to do. I was at his job everyday when he got off. Never late. I called him at least twenty-two times a day just to let him know I was thinking about him. And I stood outside his window night after night just to watch him sleep.

Milan leaned back into her chair. She gawked at me strangely.

"After doing all that for him to show him that I was devoted to his ass, do you know what he said?"

Milan just stared. Probably mocking my honey colored skin and pouty thick lips. Both my hands crashed down on the table loudly as my body rose over her and my anger filled face looked this scary bitch dead in her eyes. "He said he needed space. He said I was smothering him. Can you believe that bullshit?"

"Maybe you were," Milan reasoned but in a soft non-threatening tone, careful not to set me off even more.

I hopped up, began pacing the kitchen wildly with no memory of ever getting out of my chair. "Men say they want a good woman but when they get one, what do they do? They get intimidated. They want space!" The shaking of my head in utter disbelief was all I could give after thinking that bullshit.

Milan's eyes watched me closely. They hadn't blinked in minutes and her mouth fell slightly open. She'd seen me act wildly before but Jamal had really ticked me off. I thought about what Miss Celie said to Mister in the *Color Purple,* when she told him, "Til you do right by me, everything you even think about is gonna fail." That's how the fuck I felt about Jamal. I wanted that muthufucka to fail. Tremors ran through every inch of my frame uncontrollably as memories of my revenge now began to fill me from head to toe like the best orgasm I'd ever had.

"I keyed that bastard's car every chance I got," I revealed proudly. "I cut up all his clothes. And I got him fired from that job at the Sportsplex that was always taking him away from me."

I closed my eyes and let complete darkness blanket me, my body relishing every act of my vengeance. Everything inside me finally calmed. My eyes opened, but for some reason not to a feeling of relief but more to a feeling of hurt and a need to be comforted.

"How could he do that to me?" I asked Milan, sincerely needing an answer. Tears welled up in my eyes. "How could he file a restraining order against me? I just wanted him to know I missed him. I just needed him to know that."

Milan stood up and quickly made her way around the table, wiping my tears away with the palm of her hand. "He's not worth your tears, Zaria," she whispered. "The relationship has been over for a few months now. Let it go and move on."

"But it's hard."

"You guys only dated for a few weeks. Think about that. It's crazy to let it beat you up like this."

Milan's words were filled with sympathy and the type of caring a mother had for her child. They made me think back to the day I met her two years ago. Milan answered my ad in the paper for a roommate and came by to see the apartment. It was hard to believe that two years had passed. For hours we stood in this same kitchen and talked.

Right off the bat the both of us could see that we were as different as night and day. She was tall, extra light skinned, and slim. I was of average height, thick, and had slightly darker skin. She preferred skirts and manicures. I preferred jeans and bit my nails constantly. She wore make-up daily and I could only rely on the natural beauty of my long lashes that everyone adored. Milan loved to hang out at clubs. I liked to just curl up on the couch with a good book, or a good man. She had plans on being a famous fashion model. I just wanted to continue to be the best elementary school teacher I could be. We were so different but something inside us made us feel like kindred spirits and sisters. We couldn't stop laughing, sharing secrets, or enjoying each other's company that afternoon. And had been roommates ever since.

The ringing of Milan's cell phone brought me back to reality. She answered and told the caller that she was on her way downstairs.

"I've gotta go, Zaria," Milan told me.

"You coming back before evening, right?"

"Probably not."

My face bawled up instantly. I hadn't told Milan that I'd been having those nightmares again lately. Being alone tonight suddenly made my blood run cold as Milan's phone call reminded me that she had plans to hit a new club with Mia and Jazmine tonight. "Are you gonna be out all night?"

"I'm not sure. But I'll call you," she said, grabbing her red Prada dress wrapped in plastic, fresh from the cleaners.

I looked hard at the dress. "Please don't go out tonight," I begged. "Come back before it gets dark. You have the whole day ahead of you." I paused to give Milan my puppy dog eyes. "I'm having those crazy dreams again and I'm afraid someone will break in again. I feel it. I really do."

"No one's gonna break in, Zaria. Everything's gonna be alright," she reassured me. "Nothing's gonna happen."

Milan headed out of the kitchen with me in tow like a little sister trying to convince her big sister that there really was a boogieman hiding in the bedroom closet. But my pleading fell on deaf ears. I realized it when Milan didn't even glance back at me, and the living room door closed in my face.

"Bitch!" I shouted, and threw a glass vase against the door behind her.

4 · · · *Zaria*

Clubs were never really my thing. The act of being in an overcrowded room smashed between hundreds of people like sardines, as germs hover over both myself and my drink, had never really got me off. But tonight I chose to make an exception. Being in that apartment alone and on a Saturday night wasn't gonna happen.

Some kind of new age retro music poured from the club's speakers as skinny model types and preppy looking men, black and white pranced around, danced , and talked loudly over every song the DJ threw on the turntable. Not one single true hip hop song would get any airplay up in here as far as I could tell. There was no way in hell I could ever see myself getting use to this futuristic sounding bullshit.

My eyes searched the entire club from the dance floor to the bar repeatedly as I made my way throughout hundreds of people for nearly half an hour until I finally saw Milan standing at the bar with her friends. I walked up behind her and tapped her on the back. As she turned, I could see Jazmine choke on her drink when she got a look at the dress I was wearing while Mia only eyed me silently from head to toe.

"Zaria," Milan said, with surprise. Her eyes quickly ran

from my freshly washed weave to my three-inch heels.

Jazmine whispered something to Mia and they both began to laugh. It could've been about my shoes since they didn't cost very much. I was never one for spending big money on material things. Money didn't mean much to me. Nonetheless, it was probably something slick they were saying. But I was a hard-core girl and would beat them both at the same time if needed. I ignored their ignorance with everything inside me, though I just wanted to spaz out on both of their prissy asses. Undoubtedly, I looked fabulous. And they hated me for it. That's all.

"What are you doing here?" Milan asked, still surprised.

"A girl can't go out sometimes?" I countered, smiling.

"Of course. I just didn't know you were coming."

"How do I look?" I took a step back and placed my hands on my thick, rounded hips, hoping they'd grow envious of my toned arms.

Both Jazmine and Mia began laughing again.

Milan smiled and hit me with phony talk, "You...You look great."

Her compliment really wasn't needed at all. I knew I looked hot. My weave hung past my shoulders and I'd painted my nubby nails bright red. The little bit of makeup that I'd managed to apply was flawless. And to top it all off, I rocked the same exact, red Prada dress and accessories as Milan. That's probably why Jazmine and Mia kept laughing. They were probably laughing at how ridiculously skinny Milan looked in hers, while the thickness of my hips and C cup breasts filled mine perfectly.

"I'm glad you're here," Milan said, taking a step forward to hug me.

Both Jazmine and Mia finally walked closer and greeted me with hugs also, but I knew it was fake.

"Milan, I didn't know you had a sister," a young handsome, distinguished looking brother said out of the blue. Milan introduced me to her date.

"Marcus, this is Zaria."

Marcus extended his hand and shook mine. "It's a pleasure to meet you, Zaria."

"You too," I returned with a juvenile blush.

"So you guys are sisters?" he asked, assuming we were because of our dresses.

Jazmine and Mia laughed again. I could feel them plotting on me. So inside, I pondered ways to torture and kill them both.

"No," Milan said quickly. "We're just roommates."

Why couldn't she lie? Was she trying to say I wasn't cute enough to be her sister? I had to admit, my feelings were a little hurt. My skin-tone had always made me feel ugly no matter how hard I tried to front. Some folks considered me to be light-skinned, and just a little bronzed but not me. I wanted that skin like Milan, almost white. Something inside me had always told me that my complexion wasn't pretty enough to compete with fair skin women. Just think, Milan probably felt like I wasn't good enough to hang out with her and those other two skinny, light bitches. How could she do that to me?

"Are you here with someone, Zaria?" Marcus asked me.

"No. I'm not," I spat, obviously heated.

"I think I can fix that."

How could Milan embarrass me like that? My mind wouldn't leave it alone.

"Do something about it, Zaria," my crazy inner voice ordered.

That voice hadn't showed its face in over eleven months; not since my psychiatric meetings had ended. And now wasn't a good time for the voices to resurface.

"Not now," I said out loud as I watched Marcus wave someone over to the bar. Within a few seconds a man even more handsome than him walked over.

"Damon, this is Zaria… Zaria, Damon."

"Hey, Zaria," Damon greeted with a bright smile and extended hand. "How are you?"

"I'm good now," I returned with major sex appeal. With the heavy flirting, my anger at Milan disappeared for a moment.

He chuckled. "Can I get you something to drink?"

"A Corona would be nice. I'm not a heavy drinker."

"That's no problem." Damon softly placed his left hand on my arm. He waved for the bartender and ordered my drink.

I couldn't help but give him a few sly once overs. He was gorgeous: Big brown eyes, pearly white teeth, well dressed, well spoken, toned, and a wide, warm smile.

"Do you mind if we sit at a table?" Damon asked after I got my drink. "I've been on my feet at the office all day."

He has a job. Shit! That's always a plus.

"Sure," I responded softly, batting my eyes.

"Wow, you have beautiful eyes. And those lashes," he said almost amazed. "Are they naturally yours, or yours because you paid for them?"

I laughed. "Naturally mine," I boasted.

Before I knew it, the two of us were bunned up at a booth in the corner of the club trapped in conversation like we were the only two people in the club. I loved the feeling even though I hadn't planned on meeting a man tonight. I simply didn't want to be at home alone just in case there was another break-in at our apartment.

Within just a few hours I felt his body wanting me. And I wanted everything about him to be mine; his smile, the soft touch of his hand when it brushed against my own, and the smell of his cologne. I could feel it. And I didn't need months or years to realize it like most women. I was so deep into Damon that I didn't notice him wave to a passing waitress.

"Could you please bring her another Corona, please?"

My eyes caught her give him a lightning fast inspection, thinking that I hadn't seen her. "I can't believe this bitch," I said in disbelief. Letting her get away with that shit was not an option. I wouldn't be labeled a push over. "I don't appreciate that," I stood and said sharply.

"Excuse me?" she responded sassily, like I was some fool.

"Zaria, what's wrong?" Damon asked me with creases in his forehead.

"She knows what's wrong." I lunged forward, ready to rumble. I looked the big tit waitress directly in her eyes. "That was very disrespectful, hoe!"

"Miss, what are you talking about?"

Damon stepped between us just as Milan rushed over.

"What's going on?" Milan asked, followed by Jazmine, Mia, and their dates.

"This bitch right here!" I shouted, pointing my finger in the waitress' face. "She just tried to make a pass at *my* man!"

Several club goers turned to see what had kicked off.

"Bitch, do you think I'm a fuckin joke?" I asked, anxious to show her I was not the broad to test. I may have been twenty-nine, but had muscles, and the strength of a weight training twenty-two year old. Before I knew it, I'd kicked my PayLess heels off.

The waitress was still trying to lie, "I never said…"

Before she could say another word, I grabbed Damon's glass from the table and slung Vodka in her face, followed by two half-empty glasses that shattered, and flew in all directions. My first thought was to grab the sharpest piece of glass I could find, and slit her face wide open just to send her a message about messing with any man of mine. Then, just like that, the DJ cut the music and shouted for security, turning the entire Club's attention in my direction.

The waitress lunged at me attempting to retaliate.

I ducked her lousy punch. Little did she know I had a past where I always had to fight. "Don't lie about it!" I screamed. "Be a woman, not a mouse! Admit what you did!"

"Zaria, Calm down," Damon said, with his eyes beyond

wide.

I got even more pissed. Why was he protecting her? Were they fooling around before I got to the club? I'll bet she sucked his dick in the bathroom stall just before he came and talked to me. Fuck that shit! I'm nobody's fool. I grabbed the empty Corona bottle by the neck, intending to tear his mutha-fuckin' head off. But before I could swing, security had me by my arms and drug me outside while I kicked and screamed like a lunatic.

Dumped onto the street, I saw people outside pointing fingers and wondering why I got thrown out, but then reality disappears in an instant. The club is gone. The bouncers are no longer carrying me. Everyone around me is gone.

I found myself standing outside on a very dark night hold-ing a bag full of my clothes with rain pouring from the sky, drenching my body, lightning and thunder nearly deafening me. Why am I here? Where is everyone?

Footsteps come quickly from the distance, splashing water underneath them. They're getting closer and closer quickly with each step. Something inside me knows they're coming for me. Something inside me knows they're coming to hurt me. I look into the night to see a tall shadowy figure dash-ing up the street towards me, the sight of him scaring me more than the sight of the devil himself.

I run to the nearest house and begin to beat on the door, feeling that I belong there. I've been there before hundreds of times. I can feel it. It feels like home. Someone here will protect me for sure.

"Please let me in!" I scream, turning to see the stranger quickly getting closer. "Please help me! I have no place else to go and I need help!"

Tears fall from my eyes. Why won't they help me? Even over the rattling of thunder and lightning their voices can be heard inside. Why are they ignoring me? Why don't they love me anymore? What did I do to make them leave me out here to die?

The stranger's hand grab's my shoulder.

"Zaria!" Milan shouted, snapping me from my daze.

Current reality surrounds me again just as quickly as it disappeared before. I'm outside the club with the bouncer standing in front of me.

"Sweetheart, you might've had a little too much to drink," he said. "You really need to go home before I call the police."

"Hit him! Hit him now." That voice was back and he wouldn't stop. "You're such a punk, Zaria. Either hit him or go home."

"Zaria!" Milan called out again. She got close enough to touch me and offered some encouraging words. Next thing I knew Mia and Jazmine were outside too, adding to my turmoil.

"Single black female is on a roll tonight," Mia said with the intent on hurting me.

I blocked her out. "My shoe. I can't find my other shoe."

"They were cheap, old, and too little anyway," Jazmine joked.

"Hit her!" The voice told me.

I turned away from them all, and hopefully that annoying voice. With the quickness, I stormed to my car, with one shoe in hand, and the other lost. I hurried into my Honda Accord and slammed the rattling door, hard. Very hard.

"Zaria!" Milan yelled again, hoping to catch me before I started the car.

It was too late… nothing left for her to see now but my tail lights and the invisible horns on my head. At that moment, I knew I needed to see a doctor.

5···*Hardy*

The beer's bitter acidic taste was heavily needed. I took two huge sips from my Heineken, placed the mug back on the bar, and looked up at the Knicks game playing on the overhanging flat screen television. Although my eyes were on the screen, they weren't watching it. I didn't even know what the score was. My mind was too stressed right now to think about the game.

My neighbor had called me this morning and told me that my wife had thrown all my clothes out on the front lawn and turned on the sprinklers after my sister failed to cover for me this weekend. When I called my sister to find out what happened, she gave me some bullshit about me needing to grow up and about Dana being a good woman who deserved to be treated right.

My sister had always liked Dana and had always taken her side over mine no matter what. But damn, isn't blood supposed to be thicker than water? Isn't she supposed to ride with her brother before anyone else? At least that's how I had always thought a sister and brother were supposed to get down. But I guess not.

"Damn, your sister played the shit out of you." My boy,

Kyle said, sitting beside me and shaking his head.

"No, she didn't," my other partner, Mario added, sitting on my other side. "It served his ass right. Hardy, man, you not worth shit, dog."

Both Mario and Kyle had been my best friends since we were kids, although they were as different from each other as night and day. Mario was highly educated, was a lawyer, had A-1 credit, and drove a Jag. Kyle, on the other hand still lived with his momma, had dropped out of high school, rode the bus, had six baby mommas, and if was ever offered a job he'd probably run from it.

"Why are you married anyway?" Mario asked. "It defies logic. People are supposed to get married because they want to be married; because they want to belong to someone."

"Oh, boy," Kyle moaned, annoyed at the upcoming sermon. "Here goes Mr. Holier Than Thou."

"Fuck you, Kyle. It's not about being holier than thou. It's about doing the right thing. That's something I wouldn't expect you to understand, Kyle. What you up to now anyway, your tenth baby momma?"

My mood wasn't really up for laughing right now but knowing that Kyle was quickly approaching ten brought a chuckle. For him, strapping up while getting his fuck on was unheard of. Me, on the other hand, I rarely fucked bareback.

"You're trying to get a nice little collection going, ain't you?" Mario asked him.

"Yup," Kyle responded proudly. "As a matter of fact, I've been thinking about adding your fine ass sister to the list. Tell'er to call me."

Mario laughed, knowing that his friend stood absolutely no chance with his sister. If your bank account wasn't holding six figures or more, you could forget about it. I tried to listen to their conversation but I kept thinking about Dana and the wrath I would face when I got home. All of a sudden the bartender sat a plate of hot wings in front of Kyle breaking me from my trance. She was short, half-way cute, but toted a humongous ass.

"You're married, Hardy," Mario belted to me loudly.

"So, if you were married, you'd never step out even once?" Kyle asked Mario, as he grabbed a wing and tore into it like a Viking.

"No, I wouldn't," Mario said matter of factly. "And especially if I had one as good as Dana."

"Nigga, whatever," Kyle said, shaking his head and mumbling something under his breath.

"So what are you going to do?" Mario asked me in a more serious tone.

"I'm going to go home," I said sharply as if he should've known better.

"And then what?"

"The same thing I do every time she starts tripping." I stretched, then placed my hands on my bald head, noticing that I was sweating. "I'm going to sweet talk her real well, eat the pussy real good, and make her forget about whatever she was mad about in the first place."

"That's my nigga," Kyle said, giving me a pound. He kept shaking his head up and down like he was proud of me.

My statement was meant more to convince myself rather than my friends. Dana had caught me cheating several times before and forgave me. She'd cursed me out more times than I could remember and threatened to leave a few times. But threats and curse words were about as far as she ever went. I always knew she loved my black ass too much to ever really leave no matter how much bullshit I put her through. But this was the first time she'd ever thrown my clothes out. This one was uncharted waters. I honestly wasn't sure what my next move would be.

"And that's going to make everything better, huh?" Mario asked. "That's going to fix your marriage?"

I couldn't answer.

"I didn't think so. Despite what that goofy ass nigga over there tells you," Mario said, pointing over at Kyle. "You know I'm right. I'm your dog, and I got your back."

For as long as I'd known Mario he had always been the voice of reason. He'd never believed in telling me what I wanted to hear, only the truth. That's why I loved him like a brother and chose him to be my best man at my wedding. Even though we were both twenty-one at the time he kept giving me words of encouragement, hoping I wouldn't back out.

"And I'm not a divorce attorney," Mario added. "I'm a criminal attorney. So don't come asking me to come represent your ass when she decides to take everything."

The bar cheered as the Knicks took the lead for the first time of the evening. I had nothing to cheer about, and could only take another swig of my Heineken. I could see out of the corner of my eye Kyle smashing his bowl of hot wings, occasionally licking sauce from his fingers with no shame at all. I remembered when my life was like his; no cares, no responsibilities. Sometimes I hated to admit, I yearned for those days. But at the ripe old age of thirty-two, those days were gone for me.

Why the hell did I have to go and get myself married anyway? I mean I knew that when I walked down the aisle, side by side with Dana like a square, being faithful was going to be a challenge. But my love for her was so strong that I thought it would win. It had me honestly believing that it would curb my desire for other women. Damn, I couldn't have been any more wrong in my entire life. Immediately after our wedding day it seemed like pussy began to rain from the sky on my head. It was as if every woman in New York had discovered I was married and wanted to see if they could change it.

Nowadays I'm not sure if marriage is for me. I'm not sure if it ever will be. Dana sleeps in the bed while most nights I choose to sleep on the couch. My body is usually so drained from the constant amount of pussy I get in the streets that making love to her has damn near become non-existent. And when we talk it's usually guaranteed to turn into an argument. We've become more enemies these days than friends.

I do have to admit though; she does make an attempt at trying to make the marriage work. She tries her hardest to explore all possibilities. She's always doing things like trying to keep the lines of communication open or surprising me with a candle light dinner. But for some reason the ability to want to be married is no longer inside of me. I still love her and forever will. But being in love with her is a totally different matter. I'm not sure if that part is still there. I guess that's what keeps us butting heads constantly. Sad to say, if it wasn't for my son, I would've probably asked for a divorce a while ago. But turning Terrell into one of those angry kids who'd been made bitter because his parents divorced was something I just couldn't do. My son had my heart.

"So, did you fuck that big-bootied girl at the school yet?" Kyle asked me, wiping sauce from his mouth with a napkin.

I was sorta still in a daze but caught the end of what he was saying. "Which one you talking 'bout?" I asked, honestly not knowing who he was speaking of. So many teachers at my school had become my victims.

"The one you said looks like Tyra Banks."

She'd already got the dick twice but I had to put the brakes on it because she started getting a little too possessive.

Kyle laughed.

Mario looked at me in disbelief. "Don't tell me you're fucking your students' mothers."

"Bang, Bang, Bang!" Kyle joked, taking a sip of his Hennessey and Coke and smacking a passing waitress on the ass.

"Is he serious?" Mario asked me, not believing Kyle was telling the truth.

"I only hit a few of them; only three or four," I said,

shrugging off the numbers.

Mario threw his hands up in defeat and shook his head. "Is there anything sacred? Hardy, you're a lost cause."

I understood where he was coming from. He was the product of a two parent family who were celebrating their 50th anniversary this year. Me on the other hand, all I had seen was my father cheat on my mother my whole life. And in my defense, I've always been a sucker for hoes with fat asses. And just because one or two happen to be on the backs of my students' mothers doesn't make them off limits. Shit, mothers need some good dick too. That's how they became mothers in the first place, right? I reasoned with myself and ordered another drink.

"A wolf among sheep," Mario said, taking a sip of his beer. "But I don't even know why it amazes me. Nothing should amaze me more than the fact that you of all people became a teacher in the first place."

"C'mon now. You're saying that I don't take my profession seriously," I told him, "true enough I'm a player but being a good teacher will forever be important to me. I understand that I'm the closest thing to a father figure that most of my students have, so I take my job seriously."

"Don't get me wrong," he said quickly. "I know you take it seriously. I remember how hard you worked to get that degree in mathematics. And teaching is one of the greatest services any human being can give. I respect it. I'm just saying that of every occupation on earth, teaching was the last one I expected you to go into."

"He's right about that one," Kyle chimed in. "Look at you, man. You don't dress like a teacher. You don't talk like a teacher. And you've got more tats on you than every nigga I know put together. Shit, nigga, you look like a bad influence."

Mario laughed.

"Aint that a bitch." I was slightly offended. He was right, but damn. The part about me looking like a bad influence was a little harsh. I mean, I did have swag, and loved to dress in my hip hop gear, but was that a crime?

"You're still my nigga though," Kyle commented.

"But I'm a bad influence, huh? I asked him, really wanting to know what he thought of me.

"Just keeping it one hundred."

"They don't come no more of a bad influence than you; a thirty something year old man still living with his momma," I told Kyle trying to retaliate.

"But I'm not a teacher though," he pointed out.

"Thank God!" Mario shouted, seeming relieved. "Anyway, I'm not a player but doesn't it say somewhere in the imaginary player's handbook that you should never fool with women at your work place?"

"That's only when you're dealing with crazy hoes," I told Mario as if I had everything under control. "I only deal with women who know the rules, dog."

Both my homeboys looked at me.

"You prep them first?" Mario asked with a smirk.

"Yep." And crazy broads were off limits to me. "You know how I roll," I bragged.

"What about Sarah?"Kyle reminded, while laughing so hard, almost falling off his seat.

"Yeah, Hardy," Mario said. "What about Sarah?"

Both of my friends began laughing even harder.

"She was the only one," I said, meaning it. I slid my hand over my head as I always did when things troubled me.

"Are you sure?" Kyle asked.

"Hell yeah. I'll never get caught slipping like that again."

"I hope not," Kyle commented. "Man, that white bitch was nutty as hell."

Sarah was a white girl I'd met a few years ago. She was real cute; made me think I was fucking Brittany Spears. After fucking only a few times, and making her scream so loud each time the cops came knocking, she became dickmatized. That's the only way it can be explained. *Dickmatized*. She was so gone from the whipping I'd put on that little, tight, pink pussy of hers she developed the strange notion that we were a couple and that I was in love with her. She even went as far as to start telling my friends we were moving in together. The problem was, Sarah was the only one in the relationship who was in love. She was nothing but a jump off to me.

When I finally cut her off, she took it bad. She took it more than bad. It was like her entire world had crashed and burned at the bottom of the ocean. She cried so much I thought her eyes were going to stay red permanently. She begged me to come back to her, keyed my car, and called my phone so much I had to change the number twice. The bitch even hid in the bushes outside my apartment night after night, having me look both ways nervously for her every morning before I left out for work. When she'd finally get a chance to see me, she would threaten suicide, saying that life wasn't worth living if she couldn't have me to share it with. "Damn, the power of the dick is incredible," I finally said out loud.

"Yeah, Sarah was fruity for real," Kyle said, nodding his head back and forth.

"See, now I watch the mannerisms of my newest victims a little more carefully. If something comes off even the slightest bit crazy about one the very first moment I see them, I place them on my *no fly list*." I slammed one fist into the other and threw a couple of jabs like I was a prized fighter in the cheating category. "That means I simply do not fuck with them."

"I hope so, 'cause the last thing you want is a nutty bitch coming up to your job," Kyle continued, like he had a job for a crazy bitch to come to in the first place.

"He's right about that one," Mario agreed. "You can learn a lot from a dummy."

"Fuck you," Kyle told him.

I shook my head and laughed at my boys. After another

hour, I finally slipped my wedding ring back on, downed my last beer to the suds, and mustered up the strength to go home. Dreading the trip wasn't the word, I thought to myself, climbing off of my stool. But there was no other choice. My nympho Brazilian jumpoff had spent the entire weekend sucking the life out of me, literally, leaving me sluggish and lazy. But since the board recently approved my transfer to Terrell's school in Brooklyn and tomorrow was my first day, getting home and getting some rest was high priority. The sooner I got home and faced the music the better. *Damn, what will I wear? Dana has fucked all my shit up!*

6 · · · *Zaria*

Monday rolled around with me in a sour mood and off to a bad start for the week. My day at school was horrible and I found myself waiting in the lobby by the elevator for nearly an hour after not seeing Milan's Toyota Camry parked outside. It was assumed that she was still tripping about that shit that happened Saturday night as if it were all my fault. I'd be willing to bet Brent had pumped her up to think so. My plan for him was already in action. My guess…she was probably with him at the moment, laid up with her legs spread wide open like a slut. I'm so damn tired of him, I spat.

Suddenly, Milan waltzed through the lobby door as if she knew I was talking about her. Her head tilted upward showing her confidence while she strutted like she was on the fucking runway. She was dressed in a pair of thin-heeled black leather boots, a black skirt, and a black leather coat pretending to be untouchable. Well, I had words for her.

"You're so inconsiderate." I jumped in her path and roared like an animal.

"Girl, you scared the hell out of me," Milan shouted. She seemed relieved that it wasn't a mugger, anxious to bust her head open, but upset about my outfit.

47

"Zaria," is that mine?" she blasted.

"No, I bought my own."

"Please stop dressing like me. I don't like it," she told me, staring at my black jumpsuit; the same one she'd bought and worn just a week ago. "And why in the hell would you wear that with Reeboks?"

"Don't try to change the subject, Milan. I said, you're so inconsiderate," I repeated, this time with my facial expression like stone. "Where were you?"

"Huh?"

"You could've told me that you weren't coming straight home."

"Why?" she asked with a perplexed look. "Were we supposed to do something together this evening? If we were, I'm so sorry, Zaria. Bee and I-"

I knew it! "Bee and I, Bee and I, Bee and I," I repeated her words to her, aggravated and cutting her off. "Is Brent all you think about these days? What about me?"

"Zaria, calm down," she instructed, reaching for my shoulders.

I jerked away. "Don't touch me! You hate me, don't you?" I paused to reload. "You hate the way I dress but when I try to duplicate you, you still talk bad about me. What is it about me that you hate so much?"

Her eyes narrowed. "I don't hate you, Zaria. And if you want to dress like me...no problem."

She huffed, letting me know she didn't mean those words at all.

"If we had plans for this evening, I'm sorry," she commented showing that she was fed up with me. "It was an honest mistake."

"You could've called."

"I'm an adult, Zaria. Twenty-five as a matter of fact. I have a life, you know."

"Your life doesn't include me anymore? Is that what

you're trying to say?"

Milan looked confused. "What are you talking about?" She paused then began walking toward the elevators. "You know what? Never mind?"

I followed quickly behind wanting answers. "Is this about Saturday night? I already told you that I don't let NO bitch play me like that. If you're gonna be mad at anyone, be mad at Damon. He should've told me that him and that tramp had something going on."

"Zaria, I'm not even thinking about what happened that night. It's over with. And contrary to what you believe, Damon had never met that girl before. In fact, that was the first night he'd ever been to that club. Zaria, you really need to relax. Better yet, you need help." She paused to think. "Does this behavior have anything to do with why you were going to the doctor when I first met you?"

"Don't try to change the subject," I countered. "You're always taking everyone else's side over mine."

"I'm not taking sides. I'm just saying."

"I'm always the problem, huh, Milan? I'm always the one who has to be wrong? "

"I didn't say that." She huffed.

Milan pushed the up button with attitude and turned her head away from me. Was she trying to be disrespectful? If so, I wasn't going to allow that and would have to go to Plan B. I decided to give her one more shot. "You didn't say it but I know you were thinking it." My eyes rolled to the top of my head.

"Zaria, I wasn't thinking…"

I cut her off. "You know what? Don't worry about it," I said quickly, turning away and pressing the up button on the elevator again, even though she'd already pushed it twice. My eyes couldn't take looking in the bitch's face anymore without the urge to slap the shit out of her.

When the elevator doors opened, we climbed on and rode upstairs, slowly in silence, which was more than fine for me. Hearing her voice right now would probably make me jump on her and beat her like a bitch in the street. As soon as we reached our floor, I hopped off with speed, leaving her chasing my back. When we reached the apartment door, as usual, I realized that my keys were somewhere in my tote bag and I really didn't feel like going through the hassle of looking for them, so I stepped to the side.

"I really don't understand why you're acting like this," Milan remarked, taking the invitation to unlock the door herself. "It's really not that-" Milan stopped mid-sentence and turned to me with a strange look on her face. "Did you leave the door unlocked?"

"No. I haven't been upstairs yet." My expression showed my worry.

"It's unlocked."

I clutched my bag while Milan pushed the door open slowly. I could understand her fear. It had happened before…something we both hoped would never happen again. We crept inside taking two baby steps at a time. Finally, her mouth dropped and my heart felt like it had stopped.

Without warning, my feet stopped dead in their tracks. "Oh my God," were the only words my mouth could spill as both me and Milan stared at the living room, unable to believe what had been done.

The entire apartment had been destroyed from top to bottom just as it had a month ago. Both of us remained in shock for what seemed like minutes. Then Milan bravely took the first step forward while my feet stayed frozen in one spot.

Sliced furniture, scattered pillows, glass covered floors, tossed cds, shattered mirrors, shattered portraits, overturned tables, and broken lamps, all destroyed. Everything we loved-fucked up. Nearly nothing in the apartment was spared.

Wrapping my mind around the mess seemed impossible. My mouth fell open while my brain remained trapped in a daze. "Oh my God! Not my movies!" I shouted, seeing them tossed across the floor, some completely destroyed. They were my favorite possession. Milan walked away taking a closer look while the inside of my head played ping pong with thunderous thoughts. Why us, I wondered? Who did this? Why the fuck did they do this? My mind remained full of questions.

"Zaria!" Milan shouted from the bathroom.

Her piercing scream freed me from my daze. With no hesitation, I jetted toward her voice ready to fight for my girl. With glass crackling underneath the soles of my Reebok Classics with every step my courage was up. I was ready for action. But when I reached the bathroom and found Milan standing inside staring at the mirror, I settled my nerves a bit and rushed to her side. The red lipstick written words sent my heart pounding.

MILAN, U'RE A DEAD BITCH!!! PROMISE U!

Milan was completely shaken by each word. I watched on as her hands trembled and tears flowed uncontrollably. I felt bad for her. Strangely my fear wasn't brought on by the words on the mirror. The fact that I'd been having nightmares about this evening for the past few weeks sent chills through my spine.

"Milan, I dreamed about this," I whispered in fear.

Milan turned her neck like the girl on the exorcist. She looked on with terror. "What are you talking about?" she shrieked.

We faced each other.

"The destroyed apartment. The threat written on the mirror. All of this. I dreamt it. I mean I know someone broke in before, but my dream was so exact this time."

Milan couldn't say a word. She only stared at me.

"Do you hear what I'm saying to you?" My voice got louder.

"I'm going out for a few seconds. I need to breathe," she belted with resentment.

"Milan, you can't go out!" I said frantically. "The person who did this could be out there! You should take a break away from your modeling shoots for a while. You really need to lay low. Whoever did this isn't playing."

I reached for Milan but she pulled away.

"Milan, do you think Brent could've done this?"

"What are you talking about, nutty? Why would he do this?"

"Why not? He probably found out you're fucking other men and couldn't take it. I knew he was bad news."

"Zaria, you're crazy," she said with the most serious expression I'd seen in a while. Just like that she walked out of the bathroom.

I followed Milan, step for step, refusing to let up. "Why? Because you can't take the truth about your boyfriend?"

"He's not my boyfriend. I haven't committed to anyone yet."

"I can't tell. You were riding his face Saturday night like he was your man."

Milan stopped and turned to look me in my face. "Zaria, don't go there. That's none of your business."

"You fuck all of your quote unquote friends like that? Huh? I badgered."

Milan shook her head angrily, the sting of my words showing. But instead of answering me, she reached for the phone and dialed 911.

Hours passed and I found myself sitting on the ledge of the window sill watching imaginary bugs crawl along the frame. There was no need in showing Milan. She would tell me there was nothing there and talk bad about me later. I watched her talking shit and whispering to the officer about me, but I said nothing. The officer thought I hadn't noticed. Besides, the bitch flirted with him, too. Once a freak, always a freak, I thought.

"If you ladies see or hear anything, call us. Don't hesitate," the burly officer told us as he prepared to leave.

I nodded, stood up and closed the door behind him, making sure to lock it. From the living room I could hear Milan in the kitchen cleaning up. After an hour of cleaning and filing reports with the police she was still angry with me. I could tell when the officer was asking us questions. Milan spent the entire time avoiding eye contact with me and trying not to stand too close to me.

I decided to make things right with us so I walked to the kitchen, stepping over broken furniture and glass along the way. When I reached the war torn kitchen, Milan was sweeping, dressed in a pair of grey sweats and white shell toed Adidas; the plainest I'd ever seen her. She knew I wanted to talk but ignored me purposely.

"Milan, I'm sorry about blaming Brent," I stated, meaning it genuinely.

She kept sweeping.

"I'm sorry," I repeated, still meaning it and hoping she'd accept my apology. I guess I'm just jealous that you've been spending so much time with him. But I'm really sorry."

Milan continued to ignore me, making me sigh with defeat. There was nothing I could do to make her talk to me at the moment so I stormed off to my room and laid down for a nap that seemed like forever. What was supposed to be sweet sleep turned into devastation.

The first scream left my vocal chords and his first punch caught me off guard. His large hand smashed against my head so hard that it gave me a massive headache as I fell to the floor. I just wanted to lay there and die but his hand snatched hold of my weave and yanked me back up to my feet. How did he get in? And where was Milan? I wondered, until he forced me to look into his anger filled eyes. His immense dislike for me showed through them easily. He wanted me to see every ounce of his hatred, terrifying me beyond imagination.

The second punch landed violently against my right eye, closing it immediately; its force so strong that it lifted me off my feet and hurled me over the dresser as easily as a ragdoll. My head pounded even harder now and I could only see hundreds of bright colorful lights, nothing more.

"Whyyyyyyyy, whyyyyyy, are you doing this?" I screamed, wanting to know.

Tears ran down my face, each falling to the floor and lightly exploding like raindrops. Once again all I wanted to do was lay there and hope for a mercy in him that I knew with all honesty didn't exist. Not even a shred.

"Please, stop," I begged, extending my hands in weak defense. My plea was met with more violence.

The bottom of his boot dropped down on my stomach like a trash bag full of bricks tossed from a rooftop, literally taking my breath away and making me bring my knees to my chest. The impact forced me to fight for air, coughing like a child after taking his very first puff from a cigarette. I could feel every bit of food in my stomach rushing to my throat but the only thing from my stomach that managed to reach my mouth was the bitter, nauseating taste of my own blood.

I clutched my stomach. All I wanted in this entire world at that moment was for my pain to stop. I wanted the torture to end. I opened my left eye and caught a glimpse of the nickel plated gun in his left hand. God, I don't want to die! My inner voice screamed, making my heart pound against the inside of my chest like a sledgehammer.

He reached for me, undoubtedly to inflict more pain.

I refused to die tonight.

My eyes locked in on his crotch. And I let loose from the floor with the strongest kick I had, crashing both of his balls. The heel of my foot landed on target with force, sending him to the floor with a horrendous, agony-filled scream and his gun flying in the air several feet away. Once he hit the floor clutching his balls, I rolled onto my knees and crawled for the gun. I wanted to kill this monster more than words could ever describe. I made it, clutching the gun in the palm of my hands. Before I could even turn, I saw him diving toward me before I could pull the trigger. With his weight now on top of me, grabbing and reaching, everything began to happen so fast. I knew then, I would die.

The first shot rang out.

Then another.

Everything became silent and still.

Suddenly, he slowly climbed off of me and staggered backwards.

I wanted so badly to believe that I shot him but the excruciating pain in my stomach told me differently. Flat on my back, my eyes fell to my stomach where both my hands waited, desperately trying to stop the bleeding. But it was too late. Too much life poured out of me. I could feel every inch of it as it left me.

So many things left undone. So many things left to say. So much of the world still left to see. Still so much left to do. A chance at marriage would've been great. Something I always wanted.

Current reality snatched me awake. My entire body and sheets were heavily soaked in sweat while my chest heaved up and down violently.

"Zaria, I heard you scream," Milan yelled, standing beside my bed with a broom in her hand. "Are you okay?"

This time it's Milan's words that fall on deaf ears as I jump out of bed and grab my tote bag from the floor. "Get out!" I screamed, grabbing the video tape from the bag.

"But, Zaria," she pleaded, needing to know I was okay. "You were supposed to be helping me clean…but you laid down and fell asleep."

"Get out!" I screamed again at the top of my lungs,

pushing her out of my bedroom and slamming the door. It slammed so hard it rattled the entire apartment like a slight earthquake. I quickly ran to the television and turned it on. My hands trembled as I placed the evidence into the DVD player and pressed play.

Everything inside me raced. I have to watch it, I chanted. My body desperately needed to see its images like a fix, my need for it running through my veins wildly. It's the only thing on God's earth that will calm me, I told myself wondering when I would be free from it all. I fell to the floor, wrapped my arms around myself and began to rock back and forth in the bedroom's darkness, illuminated by the television screen.

7 ··· *Zaria*

Most New Yorkers hated fall and so did I. The forecast called for rain, winds, a cloudy sunless sky, and a temperature that would be lucky to reach the upper forties. The entire day would pretty much be a gloomy mess, but I didn't give a flying fuck. It matched my mood more than perfectly. It was what I needed. In fact, the miserable presence above inspired me so much that I decided to leave my car at home and walk the several miles to school this morning.

One quick stop had to be made though. I was about to open a can of whip ass. My entire body seethed with more anger than any one person could possibly feel as the wind from the brisk air hit me in my face. What Jamal had done to me had me now ready to erupt on his ass with a vengeance like a fuckin' volcano as I made my way from street to street.

"Look at that chick," a young teenager announced to her friends as I passed them with smoke erupting from my nostrils.

I ignored their laughter and kept walking. New York's early morning chaos, blaring horns, screeching tires, and foul-mouthed drivers yelling from their cars bathed my ears like some sort of sick baptism, leaving me angrier with every step of my journey. The loudness seemed to urge me on like a blood-

57

thirsty audience screaming for a young Mike Tyson to knock out his newest victim.

"Today's the day, you scary bitch! You won't go through with it!" the voice in my head screamed loudly over and over again, pissing me off even more than it did when it woke me up this morning. Ignoring it was impossible as it now began to scream so loudly that my head was starting to pound terribly with a migraine; a migraine that brought tears to my eyes, as I power walked the streets of Brooklyn with a purpose.

I wanted the voice to stop, but it wouldn't.

"Zaria, just in case nobody told you lately...you ain't shit! And will never be shit!"

I kept walking. Now even faster. I knew if I said something back, the people passing by would look at me even more strangely. So I ignored the voice. With my tote bag strapped over my shoulder, I repeatedly tossed the Louisville Slugger from hand to hand, occasionally stopping to take a few practice swings at the air. I imagined each of them connecting with my target hard enough to destroy it. My behavior caught whispers and strange looks from everyone who passed me by.

"That bitch 'bout to fuck somebody up," an old man pretending to be young again shouted.

"I bet her nigga didn't come home last night," another blasted.

I paid absolutely no attention to them. Fuck them! I told myself proudly. If they wanted some of what I was about to dish out, they could get it too. All comers were welcomed without discrimination.

A raindrop fell softly on my forehead letting me know more was to come. But nothing would stop me. It was payback time. I simply slipped my hood over my head and made my journey through street after street and alley after alley on a mission to inflict pain.

Several minutes later, a smile slipped through the side of my lips. There it is! My eyes filled with tears of joy and widened at the sight of Jamal's most prized possession. My pussy got soaking wet with anticipation and rage. Instantly, I dropped my tote bag down to the sidewalk, placed the bat over my shoulder, and got into a batter's stance that would make Barry Bonds himself truly proud. Everything inside of me began to smile.

I'd been waiting on this moment for the past several days more than anything I could remember. And being talked out of it would've been impossible. Nothing could stop me from doing this once I decided that revenge, retaliation, and get back was what I had to have. It became like the need for air in my lungs and food in my stomach. If I couldn't have it, I felt like I would die. Jamal needed a taste of his own medicine.

The words, RESTRAINING ORDER in that damn letter were forever etched into my brain. I had been thinking about it all night. And simply waiting until I saw him in court had become impossible. Every time I thought about Jamal, I felt like the world's biggest fool. He made me feel worthless and like I would never be good enough for any man. I hated that feeling. The only thing that would make me feel any better was this particular moment.

"Do it, Bitch!" the voice yelled inside my head, making my migraine pound even harder. "What are you waiting for!"

"You think I won't do it!" I screamed back, wanting the voice to continue doubting me so I could prove it wrong.

"I knew you were just a scary bitch; all mouth and no muthafuckin action!"

My heart pounded like a drum. And of course several people had stopped to stare at me crazily.

"Scary Bitch! Scary Bitch! Scary Bitch!"

My adrenaline rushed through my veins like a wild river.

"Scary Bitch! Scary Bitch! Scary Bitch!" the inner voice egged me on.

My head ached excruciatingly. More and more.

"Scary Bitch! Scary Bitch! Scary Bitch!"

"Stop it!" I yelled out loud.

This was my moment. My eyes closed tightly and I took the first swing, hearing the windshield of Jamal's silver Chrysler 300 crush underneath the bat's force. I didn't care who saw me or heard me, even the police. I opened my eyes and swung again, this time at the passenger side window, shattering it easily and loving how it felt to get back at Jamal's non-appreciative ass.

"What the fuck!" someone shouted from an apartment window.

"That bitch is tearing up Jamal's whip!" another person yelled. "Somebody go upstairs and tell'em!"

As a huge crowd began to gather on both sides of the street and cars stopped. Their "Ooohs" and "Ahhhs" only fed my urge to do much, much more damage. I slowly circled the car like a warrior and swung like Babe Ruth at everything; tinted windows, side view mirrors, headlights, tail lights, bumpers, and the custom Bentley grill. It didn't matter. I swear it didn't matter at all. Nothing was off limits to my rage. I swung and swung, sending everything landing loudly on the street. Each swing felt like the constant stroking of an experienced lover during a night of unbelievable sex.

When Jamal finally made it out into the crowded street in only his boxers and a pair of Timbs, it was too late. His pride and joy was destroyed completely and I was on my way up the street headed to my class. I shot him a devilish grin over my shoulder, ass swinging side to side, and my bat thrown into one of his neighbor's trash can.

"You loony bitch!" Jamal shouted, looking like an idiot in his boxers.

Yeah, I'm a bitch, I thought with a smile. My mind flipped back to the old movie, *Misery* with Kathy Bates that I'd watched a thousand times. I loved it when she said, "Sometimes being a bitch is all a woman has to hold onto."

"I'ma see your ass in court next week!" Jamal continued

to shout from behind.

I wanted to turn around and see the simple look on his face so badly but instead, I simply threw up the deuces and kept it moving.

My adrenaline was still pumping savagely when I walked into my classroom, my face twisted into a smirk that seemed like it would never go away. I placed my jacket on the back of my chair and began to grab papers and notebooks from my bag, not paying attention to all of the chaos around me. My mind was too busy playing back my revenge over and over again.

When the bell rang, it sent my migraine through the roof. I finally snapped out of my trance just in time to look up and see Andre, a seven year old future goon, standing behind Shauntey pulling her by her ponytail. The rest of the class had already cut out the bullshit at the sound of the bell and took their seats, knowing that I wasn't the one to be played with. I had a reputation as the toughest second grade teacher that my school, PS 174 had ever seen.

"Andre!" I shouted so loudly he and the entire class jumped.

Andre stood straight up in fear, knowing that he'd just been caught with his hand in the cookie jar.

"Do you have a problem," I asked. My eyes narrow and locked on only him like a heat seeking missile with no other intentions but putting his little, narrow, black ass in check.

That voice came at me again. "You don't even know how to do something as simple as put second graders in check. What are you teaching them anyway? Are you giving them a special education course on how to be stupid just like you?"

I breathed heavily knowing I had to ignore that voice inside my head. I had a job to do.

"Sit down, Andre. Now!"

"But Shauntey hit…" he attempted.

My head was now aching so badly that my hands crashed down on my desk hard enough to nearly drop it to the floor. "Do you have a fuckin problem!" I shouted. After what I'd just done to Jamal's car and the pain of my headache, I wasn't in any mood whatsoever for games and bullshit.

"No," Andre answered sharply, his answer filled with frustration.

"Then you need to apologize to Shauntey."

"But she hit…" he attempted again.

I stared at the little hardheaded, future-convict-looking bastard with a look that let him know the order wasn't opened to debate. Period.

Andre sucked his teeth angrily. "I'm sorry, Ms. Hopkins," he whimpered, then slung himself down into his chair.

Is it wrong to hate a child? I'd wondered that over and over again ever since I'd become a teacher. I wasn't sure how it worked in white schools, but down in the trenches it was rough being a teacher. Most of the parents weren't too much older than the children and are still immature, disrespectful, and childish themselves, so they don't know what it truly means to be a parent. They don't understand what it means to teach a child to clean up after themselves, to say thank you, respect authority, and all the other bullshit because they as parents haven't grown to understand themselves. They just figure the teacher is supposed to put up with their bad-ass, back-talking children like it's okay. Well, other teachers might. Not me. I ain't going for it. I get in their asses whenever and wherever necessary. And I don't give a damn about what the parents have to say about it.

"Get out Friday night's homework," I instructed as I sat down behind my desk.

"Ms. Hopkins," Rosie, a little Puerto Rican girl called. "Ms. Johnson is taking her class on a fieldtrip today for Halloween. Can we go on one?"

The entire class lit up. Everyone had a suggestion: trick or treating, the haunted house, etc, etc. Suggestions bombarded me from all directions, aggravating my headache. I just wanted everyone to shut the fuck up. Honestly, I had forgotten it was Halloween.

"No," I said sternly, expecting my answer to be the end of it all. My eyes were on the pages of the math book as I flipped through it to the page that I'd assigned for homework.

"But Ms..."

My eyes rose. Then my nostrils spread.

The whole class understood what the look on my face meant. They sighed in defeat and began to grab their homework out of their desks in disappointment. I had them each trained enough to clearly know that with only a look nothing else needed to be said. I stood and turned to the chalkboard.

Shauntey pressed the issue. "But, Ms. Hopkins..."

I turned quickly and reacted to her whining without thinking. "Can you hear?" I shouted. "I said no! Hell no! And tell your mother you need a perm!"

Shauntey began to cry.

Before I knew it, I had charged her desk like an angry Rottweiler. As soon as I reached her I dropped to one knee, grabbed her desk, and pulled it towards me so quickly her body jerked to one side like a rag doll. Our faces were now so close to one another we could smell each other's breath.

"Listen," I said to Shauntey through gritted teeth. My head was now pounding behind my eyes so hard I could barely see. Both of them felt like they were going to pop out of my head from the pressure. "Life isn't fair. And the world we live in is a cruel place. It won't allow you to have your own way whenever, wherever, or however you want it. That's the way it is. Your tears can't change it. They only make me want to hurt you even more. Do you understand me?"

Shauntey was horrified and silent.

"And I was serious about the perm. Your hair is nappy and the little balls surrounding your hair line distract me when I teach." I moved in closer, my face showing no compassion or sympathy. "Do…You…Understand…Me?" I asked again, my eyes silently demanding an answer from her.

"Yes," Shauntey answered finally.

"Then wipe those tears away."

Shauntey slowly did as she was told.

My teaching methods may not have been by the book but they'd always gotten me farther with my students than kind words and a soft voice. Sometimes a loud voice and no sympathy was the only thing they understood. Most times it's what they needed.

"Excuse me," a man's voice came from the doorway.

I looked over to see a handsome, mocha-looking brother standing there in jeans, Timbs, and an untucked button down. He was athletically built, his head was freshly shaven, and his thinly trimmed beard outlined his jaw line perfectly, connecting it to his goatee. The shape of his bald head reminded me of Michael Jordan, but he definitely had the body of 50 Cent. Whose daddy was he? I wondered.

"Can I help you," I asked, standing and sliding my hands into the back pockets of my jeans. I didn't believe in coming to work dressed like a church girl; it's always tight jeans and sneakers for me. His eyes checked me out quickly, making his face smile at what they'd just taken in. As he stepped into my class and made his way towards me, I couldn't help admiring his thuggish-like swag. He wasn't loud or blatant with it like most thugs I know. But it was there. And it was etched in stone when I got a glimpse of the tattoo near the top of his neck line.

"I'm Hardy, Gerald Hardy," he said, extending his hand for me to accept. I obliged him, liking the warm feel of his hand inside mine.

"I'm Zaria Hopkins," I told him. Suddenly my head didn't ache anymore. All traces of it had disappeared.

"It's nice to meet you," he returned. "I'm sorry to interrupt your class but I'm trying to find room 237. There's so many hallways I got lost just walking from the office. I'm sorry if I bothered you."

"It's okay," I assured him. "Are you a parent?" *A black man being a father to his child; that's the ultimate turn on.*

"Actually, I'm a teacher. I'm new here. My first day. I was transferred to take Mr. Leonard's place."

Damn, that's an even bigger turn on.

My face lit up immediately. Before I knew it, I'd left my own class and walked side by side with him to his. Fuck giving him directions, I had to escort him personally to his destination like a drug dealer watching his package as it traveled from point A to point B. There was no way in hell I was going to let any of these other lonely dick hungry, female teachers get hold to him before me. He was mine.

8···*Hardy*

"That's right, baby. Cum for Daddy," I told Yvonne. "You sexy muthufucka," I added, while listening to her moan.

"Ahhh….ahhhh…ahhh, Hardy," she groaned, letting it all release.

I smiled while sitting on the toilet, holding the house phone to my ear. Sex was sex and even if I'd been demoted to having it on the phone it was fine with me. I'd always been curious about the answer to this one question though…why are men such horrible cheaters? I mean, we're catastrophically terrible at the shit but we do it anyway, leaving obvious clues all over the place like we want to get caught. It's almost like we begin to walk around with a blinking bright light on our foreheads advertising to our wives and girlfriends, *I'M CHEATING! AND I WANT TO GET CAUGHT!*

I mean, we dramatically change up our normal daily routine. We start buying new underwear on a regular basis. We come home smelling like perfume and pussy. We leave condom wrappers in our car. We leave bitches' pictures in our glove compartments. We never thoroughly think out a lie before we tell it. We fuck hoes raw. Then go home and fuck our wives with no fear of possibly passing something incurable on to them. I mean, shit, we'll even go home and let our wives give us head although we know that we hadn't washed the last woman's pussy off our dick. It's crazy.

Dana's a muthafuckin super sleuth. Sometimes I wonder if she used to be a private detective before she met me but just never told me about it. I mean, she goes out of her way to sniff out my infidelities. She's done shit like calling in behind me to verify that I am where I say I am. And whenever she can get hold of my phone she rambles through the numbers. She'll ask me a question about where I was and who I was with. Then a few days later she'll ask the same question about the same situation just to see if I'll give a different answer. She'll go through my pockets when I'm asleep searching for numbers. She smells me when I come home late. Shit, she reminds me of that little muthafucka in the trench coat and big hat that used to follow the Pink Panther around all the time with a magnifying glass.

I stood, stripped down to my nuts and balls, and hopped in the shower thinking about how Dana's shit had gotten on my nerves to the third power. I can't stand an insecure woman. I look at it like this; Dana knows I'm cheating. She's known it for a while now. So I figure if you're not going to leave me, let me do me. As long as I pay the bills, handle my responsibilities as a father, and I don't throw my cheating up in your face don't ride me about the shit. At the end of the day I'm your husband, no one else's.

Dana doesn't see it that way though. For the past several days since she threw my shit out on the lawn, she's been giving me a mixture of the silent treatment and the extremely loud treatment. It varies from day to day. One day she's ignoring me completely and going out with her girls without letting me know that she even had plans, childishly trying to make me jealous. Other days she's slamming shit, cleaning the house with so much Pine Sol and Bleach, saying she's sterilizing her floors and furniture just in case I had a bitch in her house. Then she starts vacuuming in front of me while I'm trying to relax in front of the television after a long day at work.

Despite her childish-ass games, I started coming straight home from work every evening in an attempt to keep confusion down. Little did Dana know I would go in the bathroom and have phone sex with my broads anyway. *You can't keep a good man down.* But as long as I was in the house, she couldn't say I was cheating. I'd even started going to bed, *to our room* at night instead of sleeping on the couch like I usually did. But after all of that, I was still in the dog house.

I had to admit though; Dana did have me a little nervous about this one. I'd never seen her so steamed before. And she had definitely never thrown my clothes out before. But after hours of arguing, whining, and crying I think she silently realized that divorcing me wasn't in her best interest. Without me, who would pay the bills? Who would pay her car note and insurance? How would she be able to afford those name brand clothes and heels she likes so much, or those trips to the hair salon to keep that short, sassy hair-do perfect?

I had pretty much paid for everything in the house. And I always kept a side job or a hustle. It was my skills as a teacher, landscaper, and even mechanic that had laced our home, from the expensively furnished living room to the fully carpeted basement downstairs, laced with a pool table and plasmas. Dana knew what side her bread was buttered on. She wasn't dumb. She understood that if she let me go, it would be hard to find another black man who'd take care of home base the way I did. Hell, it would be almost impossible just to find a black man who wasn't toting guns and selling work on the corner. Dana would never admit it. But the two of us knew. What's understood doesn't need to be said.

When I stepped out the shower, slid the curtain back, and opened the door to the bedroom, as usual I was expecting either the silent treatment or the extremely loud treatment. Whichever it was going to be, I wasn't going to let it get to me. The Knicks were playing tonight and I was going to watch.

"Who is Lisa?" Dana asked angrily when I opened the bathroom door. As usual, a question like that was accompanied by her patting her right foot on the floor and holding her hands on her hips. The only thing different this time was that one of her hands was hidden behind her back.

"What are you talking about?" I asked, standing there in only a towel. I knew who Lisa was, but I wasn't going to just walk right into a trap like a dummy. I wasn't going to volunteer any information until I knew exactly what was going on.

"You know what I'm talking about, Hardy. Forget Lisa, who the fuck is Angie?"

"I don't know," I lied.

"Oh, you don't know, huh?"

"No, I don't, Dana."

She whipped my cell phone out from behind her back and began to read off Angie's phone number.

"Ohhhh," I said, getting over my amnesia. "That Angie."

"Don't play games with me, Hardy. Why is she calling you?"

"I don't know," I said. I honestly didn't know. I hadn't fucked Angie in months.

Dana was sick with her detective game. I'd left my cell on the dresser and taken the house phone in the bathroom thinking she would chill and give a brotha some breathing room if she saw my phone on the dresser. But not only did she tamper with the evidence, she went a step further. Within seconds, she typed in my code and played a voice message. Lisa's voice came from the phone's speaker suggesting that If I wasn't busy, I should stop by and let her suck my dick. When the message was over, Dana just stared at me, super pissed off.

"Look, Dana," I tried to explain. "I never did it. And how'd you get my voice message code?" I knew I had about thirty wrinkles in my forehead tryna figure that shit out.

"Fuck that, Hardy! I should throw your ass out!"

Here she goes with that shit again, I thought. "Dana," I

70

said, trying to grab her arm.

"Get off of me!" she shouted, snatching away. She turned around and stormed off to the bathroom. "I'm tired of your shit!'

"Baby," I said, following her. "I haven't spoken to that girl in months. I've been cut that girl off."

"Then what is she still calling you for?" she asked, brushing past me, heading back to the bedroom.

I shrugged, looking stupid as usual. "I don't know."

"She's a nasty fucking bitch, too. Talking about she wants to suck your dick. She's a fucking ho, Hardy. That's what you like? Hoes?

"Baby, I told you the other night that I'm through with all that. I'm done cheating." I reached for her arm.

"Hardy, you were lying then and you're lying now," she blurted out, attempting to snatch away again.

"Dana, I love you, girl," I confessed, not letting her break my grip. The words weren't one hundred percent true, but I knew it was what she wanted to hear. "How are we going to move on to the future if you keep tripping on the past?"

"Because phone calls like that one keep throwing the past back up in my face."

I took her in my arms, knowing she was weakening. "I'm not thinking about that girl," I assured her. "That's why I haven't called her in months."

"Hardy, you always say stuff like that," she said weakly.

My lips planted a soft kiss on her neck. "But I mean it this time," I whispered.

"Hardy, stop," she said, halfheartedly trying to fight her way out of my arms.

"I love you, Dana," I said even softer, kissing her on the neck again.

"No, Hardy, stop," she belted, this time raising her chin to give me better access to her neck.

"Let me have you tonight," I begged, slowly sliding my

hand underneath her nightgown and between her thighs. "Let me taste you."

"Hardy," she whispered, placing a hand over mine and rubbing herself through her panties. She raised her head and let out a soft moan.

"That's what I'm talking about," I said, feeling her begin to dampen her panties. "Let me eat that pussy for you." My words enticed her.

"Hardy, I'm still mad at you," she moaned, her eyes closed and her pussy slowly working itself against my fingers through her panties.

Ignoring what she just said, I slowly pushed her to the bed and laid her on her back .She tenderly bit her lip as I lifted her nightgown and removed her silver, silk panties. Her anticipation for what was coming was obvious as she spread her thighs and placed her right hand on my muscular shoulders, urging me to feast on her.

My face was now only a fraction of an in inch away from her furry tunnel, my eyes admiring every curve, and my nose taking in its glorious perfumed scent. I could feel her body quiver from head to pedicured toe, at just the feel of my warm breath against her most private place.

Dana placed another hand on my head and pressed herself towards my mouth. She wanted it desperately. "Eat it for me, Hardy," she whispered, arching her back, and spreading her legs as far as she could.

I gently took her clit into my mouth and sucked softly.

"Oh, shit,' she moaned, eyes still closed.

I moaned myself at the taste of her clit and for several minutes pleasured it beautifully, not allowing my attention to leave it for even a second. Dana gently reached underneath her nightgown and began to squeeze the now hardened nipples on her breasts. "Oh, Baby," she moaned. Then let out a long, yelp, "Ahhhhhhhhhhh, Hardy, damn!"

I knew what she wanted next and was more than ready

to give it to her. I wanted it too. "Stick your tongue in it," she begged.

My tongue slithered slowly out of my mouth and deeply into her steaming hot pussy as I spread its lips with my fingers. Repeatedly, I began to work it in and out, lapping up and swallowing all her juices.

Dana moaned and groaned even louder and began to twist and turn her nipples as if she were using them to find her favorite radio station. "Oh shit," she moaned.

I stuffed two fingers inside her wetness to accompany my probing tongue. They slid easily deep inside of her, massaging and exploring nonstop. Dana finally let go of her nipples and grabbed my head again. Thank God I had no hair the way she yanked and pulled, tryna take my head off. She tightly pressed herself against my face, now wanting all of my mouth and everything it had to offer. She began to work her hips, grinding and riding my face like rodeo, refusing to let me breathe.

I moaned appreciatively at the feel of my wife's assertiveness and began to munch on her pussy wildly. It had been so long since the last time I'd eaten her, I had almost forgotten how good she tasted. My mouth was now savoring every lick, enjoying every drop.

"Oh, God!" Dana screamed, finally turning my head loose and gripping the comforter, tightly gathering it into the palms of her hands.

The two of us knew what was coming next.

"Hardy!" she shouted as I began to let my mouth work on her insides like a machine, trying to get so deep in her stomach. It was a wonder I couldn't taste her ovaries.

"Oh, Baby, I love you!" she hollered with tears in her eyes as she gushed all over my tongue, and the trim line of my beard. She flowed like a water fountain then sprawled across the bed, nearly lifeless.

I scooted beside her with a wide grin. It had been a long

time since our bodies had been this close and this time it honestly felt good to be near her. Dana's cell phone began to ring on the dresser beside me. The two of us ignored it and let it go to voicemail. Seconds later, it began to ring again. It was weird how all of a sudden, every night she had an abundance of calls. It was also bizarre when I looked over at Dana and saw that my wife had begun to get nervous. My intuition kicked in, so I grabbed it without asking her.

"Hello," I said, answering the tiny beat-up phone.

The person on the other end was silent but I could hear some sort of slow music playing in the background.

"Hello," I said again.

CLICK! They hung up.

I pressed the end button and sat the phone back on the dresser. When I turned to Dana, she had either fallen asleep or was pretending like hell.

9···*Zaria*

For the last two years my love for teaching had evapo-rated from my heart. Somewhere along the way it became just a job and just a paycheck. More often than not, I dreaded going in to teach a bunch of young hoochies in training, and a bunch of young fatherless bastards who were going to grow up to be nothing more than drug dealers. Most of them were going to drop out by high school anyway. That's what my no-good father had always taught me. But over the past week just seeing Hardy's face each morning made it fun again. He gave me life. Just his presence alone gave me something to look forward to. It gave me something erotic to dream about at night, and some-thing wonderful to roll out of bed for every morning. I even re-alized over the past two weeks, I'd started treating my students better.

Wanting Hardy was an understatement. My body yearned for him so badly that lately my dildo got no rest. Whether lying on my back with my legs spread wide, or on my hands and knees stuffing myself from behind, I had to have it. Packs of batteries got ran through like water as I forced my toy to probe my pussy deeply every night, while imagining it was Hardy's super-sized dick pleasing me. My hips rode it mercilessly, creaming all over every inch of it and staining my sheets over and over again.

While my nights were filled with imaginary pleasure, during the day I flirted and teased every chance I got; striking up conversations with him in the teacher's lounge, saying good morning to him in the hall at the start of each school day, rocking my jeans extra tight and wearing make up, and always making it absolutely clear to him that I had no children or boyfriends. And just like expected he showed interest. Several times I'd turned around and caught his eyes locked on my ass as I swung it extra hard just for him. During our conversations he always seemed to find a reason to touch my hand. And no matter what time of day or how trying of a day, he always had a smile for me. Then today, finally, my flirting paid off. He asked me to go out on a date with him.

Immediately, I tried to play hard to get. " I'm not sure if I can break a prior commitment," I lied. Then I added, " I'll try."

"C'mon now. Just for about an hour. I know this nice restaurant on 44th."

I grinned. "Hardy, I'm trying to focus on me for a while, but I like you. So an hour will work. Are you seeing anyone?" I asked abruptly, catching him off guard.

"Does it matter? A girl like you could change all that. Besides, I haven't been around a woman in years who makes me smile like you do." He paused before leaving my presence, then rubbed the top of his slick, bare, head. "Text me your address, I'll be there by eight."

Those words stuck with me the rest of the day. Cloud nine couldn't explain where my head was during the drive home. I played slow CDs the entire trip and sang every word of every song with passion, embracing how it felt to have someone interested in me again. The feeling made me feel so alive that something about the air I breathed seemed different. It seemed sexy and filled me with a pleasure that I'd almost forgotten existed. I never wanted it to come to an end or fade.

Hardy was the only thing on my mind as I stopped on my way home to buy a new dress for my date. I usually waited to see the dresses Milan bought then copied her style. But things were different now. I was top dog, and the best looking guy in the school wanted me. As I tried on the short, black one-piece that made my breasts sit up high, I stared at myself in the store's full length mirror. "Yes," I mumbled, impressed with the firmness of my body. I imagined his eyes admiring my every curve. The thought of his good smelling cologne and muscular frame intoxicated me heavily; so heavily that my pussy moistened. I couldn't wait for tonight.

Nothing could get me down or piss me off this evening, I thought until an hour later, I opened my living room door and found Milan sitting with her sister on the couch. Something about their facial expressions didn't seem right. Something about them just made me feel like they were going to spoil my happiness with some unnecessary bullshit. It was obvious that I'd walked in the door during the middle of a conversation about me.

"Hey, Zaria," Milan said, standing up from the couch.

Her face was serious, and looked as if she'd been crying. She still hadn't gotten over the threat written on the mirror two weeks ago, and had barely left the apartment. But I understood why. It was crazy how she'd been staying in the house night after night, almost afraid to go out.

"What's up, Milan?"

"I'm glad you're home. I need to talk to you."

"Hey, Zaria," Tiffany, Milan's sister greeted. The two of them looked so much alike they could almost pass for twins.

The sight of Tiffany sent a silent rage through me. I had always felt jealous of her because over these past couple of years I had been more of a sister to Milan than her. I deserved to be a part of Milan's bloodline much more than Tiffany. But right now letting that shit get to me wasn't an option. I ignored the two of them and headed for my bedroom, hoping neither of them would follow me.

"Zaria, I need to talk to you."

Milan's voice annoyed the shit out of me. I didn't want to hear it right now. Without looking behind me I closed the door, hoping it would slam dead in her fuckin' face.

"Zaria," Milan called, catching the door with her hand and pushing it wide open before it could close. "I'm trying to talk to you."

My eyes zeroed in on her ring finger. Strangely it now had a ring on it. Nothing fancy, but it was still a ring. "What?" I finally answered, turning to her obviously aggravated.

Milan held out an envelope.

"What's this?" I asked, accepting it.

"It's November's rent. Sorry it's late. For two weeks now my agency said they sent checks but I never received them." She sighed, looking for me to accept the fact that her rent was now 14 days late. "Anyway, I'm moving out on the 30th of this month."

So that's what her and Tiffany were out there plotting on when I came in. What is it with haters? Why is it that when they see you happy, their first reaction is to destroy your happiness? Why can't they just live and let live?

"Brent helped me find a nice apartment. He thinks it's time I …"

"Milan, I don't care," I told her, interrupting whatever meaningless rambling she was planning on boring my ears with. "Fuck Brent!"

Milan stood in silence for moments then said, "Well, we're engaged."

"Who cares," I blasted. As I looked into that yellow bitch's eyes, something inside of me was now sincerely hoping that whoever left that threat for her would make good on it. It would probably serve her ass right. It would teach her to be more appreciative of the people like me who've looked out for her instead of betraying them like she's doing now.

"Okay, fine. Did you hear me say I was leaving on the 30th? That's two weeks from now."

"So. Were you expecting me to beg your ass to stay?" I asked. "Were you expecting me to cry or something?"

"I wasn't expecting any of that, Zaria," Milan finally said. "I was just being courteous. I just wanted to give you a thirty day notice."

"You mean two-week notice?" I said straightforwardly, making it clear to her that her presence was getting underneath my skin. "So now you've given it. Is there anything else?"

Milan could only look at me, wanting to say something but reluctantly decided it was best not to.

"I didn't think so," I told her. "Now could you please get the fuck out of my room? I have to get ready for my date."

"Zaria, I really don't understand the person you are sometimes," Milan said harshly.

"That's because fake bitches like you were never meant to understand real bitches like me," I said then slammed the door in her face. I began my chant, Smiley face…Smiley face… Can anyone see my Smiley face?

New Yorkers roamed through the night as Hardy, like a gentleman, opened the door of his tinted out black Tahoe, placed his hand at the bottom of my back, and helped me inside. That act bought him cool points with me immediately. Men just didn't do gentleman-like things like that anymore.

"You look beautiful tonight," Hardy complimented when he climbed into the driver's seat.

"Thank you," I returned, trying not to look into his exotic looking eyes, or at his thick lips for too long, knowing that they would hold me hostage so badly that I'd probably get tongue twisted and ruin the rest of the night. Being around him any other time never made me nervous but tonight was different.

"You like poetry?" he asked.

"Sure do."

"That's good. There's a spot in Harlem that I want to take you to tonight that has excellent poetry readings. It's on 125th street."

Is he serious, I thought to myself? Wow, A black man who actually likes poetry? This had to be a dream. "I'd like that," I told him.

"From there we can go out to dinner. What do you have the taste for?"

"Chinese."

"Good choice," he said with a smile. "Chinese is my favorite."

"So what else do you like doing?" I asked trying to make small talk.

"Spending time with my son."

"Aweeeeeee, that's so sweet," I told him, thinking about my own father, my only surviving parent. I'd never gotten the attention that Hardy seemed to give his son. Strangely, at that moment, I became envious of Terrell.

"Oh, and I love to work out when I get the time."

"I can tell," I joked, glancing at his bulging arms. *This nigga is sexy as hell*.

Robin Thicke's 'Sex Therapy' came over the radio causing me to nod my head slowly to it.

Hardy reached over and softly placed a hand underneath my chin, turning my face to his own. Now I was forced to look into his eyes. "You're a beautiful black woman," he whispered genuinely. "And those full lips, so damn sexy. I'm glad you allowed me to take you out tonight. I've wanted to ask you since the moment I saw you."

"Why'd you wait so long?" I asked, smiling at him. My

hormones were raging.

"I don't know. I guess I had to be sure you weren't going to say no. I haven't dated in a while and damn sho' don't like rejection."

His cologne was doing wonders to me. I twitched in my seat, switching up the way my legs were crossed about five times repeatedly. "Why would you think that?"

"Because you look like the type of woman who has men beating your door down constantly."

I laughed. "Trust me. I'm not that type of woman."

"I realized that. That's why I finally decided to ask. I like chill type women."

Our eyes began to stare into each other's for what seemed like forever. Hardy's eyes and lips began to stir something inside of me. They seemed to be calling my own to them like a moth to the most enticing of all flames. Before I knew it I was heeding their call. My eyes closed and my lips pressed against his softly. Their taste was unexplainable. I needed more. He obviously did too. My tongue slipped between his lips and tasted his mouth from top to bottom, sucking him like they were my last meal on earth.

Seductively, Hardy grabbed my hand and placed it over his crotch. I squeezed it and squeezed it until it became a huge bulge throbbing in his jeans. My hand unzipped him hurriedly and reached inside. My pussy throbbed as I wrapped my fingers around Hardy's dick causing him to moan.

God, it was huge.

Robin Thicke's rhythmic words of seduction were truly taking me over. My body wanted to give Hardy the most amazing sex therapy possible. He realized it as he pulled his lips away from mine and placed his hand inside my weave, guiding my face down to his dick. With no fear of choking on his thick massive pole, I took it deeply into the back of my throat. Within seconds I was sucking it wildly; slobbing on it and thickly covering it completely with every bit of saliva my mouth could manufacture.

"Suck that dick, Zaria," Hardy softly ordered with his head titled backward.

I accepted his command with pleasure. I placed my hands and knees into the passenger seat and my ass in the air so I could please him even better. Moans left my mouth as his hips began to fuck my mouth and throat.

"You like that dick, Zaria?" Hardy asked, pressing my head so far down on him that my lips were no more than a half an inch away from his huge balls. It surprised me at how skillfully I could take a dick that size. I hadn't had practice in a while.

I answered with a mumble as best I could; my mouth filled to capacity and more making it impossible to talk. Seconds later I could feel Hardy's hand squeezing my ass and pulling my dress up. There was no shame in me at all. Since the windows of his truck were tinted, I knew that no one could see inside. With only his fingers he slid my panties to the side and inserted his forefinger inside me making me moan with immense pleasure. The taste of his dick and the feel of his finger inside of me sent shudders throughout my body. I finally raised my head and looked into his eyes.

"I want you inside me," I begged.

Hardy obliged me by lifting me by my hips and placing me onto his lap. I was face to face with the tattoo near the bottom of his neck. It was weird, resembling a cross with some acronym I didn't understand. The plan was to ask about it, but before I knew it, he'd slid inside of my wet pussy. Easily. The fact that he didn't strap up first meant nothing to me. In fact, I wanted him raw. He was the kinda nigga who was worthy of me having his baby. A heavy groan left my lips at the feel of how wide his monster split me open. I could feel the head damn near inside of my chest but Hardy showed no mercy. He made my body take all of him, stroking himself inside of me wildly. My pussy had never taken a dick his size.

For what seemed like eternity, Hardy punished me. It was like we were fighting, but fucking. I loved it. I loved the pain as well as the pleasure. He fucked me in more positions I knew a truck could accommodate, making me cum several times like I'd never done before. Somewhere along the way we found our way to the backseat. He pounded me so hard my head was banging against the door. But I didn't care. All I wanted to do was make him cum like he'd done for me. I placed a hand underneath myself and in-between my thighs to softly grab a hold of his balls. With both of them in the palm of my hand, I slowly massaged them, knowing he wouldn't be able to hold out for too much longer. He couldn't. I knew it. I knew balls well…just hadn't practiced in a while. Within seconds he released inside of me. Damn, I wanna have his baby!

10 ··· *Hardy*

Eight a.m. Monday morning.

Windy and brisk.

My Tahoe hadn't even come to a complete stop in the school's parking lot before Zaria was up on it. I swear it was like the broad had just jumped out of the bushes or dropped from a tree. She just appeared out of nowhere like *The Phantom of The Opera* or something.

Since Friday night I hadn't spoken to her. There was no reason to. She gave up the pussy on the very first date. There was no reason to sweat her anymore, or answer her calls. Her pussy wasn't all that spectacular anyway; grade C- at the most. I've had a whole lot better. So obviously a possible second date wasn't anywhere on my agenda. If anything, she'd been relegated to the type of hoe I'd only call at about three in the morning when I couldn't get any of my other jumpoffs to come through for a nigga.

My phone had rung so much over the weekend I had to cut it off, hoping Zaria would get the message. Evidently she didn't. Every time I turned it back on, it was filled with her texts, voice messages, and missed calls. Damn, I hope she doesn't turn out to be one of them stalker hoes I see on *Lifetime*.

Dana was already clocking me; and now me clocking her, so I had to play things safe.

I slipped on my coat, grabbed my bag, and looked at Terrell in the back seat, sleeping. "Wake up, baby boy," I told him before opening the door of my truck; nearly hitting Zaria in the side, forcing her to stumble back.

Damn, bitch, back up, I thought to myself.

"Hey, Gerald," Zaria said happily, with her hands stuffed into the pockets of what looked like blue, work khakis. Her face was covered with more make up than usual, bringing to mind Joan Crawford in that old black and white movie, 'Whatever Happened to Baby Jane'. And that red lipstick was on blast. Ugh, I hated the way she dressed. No sense of style.

"What up, Zaria," I responded, rushing to open the back door for Terrell. He hopped out rubbing his eyes like he hadn't gotten any sleep in days. Not wanting him to witness any drama, I patted his back, ran my fingers through his curly hair and told him to run off to class without me. "I'll come pass your class in a few, Lil Man," I shouted, watching him run toward the building. "So what's up, Zaria," I asked again, hitting my alarm and making a B-line straight for the school.

"I really enjoyed Friday night," she said breathlessly, walking beside me step for step.

"Yeah, it was cool." I said, shrugging it off and now walking even faster. Last night's rain splashed from beneath my Timbos with each step.

"Is something wrong with your phone?"

"Huh?" I asked, as if I hadn't heard her question but knowing I had heard it loud and clear. Shit, the trip from the parking lot to the school never seemed this far before, I thought to myself.

"I tried calling you this weekend but I couldn't get through. Didn't you get my text messages or my voice messages?"

"My phone has been acting up lately," I said. The lie fell

from my lips without even being previously rehearsed. "It's been in the shop all weekend. I just got it back this morning."

"Did they fix it?"

All kinds of thoughts crossed my mind. If I say yes, she'll keep calling. If I say no, she may buy me a new one by mid-morning. Damn, why does it feel like we're walking further away from the school instead of towards it? "No," I lied. "It's still acting up. I'm probably just going to have to buy another one."

"That sucks."

I didn't say anything, although a fraction of a smile crossed my face. Zaria's pestering brought back a childhood memory of an old Bugs Bunny Loony Tunes cartoon. The one where the puppy nags Butch the bulldog to no end as they're walking down the sidewalk; the puppy repeatedly leaping back and forth over Butch and asking him thirty million questions.

"I was thinking we could go out tonight," she attempted. "My roommate won't be…"

"I've got plans." My answer cut her off in mid-sentence.

"Well, tomorrow night we…"

I stopped her again. "I've got to take my mother to Jersey tomorrow as soon as I leave here."

Zaria's disappointment showed on her face, leaving me feeling a little bad for her. But despite my sympathy, shrugging her off had to be done. We fucked and that was the end of it. Anything further was out of the question. She was now on my *no fly list*.

"I could ride with you," she suggested, "I need to meet her anyway."

Why can't this bitch get the fuckin' picture? I asked myself. "I won't have enough room," I firmly announced. "Some of her church group members are riding with us."

"Oh," she said, now even more disappointed.

Hopefully she got the hint. Before she could even form her lips to suggest another date, I sped up my pace, leaving her worrisome ass behind, directly in front of her classroom door. "I'll call you, Zaria," I said, lying over my shoulder, "I've got to stop by and hug Terrell before he starts his day, then get to my class."

Within minutes, I'd finally pulled the duck move on Zaria and made it to the lower grade hallway. My mind calmed now that I was free from my stalker. I stood near the front door watching Terrell chat with a few classmates, and taking a bunch of messy papers from his desk. His innocence always made me smile.

"Hey, Dad!" Terrell screamed excitedly after seeing me standing in the doorway.

"What's good, Little Man?" I asked. "You awake now?"

He simply laughed.

Seeing my son's eyes light up every time he sees me never grows old. From the moment he was born until now it has been the highlight of my days, let alone my life. My faults are numerous but if I've ever prided myself on anything, it has definitely been trying my hardest to be a better father to my son than my deadbeat-ass daddy was to me.

Terrell quickly stepped out of the classroom into the crowded hallway and quickly began to bombard my ears with highlights of his plans for the day. Hearing him show any sort of enthusiasm about learning always excited me. And it was obvious that since my transfer to his school Terrell had grown more enthusiastic about his education. I just hoped it would last throughout elementary and well past high school. Seeing him drop out would break my heart. And I was willing to do anything to prevent that.

As Terrell spoke so fast, not even finishing one sentence before he started another, his teacher, Ms. Ellis stepped out into the hallway and stood beside him, placing a hand on his shoulder. My eyes slyly and quickly traveled up and down her youthful looking body, admiring every curve like the design of a new Lamborghini. Knowing that I should've been ashamed of myself for lusting over my son's twenty-two year old teacher, it couldn't be helped. I'm a man first. Besides, it wasn't like I hadn't caught her doing the same to me. It was always obvious to me when a woman was feeling me. Just like Zaria before her, she had also started striking up conversations with me in the teacher's lounge and throwing an extra switch in the rhythmic sway of her perfectly thick hips when she knew I was looking. She'd bought me lunch a couple of times. We were now even calling each other by our first names. I'd known from the first day I started here that drawing her interest would be easy. And just like every other woman I set out for, she proved to be predictable.

As the three of us stood in front of her classroom talking about Terrell's academic performance it was obvious to me that she wanted to ask me for a date. Her enticing smile and sly looks whenever Terrell wasn't looking were a little more extreme than usual. But out of respect for Terrell, she chose not to ask. I knew that if it was going to happen, I would have to initiate it myself. Sending Terrell back to his seat, I stepped a little bit closer to his teacher and leaned my shoulder against the wall.

"Wanda, I was thinking," I said, using her first name and no longer wanting to beat around the bush about where I wanted to take things with her. That pussy was calling me. "Could we go out to a movie or something this weekend?"

She leaned against the doorway of her classroom. "A movie, huh?" she asked.

"Yeah," I said, placing my thumbs in the pockets of my Rocawear jeans. "Maybe after that we can go to a poetry reading; whatever you want. You like Chinese?"

"Gerald, I admit that I like you but you're a married man," she said; both her face and voice showing uncertainty about fucking with a nigga like me. "I'm not sure if that would be a good idea. People around here talk." She glanced at my ring finger, but I was one step ahead. It was bare.

Accepting no for an answer wasn't going to happen. From her ear length hair, double D breasts, and an ass even Jennifer Lopez couldn't compete with, I had to get a taste of it all. My tongue slowly slid between and across my lips as I decided to step my game up and hit this hoe with some well seasoned game. As my mouth opened, Zaria appeared beside us out of nowhere just like this morning with a look on her face of indescribable anger.

"Zaria," I shrieked, surprised at her sudden presence.

Zaria's eyes narrowed but stared through me with undisputed scorn. "Everything okay?" I asked, trying to get a read on her and hoping she'd answer. Her stare was creeping me the fuck out. "Class is about to start."

Zaria remained silent. Her nostrils flared and her breasts repeatedly rose up out the tight v-neck top that should've never been worn to a school. With every breath she took, her fists clenched at her sides so tightly it was a wonder that her nails hadn't drawn blood from her palms. Beginning to feel uncomfortable, I attempted to introduce Wanda. "Zaria, I'm not sure if you two have met. This is…"

"I know who this bitch is already," Zaria finally spoke, her words dripping with spite. Her gaze stayed locked on me as if there was no one else in the crowded hallway but me and her.

"Excuse me?" Wanda gasped in disbelief while stepping away from the doorway and placing her hands on her hips.

The fact that Zaria had just come at Wanda like that had me in shock. I didn't know what to say.

"Zaria, I don't know what your problem is. But my name is not, Bitch. It is Ms. Wanda Ellis," she said, looking Zaria in the face as if she were going to knock her ass a few feet if Zaria didn't fix her attitude.

Zaria dropped her tote bag and stepped to Wanda, leaving no more than a half inch between their faces. "You are a BITCH." She said, placing heavy emphasis on her chosen name for Wanda. "The reason why you are a BITCH is because I chose to call you a BITCH. You fit the description of a BITCH. So I see you as being nothing more than a BITCH. Now take it however the fuck you want to take it, BITCH!"

Passing children stopped and stared in awe as Zaria rolled her eyes, popped her neck, pointed her finger in Wanda's face, and used the word bitch as if she were standing in a bar full of drunken soldiers. Even the students in Terrell's class began to crowd the doorway. I panicked, not wanting my son to see any of it.

Out of fear of losing her job Wanda backed down. "Zaria, this is not the proper place to do this. I…"

"Awwweeeee, contraire, Bitch!!" Zaria cut her off, now raising her voice. "You were just all up in my man's face. It was the right place for that, right?"

My face was flushed with embarrassment, looking around at the gathering children, parents, and teachers. I hated to be a punk, but I needed to jet. I peeked inside the class again and saw that Terrell was now one of the nine students crowding the doorway, watching the show.

"This is the perfect place to tell you to stay the fuck away from my man!" Zaria continued.

My eyes bucked open like Scooby Doo. Her man, I asked myself? What the hell was she talking about? She was the white girl that Kyle and Mario were teasing me about all over again. This had gone on long enough. I wedged my body between Zaria and Wanda.

"Zaria," I said, placing my hands on her shoulders. "You really need to calm down."

"No, Gerald!" she screamed, snatching away from me. "You tell her about us! Tell this bitch!"

"What do you mean *us*? What are you talking about, Zaria?"

"I'm talking about *you and me*, Gerald," she said passionately, now calming just as quickly as she'd snapped in the first place. She looked into my eyes like we were newlyweds.

"I'm talking about you and me," she continued; her voice now a caring whisper. "I want to make things between you and me work. I really do. "

My body jerked from her hands. This broad is straight cucko for Coco Puffs, I thought to myself. "We went out. That was it. Zaria, there's no you and me," I assured her in front of Wanda and about three co-workers who were now laughing like crazy. I then made eye contact with Terrell.

"Fuck this Mickey and Minney Mouse bullshit!" she shouted.

"Zaria, not in front of the kids, "I warned softly.

"Go back to your seats," she roared, even jerking her body and balling her fists as if she would hit them if they didn't obey.

Wanda said nothing. She could only look on in amazement.

Zaria darted into the classroom when she heard all the complaining inside. "And shut up!" she shouted, taking over Wanda's class. "Turn to page fifty-four in your math book and do the whole page." Steam seeped from her nose.

"We already did it," a little girl chimed.

Zaria was headed back to deal with me and Wanda when she stopped three feet away from me. She turned to the children and spoke slowly over her shoulder, with venom in her tone. "Well, take out a piece of paper and write, I am an idiot sixty-five times. I'm serious!" she shouted. "Do it!"

Withing seconds, she managed to switch back to the calm Zaria I'd met my first day on the job. "Gerald, I know she's a beautiful woman. But she can't give you what I can. Don't let her fool you," she told me, pointing to Wanda." It's me you're supposed to be with. She knows it. That's why she's trying to come in between us."

It was like she wasn't hearing me. She paused then gave Wanda another evil stare. Zaria placed a hand in mine. "I can treat you so much better. You'll see. I promise."

"Zaria, stop!" I ordered, snatching my hand away.

"Gerald, we can make it through this. Baby, I swear."

"Please stop!" I shouted, finally fed up. "Stop it right now. This is crazy."

Zaria looked as pitiful and brokenhearted as a child who'd woken up Christmas morning and realized there was absolutely nothing under the tree for her. "But…But you made love to me," she reasoned weakly. "We made love to each other."

Embarrassment was no longer the word for how I felt. It was somewhere beyond as Zaria laid our personal business out in front of our co-workers like that. Thank God Wanda had finally closed her classroom door so the children could no longer hear.

"Zaria, I don't know what you're talking about." I lied.

Zaria shook her head. "Gerald, what do you mean?'

"I mean you should stop acting like this in front of all these people."

Zaria stared at me in utter silence for several moments, leaving me nervous at how she would react next. Suddenly, she raised her head to the ceiling, opened her mouth, and let off an ear piercing scream so loud everyone in the hallway grimaced and covered their ears. Its volume was the loudest thing I'd ever heard come from a human being before in my entire life. She held the torturous sounding note for what felt like an eternity and then some. I thought she was going to burst my eardrums or even set off the fire extinguishers. When she finally stopped, her eyes sent chills down my spine as they sent burning daggers of her hatred through me. For moments she just stood there shaking; her lips trembling as the entire hallway stood silent; their attention focused on her like a sideshow freak. Suddenly, Mr. Carter, the principal, came blaring down the hall wondering what all the commotion was about. Awe shit, I thought, I didn't want to lose my job. Finally, Zaria retreated. She snatched her tote bag from the floor and stormed passed me. But not without

parting words whispered in my ear…
"THIS ISN'T OVER."
Just like that she left the building as I heard the principal tell someone to put a substitute teacher in her class for the day.

11 · · · *Zaria*

My body wouldn't stop shaking. And the tears wouldn't stop running from my eyes, blurring my vision. They, along with mascara rolled down my cheeks so heavily they stained every page in the notebook I wrote on. Sweating and dressed in only my Walmart brand bra and panties, I rocked back and forth on my bed with my legs spread wide open and my notebook wedged between them. Beside me and around me sat the infamous DVD, ink pens, and dozens of crumpled up pages. I'd been trying to regain focus for hours, but couldn't shake what had happened two days ago between me, Wanda, and Hardy.

THE VOICES! This time it wasn't just the one that I hated filling my head with noise. There were more; each taunting me and teasing me to no end. My mind over ran with chatters, echoes, and screams. None of which could be controlled. They had never been this bad, not even in my years of despair. My fists crashed against the sides of my skull, trying to make them stop, or at least quiet down enough for me to concentrate. But they only grew louder.

I wiped the tears from my eyes and began to write on a new page of the notebook, hoping my tears would cease long enough for me to finish my hit list. With hands trembling so hard my writing looked hideous and unreadable to anyone but me, I wrote Hardy's name first. Lord knows just seeing his name made my eyes well up again. He had my heart already. My mind, body, and soul were his for the taking despite what had happened between us. The tears were returning but I refused to let them fall this time. Instead my fingers gripped the pen even tighter than before and I began to follow Hardy's name with more: Wanda, Jamal, Brent, Jasmine, Mia, Damon, my father, Jessie, and countless others who'd betrayed me in the past. Then I created two extra lines, leaving them blank; one purposefully left for Milan. For now, she was etched in my brain.

Each slash and swipe of my pen was swift, liberating me somehow. Seeing the red pen bleed each name from its tip gave me a feeling of power; knowing that I controlled the ultimate destiny of each person placed to paper. The only thing that would top this feeling would be seeing each name on the list crossed out one by one after I made each of their final destinys become a reality. Sadly, even they didn't know what was coming.

Although I'd been trying to tolerate Milan since the day she'd been threatened, more and more my hate for her had been growing inside of me like a fetus. The fact that she would think I would allow her to use me up then marry Brent pissed me off. What the fuck made her think that she was so special, as if the sun rose and set every morning on her ass?

Fuck her! I shouted, hoping she could hear me from the other room. What I wanted to do to Milan far exceeded everyone else on my list. My yearning for her pain and suffering was on its own level. That's why I chose to keep her name only in my mind. My focus was now locked and loaded on two others.

My eyes rose to the very top of the list again and stared at Hardy's name. Since the school had suspended me for two weeks I hadn't seen him in a few days. I knew it was a part of Mr. Carter's plot to keep us apart. He was probably rooting for that freak, Wanda. But I missed Hardy so much. And I knew it wasn't too late to make things work between us. I just needed to apologize to him. If he only knew that just seeing his name scribbled on a piece of paper made my heart race like a school-girl each time the boy she had a crush on came near her. He just needed to rethink what he'd done to me. And we'd be okay. I slung the pen, grabbed the phone, and called him. I needed his voice. I needed to hear the man I wanted to make the love of my life, even if it was only his answering machine. The fact that I'd called him at least thirty times over the past few days should have let him know that.

"Hello," Hardy finally answered his voice full of annoy-ance.

Thank God. "Hardy, Sweetheart," I said quickly, hoping he wouldn't hang up on me. "I'm so sorry. If you give me an-other chance, I swear I'll…"

"Zaria, don't call me anymore," Hardy said plainly. "I mean it."

"But, Baby I-"

"Don't call me anymore!" he shouted and hung up.

At the sound of the dial tone my entire world crashed down around me. Tears began to fall again. I told his black ass I was sorry. Why couldn't he forgive me? I'd bet it was Wanda in his ear. That bitch got into his head and turned him against me. I know she did. My pen scurried up to her name on the paper as I began outlining her name, and drawing bullet holes around each letter.

My eyes then dropped to the DVD. I had to watch it. I snatched it from the bed, slid it into the player, and sat back on the bed. As it began to play my arms wrapped around myself for comfort, a comfort that I had always longed for so much of my life and had never received. I rocked back and forth, seeing myself on the television screen at age 14. I shook my head and closed my eyes tightly, knowing the video's every sound and scene from beginning to end like an average person watching a movie they'd seen dozens of times before. But for me it wasn't a movie…it was one of the most shameful moments of my life.

As the tape's sounds and voices began to fill my ears, my mind dragged me emotionally kicking and screaming back to that moment. Oh, God, my body started to feel so, so dirty as I remembered the knock at the door and knowing what was waiting for me on the other side. My 14 year old body trembled so violently in fear and unspeakable shame.

"Answer the door!" the man on the couch ordered me, knowing the torture the knock at the door meant for me. He grabbed the video camera, took a sip of Jack Daniels, and leaned back into the couch as if I meant nothing to him.

My heart broke as I begged him like I'd done so many times before. "Pleaseeeee, don't make me do this. I promise I'll be a good girl. Please don't let him in."

"Open the door!" he shouted, scaring me half way to death.

Tears rolled down my young cheeks as I made my way to the door and opened it, my heart full with the feeling of disloyalty. How could he subject me to what what was coming after he promised so many times that he loved me and that he would never make me do these horrible things again? How could he? I thought I was his little princess.

The man who'd been knocking staggered inside the small apartment smelling heavily of cheap liquor and cigarette smoke. My stomach turned as I watched the screen remembering that awful stench. All of them always seemed to reek like they'd never taken a bath. Ever.

I remembered staring out into the night, wanting to escape into it, ignoring the frigid winter chill blowing mercilessly through my nightgown. I stared past the run down projects' endless concrete and clothes lines, wanting so more than anything else in the world to run and leave that place behind forever. But for some reason my feet stayed frozen just like each time before.

"Close the door, you dumb bitch!" the man with the camera shouted. "Are you trying to heat the whole fucking neighborhood?"

I saw myself on the screen rush over to shut the door. With a broken heart I did what I was told. As the door closed, behind me I could hear both men negotiating a price for me like I was nothing. I didn't want to turn around and face them. Seeing their faces would only hurt me more than I was already feeling. God, I wished I could've been anywhere but there. I finally felt a hand on my shoulder. It was calloused and covered with thick engine grease like he'd been working on a car before he arrived. It smelled so awful. He turned my body to him. I looked into his sunken red eyes, hating them immediately.

"Yeah," he moaned, eyeing me lustfully from head to toe like I was a grown woman. "I like her."

The way he looked at my young body made me feel so filthy, that even now at twenty-nine, I felt the same way just watching it. But I knew that no amount of showers would ever be able to wash away the filthy feeling from my flesh. It would embed itself in my pores forever.

"Come on, girl," he ordered, dragging me across the room towards the couch. "I ain;t got all night."

When we reached the couch, he turned me around and smacked me across the face so hard my entire body turned and fell across the arm of the couch. I could feel blood dripping from my nose. Through blurred vision I saw the two wrinkled twenty dollar bills he'd paid for me sitting on the end table beside the couch. He grabbed both my legs and flipped me over on my back, smacking me across the face again.

"Daddy!" I screamed as the stranger forced himself between my legs and began to unbuckle his belt. "He's hurting me!" I shouted. "Please help me, Daddy!"

I would've had a better chance at calling for my mother. But the fact was, she was already dead. Suicide was her claim to fame. She'd died when I was just ten years old. I remembered that night clearly...the night that I was now watching on the television. I especially remembered how my dad remained silent.

"Oh, you're one of those sluts who like to scream while she's getting it, huh?" The stranger asked while pulling himself free from his pants, turned on. "Well, I'm going to give your little sweet ass something to really scream about."

I turned my face to see my father standing at the door with camera aimed directly at my pain-filled face. He smirked at my humiliation while tightly squeezing the crotch of his pants in twisted enjoyment of seeing his own child suffer. A fraction of a second later everything went dark as the stranger on top of me slammed a pillow over my face and shoved every inch of himself inside of me raw, forcing me to let out a scream muffled by the pillow.

The phone beside me rang, bringing me back to current reality. I opened my eyes to see the television screen directly in front of me. The sight of my innocence and childhood being torn away from me so savagely sent anger blazing through me like lightning bolts. I answered the phone on the second ring. "WHAT!!!"

"Can I speak to Milan?" Brent's voice asked.

My blood boiled like a pot of Ramen Noodles at the sound of his voice.

"She's not here," I lied, knowing Milan was in the living room watching television and packing boxes.

"Zaria, stop playing with me. I know she's there. She's afraid to leave the house."

As my eyes continued to witness the violation of my body on the television screen, Brent's voice began to add fuel to a building rage inside of me. "Look!" I shouted into the phone at him. "You're nobody that important to me that I need to lie to. If I said she's not here, she's not here! You got that, Bee?"

"Zaria, why do you have to be so childish?"

My breathing accelerated. My rage built even more; all

while still watching the screen.

"No matter what you do, Zaria," Brent continued, "Milan and I are going to be together."

I quickly began to rock back and forth again.

"The two of us are eventually going to get married."

The screams coming from my lungs on the television as the stranger continued to brutally molest me finally set me off. I stood quickly, tightened my grip on the phone, and let loose on Brent.

"I'm going to cut your fuckin' dick off," I began through gritted teeth.

"What?" he asked.

"You heard me!" I said, now louder and beginning to pace the room. "I'm going to cut your fucking dick off, you fake ass nigga! Then I'm going to shove it in your mouth and watch you choke on it as you die!"

"Zaria, you're crazy."

"I'm going to kill you, Brent! I'm going to kill you! You hear me!"

"Zaria, whatever," Brent said and hung up the phone on me.

I slung the phone against the wall, shattering it into dozens of pieces. My head began to echo with voices again, each shouting the names on my hit list and why each of them should die. They each had hurt me in their own way. I was tired of hurting.

"Take it, slut," the perverted stranger bellowed from the television, taking far too much enjoyment in killing the innocence of a fourteen year old child.

I turned the TV off and quickly got dressed. Within minutes I was dashing out of my apartment building into the street. There were two stops on my list for the night. One was my father. I had to pay that creep a visit.

12···Zaria

My father's house…always dark, always a draft. Strangely, I chose his shower to wash away the stench of what I'd just done. How ironic. It was the same two bedroom apartment that I'd grown up in, the one that caused me so much pain. And now I'd done the unthinkable, and rushed here for cover.

I'd taken a life and was now in the presence of the man who'd essentially taken mine. I'd never been sure what it was, but something about seeing him appear to be on death row calmed me. His face was sunken in and his pores reeked of a nauseating mixture of constant cigarette smoke and cheap corner store wine. He always reminded me of Wesley Snipes' father on the movie Sugar Hill.

I'd started coming back around him when I was 21, despite Aunt Lisa's constant forbiddance. Even though we usually only sat in silence, him watching television and me staring at him, something about being in his presence always made me feel like the world outside didn't exist. To most, it sounded sick and backwards but it made perfect sense to me. Our silence together seemed to comfort me. But forgiveness for what he'd done to me would never be a possibility. That would absolutely never happen. But for some reason, I couldn't let him go totally.

Something inside me needed to keep him around.

    The couch's springs shrieked loudly as I sat down across from his chair and sat the black trash bag beside my foot, stuffed with my blood soaked clothes, and the gun I'd just stolen from the hallway closet. Even though I'd cleaned myself up good, subconsciously I smelled blood. I began to nervously ring out my hands and rub my palms against my thighs, as if trying to make absolute sure that the blood they were covered with an hour ago was gone. The murderous stench still remained in my nostrils. It would never go away. I knew it. Those types of stenches were meant to haunt a person forever. I knew it from experience.

    For moments, just like always I just sat there in his living room thinking, wishing, reminiscing, whatever came to mind in utter silence. Finally, I raised my head and looked at him. The television illuminated his face and every scar the heartless cruelty of the streets had given it. Years and years of high dosages of medications and heroin use had shriveled my father into nothing more than a grotesque gathering of skin and bones, making his clothes dangle loosely from his body like dead skin. His arms were covered with numerous tiny black scabs, each his poisonous addictions' entrance way to his soul. His legs were so skinny, mostly from malnutrition. All he ever ate were grits, and sardines. His eyes were bloodshot and buried deeply into his skull. And his skin was a horrendous shade of brown that looked hard. Hard like the outer coating of a dehydrated tree trunk.

    The tiny shoebox-sized apartment that welfare paid for every 1st of the month was cluttered with used dusty furniture collected from streets and piss filled alleys. It smelled of urine and the cigarette smoke in its walls were deeply stained top to bottom. In the kitchen dirty dishes overflowed from the sink and dozens of opened empty cans lined the table and countertop, creating a playground for what looked like dozens of scurrying roaches.

As my father sat in his chair in front of the television with his legs crossed exhaling the smoke from his Newport to the ceiling and looking so dazed and fragile he could barely hold his head up, I stared at him with a fury burning brightly inside of me. I hated him. I wanted to bash his fucking brain in.

I thought about the many shows I used to watch as a kid; *Leave It To Beaver, Father Knows Best, The Cosby Show*, etc, etc. Why couldn't I have had one of those dads? Why couldn't I have lived a life as innocent and carefree as their children? Why did my childhood have to be so fucked up? Why did he have to take it all away from me? Why?

Suddenly, my eyes dropped to the specs of blood on my Reeboks. I'd have to get rid of them immediately. The memory of what I'd done before I got to my father's suddenly made my body shake from the inside out. Its screams played inside my head in quick flashes, each always starting just before the previous one ended. Fear silently took hold of me. Did I really do it? Did I really go through with it? Or was my mind simply playing a cruel trick on me?

I looked at my father again, wondering if he had forgotten I was sitting in front of him. Did he even realize I was now wearing his sweats and an old t-shirt that belonged to him? Suddenly my anger towards him turned into sympathy for the shell of a man he'd become. Memories of how strong, handsome, and caring he was before the sickness took over his life; the days before he became a monster. I wanted to cry but wouldn't allow myself. Instead, I asked him a question I'd always wanted the answer to but could never bear to ask.

"Dad," I said with spite in my voice. An old episode of *Sanford and Son* played on the black and white television to the side of us. "Is it true that mom killed herself because she hated us?" I'd heard the rumor many times from family after she blew her own head all over the kitchen wall with my father's chrome 38 revolver when I was only ten years old. "Is it true?" I repeated.

He ignored me and just plucked his ashes in my direction onto the floor.

I still remembered my mother after all these years; how beautiful she was, the smell of her cooking, the feel of the comb running through my hair when she combed it. She was so amazing to me, the female version of what my father used to be before he started hurting me.

I missed the Sundays we spent in church as a family, the countless trips to the fair and the Amusement Park, and the rides around the hood in our Cadillac. Those memories always brought a smile to my face. But at the same time, knowing they were only memories of a life I would never be able to live again sometimes filled me with a pain I wouldn't wish on anyone. Sometimes I wondered if my father ever felt that pain or if he even cared. After all, he kept no pictures on his walls of her, or even me for that matter.

My father remained silent, still looking like he'd disconnected himself from reality. He never went out much since he thought the world was against him. And of course, no friends. Not even one.

"Is it true?" I prodded.

No answer. He only took another hit of his cigarette, swayed drunkenly in his chair, and dropped his head to his lap, leaving me to wonder if he was riding the effects of his last hit or if he was simply to ashamed to face me.

"Dad, please talk to me," I pleaded. "I need answers."

Still, only silence.

"Why did you do those things to me when I was a kid?" I asked. My body felt dirty at the thought of those foul memories. I could still smell the stench of each of those perverts' bodies as they lay on top of me.

"You already know," he finally answered, his head still in his lap and a cloud of cigarette smoke swirling over his head.

"What do you mean?"

"You and me are the same, Princess," he said through

slurred words, still sluggishly swaying in his chair so far back and forth I thought he'd fall to the floor any minute.

Hearing my father call me, Princess, both angered me and broke my heart at the same time. It had been an eternity since the last time he'd called me that. On the few occasions when I would visit him, he acted as if he barely knew my name.

"You and me suffer from the same disease," he continued. "It runs in the family."

"What are you talking about?" I asked, now beginning to grow angry and impatient.

"You know what I'm talking about," he said and snickered as if amused by my ignorance.

I leapt from the couch and snatched a hold of his heavily stained t-shirt. "Stop speaking in fucking riddles!" I screamed in his face. "What are you talking about?"

Silence.

"What the hell are you talking about!?" I screamed again, jerking him from the chair so hard he fell to the floor. "Tell me, damn it!"

He stopped chuckling and became saddened as if his heart itself had begun to hurt just as badly as my own. Tears started to fall from his eyes. "I never wanted to hurt you," he whimpered. "The voices…The voices in my head wouldn't leave me alone. I couldn't control them anymore after your mother killed herself. They made me hurt you. They told me to do it. They wouldn't stop."

"You're not making sense," I lied. He was starting to make plenty of sense. I just didn't want to believe it. I knew what 'the voices' meant. But hearing the man that I had once looked up to say that he suffered from them too was something I didn't want to digest.

"Zaria," he continued. "Schizophrenia runs on my side of the family. It's always been a part of me. There are many different forms and many different names and levels. We're not normal," he announced cautiously. "We're sick, Princess."

If the intent was to alarm me, he'd succeeded. I stood and slowly backed away from him. Oh God, no. I hated that word: Schizophrenia. Just hearing it always reminded me that something was wrong with me no matter how much I denied it. Although I'd been diagnosed with psychosis as a teenager, it was still considered a form of Schizophrenia.

"The voices…You have them too, don't you?" he asked. "Your Aunt Lisa told me you were sick. I didn't want to believe it at first but the signs were there. They'd always been there."

The trips to the psychiatrists and doctors began to play in my head. I'd blocked them out for the past year, hoping they'd never return. I'd tricked myself into believing that they had never existed.

"Zaria, I cursed you," my father confessed. "I'm so sorry."

I wanted to scream.

"I knew I should've gotten help," he rambled on. "I should have been a good father. I should have protected you. But I let the disease beat me."

The memories of flushing bottles of medication down the toilet rushed my brain nonstop. My father's admission had awakened a demon in me that I'd attempted to hide and forget. I'm really sick, I told myself.

Out of the blue, my father fell. And my reflexes did nothing to help. I now switched places with him, me staring into the air, and him trying to talk to me. He crawled to me on his hands and knees and grabbed a hold of my leg. "Baby, it's not too late," he pleaded. "We can go see a doctor together. We can go tomorrow."

He disgusted me.

"Can we go tomorrow, Princess?"

"Fuck you," I said spitefully while snatching my leg away from him. "It's because of you, Jessie, that I have court in the morning. It's because of you, Jessie, that some muthufucka named Jamal is trying to tell the world some foul shit about me.

You don't even deserve to be called father anymore," I ended with a strong kick to his chest. "I got something for his ass and you, too."

He looked up from the floor at me like an innocent child. His regrets were many and evident. "Oh God, what did I create?" he asked as I headed out the door.

I walked into the apartment expecting to see Milan still lying on the couch watching television, or asleep. It was half past midnight and lately she'd glued herself to the couch 'til the wee hours of the morning. Instead, I was greeted by darkness and silence. As I closed the door and took a step towards my room my foot bumped into something hard. And big. I flicked on the light to see boxes of Milan's stuff stacked beside the door, surprising me. She wasn't supposed to be moving out for another couple of days. Why was she packing so early? And why did she wait for me to leave before she did it?

I grabbed the lamp from the cocktail table and slung it against the wall, sending shards of glass flying everywhere. Before the final shard hit the floor my hands were already raising the flat screen television over my head. I tossed it into the dining room, sending it loudly crashing through the dining room table and shattering on the floor. Then with a swing of my forearm, I sent Milan's computer flying against the wall. Within minutes the entire apartment looked worse than the last time, thanks to me.

A smile crept across my face as I placed my hands on my hips and proudly surveyed the damage, knowing that I'd outdone myself this time. There was no way Milan would leave me after seeing all of this. She'd definitely think that it wasn't safe to leave me alone after seeing that the person who'd destroyed the apartment the first time had come back.

I rushed to my bedroom, grabbed the shoebox from underneath my mattress, and pulled out Milan's mail. My fingers trembled as I quickly sifted through every envelope, making sure that I had stolen each check the modeling agency had sent her so she wouldn't have money to move with. She would have to stay now since there was no more Brent, and no one else to finance her move. The circumstances I'd created wouldn't let her leave even if she wanted to.

Pleased with myself, I turned out all of the lights in the apartment, sat on the glass covered floor Indian style beside the living room door, and waited alone in the darkness for Milan to return. I had a bone to pick with her.

13 · · · *Zaria*

The court results had fire erupting through my nose. I was angry. Now furious. My foot patted on the floor of the elevator impatiently trying to calm down. The trip from the lobby to my floor seemed like forever today and it was annoying the shit out of me. Any other day I could make it upstairs with no interruptions. But today every muthafuckin floor had someone wanting to get on or get off. God, it was pissing me off.

I wasn't in the fucking mood for any 'hellos' or any 'how are you doings. I wasn't in the mood for any conversation. And I surely wasn't in the mood for being polite. I knew that's what the fat guy to my left wanted from me. He'd been grinning since he got on the elevator, waving, and then finally said, "Hello."

I rolled my eyes and crossed my arms. I wanted the entire world to kiss my ass; especially men. I hated them. Every one of them. The nerve of that male chauvinist ass judge, I thought to myself, fuming silently and watching number after number light up on the elevator's wall. That son of a bitch believed every word Jamal said in that courtroom today. Jamal's lying, cheating ass made me out to be the monster, and that judge believed every word of it. How fucking stupid can one person be? The fact that Jamal had broken my heart meant nothing. The fact that he'd lied and cheated meant nothing. The fact that he'd stopped taking my calls, leaving me to wonder why meant nothing; not a damn thing. Fuck my feelings, right? All that mattered was Jamal's punk ass.

When the judge said that I had to stay fifteen feet away from Jamal from now on or face charges, I wanted to explode. That black ass nigga wasn't the president of the United States. What the fuck made him so special that I couldn't go near him? So what, I destroyed his car. He had the shit coming. So what, I'd called him a lot. He should've been man enough to speak to me and let me know why he didn't want me anymore. All he had to do was be a man.

He'll get his. I swear he will, I thought to myself as I stepped off the elevator and headed for my apartment. The door was opened slightly. I pushed it completely open and walked inside the still demolished apartment to see Milan's father coming from her bedroom carrying a large box of clothes in his arms. Milan was sitting on the couch crying while Tiffany sat beside her holding her in her arms.

I bum-rushed my girl. "Where the hell were you last night?" My face was frowned up like some Mike Tyson shit. "I stayed up until four am waiting for you. Where were you? Where were you?" I repeated.

Milan lifted her swollen, tear-filled eyes toward me. Her hair was uncombed and she was wearing no make-up. Dressed in the same clothes she was wearing when I saw her laying on the couch last night, she looked terrible.

"What's going on?" I asked.

"He's dead, Zaria," Milan said through falling tears.

"Who?" I asked.

"Brent, Zaria! Someone killed him last night!" she screamed hysterically, making Tiffany hold her tighter.

I'd honestly forgotten about what I'd done last night but it came back quickly. The repeated plunges of my knife deep into that bastard's chest filled my head. I wanted to smile but fought with everything inside of me not to.

"Oh my God," I whispered, pretending to be shocked by the news.

Tiffany placed her head against Milan's while still holding her. The two began to rock back and forth like crazies in the crazy house. And it was pissing me off. I wanted to know where Milan had been and why was she leaving earlier than promised. Had she been with another man that fast? Another man she could jointly betray me with? Well, I'd kill him, too.

"What happened?" I asked, as if I had absolutely no idea. I deserved an Oscar.

"Someone stabbed him," Milan said while burying her face in her hands. "They stabbed him in his chest ten times."

I pictured my murder scene in my head; Brent's body covered in blood, the room's entire atmosphere enough to gag a maggot. The thought of him dying so brutally at my own hands pleasured me even more than sex. Instantly, I began to get wet.

Milan's father picked up another box and walked out the door, stepping over broken glass and tossed furniture along the way. He never acknowledged me, nor did he even say a word. His gaze remained focused on both the boxes and door, almost like a trained robot.

"Do the police have any suspects?" I asked, wanting to see if they were possibly on to me, although I was sure they weren't. I made sure that no one saw me grab the spare key from underneath Brent's doormat and go inside his apartment. And no one saw me come out. I replayed every detail of the murder thru my mind one last time, waiting for Milan to respond. But she was too distraught to speak. She could only cry.

"No," Tiffany finally answered for her.

"Did anyone see or hear anything?" I asked.

Tiffany shook her head.

"Wow," was all I could whisper while shaking my own head in false disbelief, trying to sound genuinely surprised by

Brent's horrific death.

The memory of straddling Brent in his bed last night, screaming, "Bleed, bitch, bleed!" as I stuck him over and over again was almost giving me an orgasm. I'd caught his ass perfectly. He was asleep when I crept into his bedroom so he never saw me coming. When he finally saw me, it was too late. That wide eyed look on his face was priceless.

Tiffany began to look around at the apartment while I stood in a mini daze. "Zaria, what happened here?" she asked.

"I don't know," I lied. "Someone broke in and trashed the place last night. I'm so afraid." Since Milan hadn't come home last night I wondered what she she'd thought about the damage.

"Did you call the police?" Tiffany asked.

"Yes," I lied again.

Tiffany's eyes widened. "Oh my God. I wonder if this is connected to Brent's murder."

Milan's head rose from her hands and looked at me with a wild look on her face. "Was it you, Zaria?" she asked, interrupting Tiffany.

"Huh?" I asked.

Milan stood. Her eyes narrowed and she was now breathing heavy. "The police said that there was no sign of forced entry at Brent's house," she explained, while looking at me with suspicion. "That meant that he knew the person who killed him. He let them in. He told me that he called here for me and you guys argued."

"Yes, we argued, but that was it." I didn't like where this was going or how Milan was looking at me.

"Was it you, Zaria?" she asked again, this time through clinched teeth.

BLEED, BITCH! BLEED! I couldn't get that chant out of my head. The sound of that fake thug wannabe choking and gagging uselessly on his own blood like he was drowning still sounded just as fresh in memory now as it did when it actually happened. I wanted to tell Milan, yes, I fuckin' did it! Instead, I meekly said, "No, it wasn't me," looking truly offended. "How could you think that I would do something like that? I'm not a murderer, I'm your best friend."

"Milan," Tiffany said, placing her hands on her sister's shoulders. "Calm down. You're…"

Milan snatched away from Tiffany and took a step towards me with more anger and spite in her eyes than I'd ever seen in them before. "Zaria, for the record, we aren't best friends. We're roommates. Secondly, I know that you've been destroying the apartment," she said. "I know you left the message on the mirror. I know about all your sadistic games. So you may have killed Brent."

"Milan, you're tripping right now. You're so hurt that you're not thinking straight," I reasoned. "You're saying things that you don't mean. But I'll forgive you for now."

"I mean it all," she assured me.

I reached for her to give her a hug.

"Don't fucking touch me, you lying bitch!" she screamed. "Something's not right."

"Milan," Tiffany interrupted. "Calm down and lets go."

"If I find out that you had anything to do with Brent's murder," Milan belted, yanking from Tiffany's grip, "I'm going to destroy you."

"Let's go," Tiffany said, grabbing her sister and guiding her to the door.

"I'm not playing, Zaria!" Milan continued. "If you did this, you'll burn in hell." Her eyes grew to the size of watermelons. "That's not a fucking threat, Zaria! That's a promise!" Milan shouted, repeating the threat I'd left for her on the mirror for her.

"Milan, stop it," Tiffany said, still pushing her to the door.

Anger arose inside me at Milan's accusations. Now all of a sudden the scary bitch has balls, making threats like she really has the heart to bang with a real bitch like me. She didn't know who she was fucking with. Threats are something that I'd never taken too kindly to. But out of respect for her pain, I didn't tear into her, at least not now. I simply smirked and called out to her just before she reached the door. "Milan!"

She turned and looked at me over Tiffany's shoulder. Our eyes locked without blinking. Silently, our anger towards each other showed itself clearly in our stare. There was no mistaking it. I hated that bitch and now she was finally woman enough to show her hatred for me.

"Milan, come on," Tiffany said, her back to me and urging her sister out the door.

Our eyes were still locked. With both a smirk and the most devilish face I could create I told her, "You be careful out there, okay." I could feel a smile stretch across my face at knowing she got the hint behind my words.

With both a smirk and a devilish look of her own, Milan returned, "No, Zaria…you be careful."

The door slammed and I jetted to my room to add Milan's name to my list.

14···Hardy

"Mr. Hardy, you sure know how to pick em'," Mr. Howard, the science teacher said, tapping me on the shoulder and laughing as he passed by me in the hall. I knew exactly what he was talking about. He laughed even louder as he got further away. It was clear that now everyone knew. But I was bonding with Carlos, the 9 year old who I agreed to mentor twice a week, so I couldn't comment.

"Kobe would eat Jordan's ass up," Carlos remarked.

My eyes lit up. "Boy, watch your mouth," I said, chuckling at both Carlos' foul mouth and ignorance of Michael Jordan's legacy as we headed down the school's bustling Thanksgiving decorated hallway. The lunch bell had just rung.

As usual, the week of an upcoming holiday meant more laughter and happiness than usual. You could feel it in the air and see it in the hallways. Everyone was looking forward to Thanksgiving break, and our two day work week.

"I'm just saying," Carlos continued, "he scored eighty five points in one game. Jordan never did that."

"True," I agreed. "But one spectacular game doesn't make him the greatest. A player's entire body of work is what dictates that. If you're going to call a player the greatest just be-

117

cause of one game, then Wilt Chamberlin was greater than Kobe. He once scored over a hundred points in one game.

"For real?" Carlos asked in disbelief.

"Yup."

"Well he was probably playing some lames," Carlos said dismissively. "The NBA had a lot of those back then."

I smiled. "Back then?"

"Yeah, Mr. Hardy. Back then; back in the old days."

"So then legends like Dr. Jay, Kareem Abdul Jabar, Earl the Pearl, and Wilt Chamberlin were lames?" I asked curious at what he'd say, and seeing Wanda further down the hall. My eyes locked on her ass like a heat seeking missile.

"Yup," he answered as if I should've known. "They had to be if I've never heard of them."

Of course I could only laugh. Dr. Jay a lame? He tickled the hell out of me with that one. "Boy, get your butt to lunch," I told him, playfully pushing him towards the lunchroom and then jogged to catch up with Wanda. "Where you headed?" I asked her.

Wanda looked around, as if not wanting to be seen with me and kept her rapid stride. "To lunch," she said plainly.

The two of us hadn't really spoken since the Zaria incident. I could tell she'd been avoiding me. I didn't blame her though. That shit was crazy. Letting the smoke die down was best. Now seeing her sexy body in heels, I'd decided the smoke had died down long enough. It was time to proceed with operation: GET in them draws!

"Can we have lunch together?" I asked. "My treat."

"Hardy, this isn't a good idea, okay?"

"What do you mean?"

"You know what I mean. My teaching record was completely clean until that thing with Zaria. And I took pride in that. But now I have people walking around whispering behind my back and stopping their conversations whenever I walk into a room. I could've even lost my job."

"Let them talk," I said, shrugging off the bullshit. People were always looking for shit to gossip about. That's a part of life none of us can control.

Since Zaria screamed on us, I'd been getting the same treatment Wanda was getting. People were acting different around me, too. But unlike her, I just decided to ignore it. Sooner or later it would fade and they'd move on to the next piece of drama.

"No, Hardy," she said. "You may be okay with that but I'm not."

"So, what are you saying, Wanda?"

"I'm saying that at least until things blow over, it's not a good idea for us to be seen together, especially at school. Hell, maybe not ever."

"Wanda, you're taking this situation too seriously."

"No, Hardy," she corrected. "You're not taking it serious enough."

"But Wanda."

"But Hardy," she mocked, cutting me off. "I don't appreciate you trying to play me like a floozy."

"It's not like that."

"Yes it is. You're a player, Hardy. You'd just had sex with her and then set your sights on me. I'm not stupid. And I don't appreciate that. People are walking around here thinking I'm a freak, thinking I just lay in any man's bed."

"Wanda, I never saw you like that," I lied, still trying to keep the ship afloat. "You're intelligent and beautiful. That's why I'm interested in you. I would never disrespect you." I reached for her hand. "Now let me take you to lunch so we can talk away from here for a while."

"I'm done with it, Hardy," she said, cutting me off and snatching her hand away from me. "My career comes first."

She quickly parted ways with me and headed up the hallway.

"Damn," I whispered, watching those curvaceous hips of

hers sway as she turned the corner. I wanted to hit that so fucking bad. But Zaria had thrown a monkey wrench in my plans.
Now it was going to take a little longer than I'd planned.

Oh well, I thought, turning the corner and approaching
the teacher's lounge just in time to see both the Special Education teacher and the school nurse coming out talking, neither
noticing me as they approached.

"She's pissed off at his ass," the school nurse said,
laughing.

"From the looks of that, she's beyond pissed off," Mr.
Edwards agreed. "That's some, 'Don't let me catch your ass in
the street' shit right there.'"

She laughed and playfully tapped Mr. Edwards on the
arm. "You're crazy," she joked.

"No," he corrected her. "Ms. Hopkins' is the one who's
crazy. I feel sorry for him when she catches up to him."

When the two saw me they abruptly cut their conversation short and walked past me, snickering. As I opened the
lounge door and looked back at them they were looking at me
smiling and whispering.

"Gossiping ass muthafuckas," I said to myself, also remembering Mr. Howard's joke a moment earlier. "Ain't got
nothing better to do than be all up in another person's business." Thank God this was only going to be a two day work
week. Thanksgiving was Thursday. I couldn't wait for the
break.

The lounge was empty as I opened the refrigerator,
grabbed a few slices of pizza I'd brought from home, and tossed
them in the microwave. Hoping to catch a few scores from last
night, I looked around the room for the remote. "Damn, why
can't they just leave the remote on the table where it belongs?"
I asked. That's when I saw the mirror above the sink.

"What the hell?" I whispered to myself. The words written on the mirror in red lipstick drew my body slowly towards
them. I couldn't feel myself walking, only floating. Now I real-

ized what the jokes I'd just received in the hallway were all about.

It read, **Hardy, tried 2 be a good woman 2 u ...but u betrayed me. U broke my heart. Now it's time 4 payback.**

The microwave beeped. Scared the shit out of me.

Immediately, I knew Zaria was on get back. Bitches never made me nervous. But *SHE* was beginning to. After that little episode in the hallway a few weeks ago, I knew she was definitely off her damn rocker and pissed off. And there's nothing worse than having a pissed off crazy bitch at your ass. Hell had no fury like a black woman scorned. But I was hoping that her two week suspension would calm her down and make her see that what we had was only a one night stand, nothing more. I guess I was wrong though.

The door to the lounge opened and two of my fellow teachers walked in, immediately attracted to the writing that was holding my attention captive. They walked over and stood beside me.

"It's from Zaria, isn't it?" Mr. Ramsey asked.

I nodded.

"I'm glad I never fucked her," Mr. Thomas said. "She always seemed like she had a screw loose somewhere inside that head of hers.

"Isn't she suspended?" Mr. Ramsey asked me.

I could only shrug my shoulders.

"Not anymore," Mr. Thomas said, "she was supposed to come back today."

I knew she was scheduled to return today but hadn't made any effort whatsoever to see her crazy ass. As far as I was concerned, out of sight out of mind.

Mr. Thomas shook his head and patted me on the back. "Good luck, Hardy," he said. "Those crazy ones are hard to get rid of. They don't go away easy. They just pester you like a fly."

"You got that right," Mr. Ramsey agreed. "But she seems far worse than a fly. Persistent too. Two words for you,

Hardy...Restraining order."

Both men walked out of the lounge, leaving me alone with my thoughts. With a passion I was now hoping against all odds that this situation wouldn't go any further. The principal had already warned me that his school was not a divorce court. He had no tolerance for lover's quarrels. If I got caught up in another one, I would be fired.

Maybe I should talk to her, I thought. Maybe talking to her could smooth things out between us. Maybe if I offered friendship, the bitch might be satisfied with it. Why not? I've never had a problem before with getting a woman to do what I wanted.

The door to the lounge opened again. I didn't want any-one else to see the words written in red lipstick. Quickly, I grabbed a paper towel and wet it underneath the faucet to wipe the words from the mirror. But when I raised my head, Zaria's reflection appeared, standing directly behind me. Nervous and surprised at the sight I turned around quickly, jumping as if I'd seen a ghost.

"Zaria," I said. "I don't know what you meant by this message but..."

Zaria hocked up a glob of thick saliva from her chest and throat and spit it directly in my face.

Out of reflex, I grabbed her by the throat, clenched my fist, and took aim. "You crazy bitch!" I shouted, ready to tear her ass apart.

"Hit me," Zaria defiantly begged.

I wanted to grant her wish so badly. Visions of her soon to be destroyed face filled my head.

"I dare you," she urged.

I realized I couldn't. Hitting women wasn't my thing. Besides, if I hit her, the police would toss my black ass in jail with no hesitation. That's what this bitch wanted, and I refused to give her the satisfaction. I released, then shouted, "What the fuck?"

"I didn't think so, you weak ass nigga," she said as I snatched a paper towel from the dispenser, and began to wipe her spit from my face. "You know better."

Pushing her out of my way with a forearm, I headed towards the door. Her mere presence was angering me more and more. Keeping control of myself was becoming more and more of a struggle every second. I was seeing nothing but red. Damn, I needed to get away from her.

Zaria rushed in front of me, blocking my path. "When did you get married, Hardy?" she asked.

"Move out of my way, Zaria!"

"You never told me you were married. Did that very important piece of information just skip your mind? Did you think I wouldn't find out?"

The anger inside me had my muscles tensing. An eruption was surely only seconds away. I was holding onto my self control by my fingertips.

"I have eyes and ears everywhere," she warned. "How you thought you would be able to keep that away from me I'll never know. You must think I'm a slow bitch."

"Zaria, move out of my way!" I shouted again.

"Or what?" she loudly returned, while placing her hands on her hips and looking defiantly into my eyes.

I wanted nothing more than to knock her ass out with one punch and leave her laid out in the middle of the floor.

"Or what, Hardy?" she shouted again.

I could only stare at the crazy bitch. The consequences for hitting her were just entirely too steep. The thought of jail time and the loss of my job and career rationalized with my anger. Besides, I wouldn't be able to live with myself if I were in jail, leaving Terrell without a father.

Zaria smiled. "Just like I thought," she gloated. "You're more than just a liar. You're a coward, too."

"Don't push me, Zaria," I warned.

"Fuck you, Hardy," she said. "I don't like being made a

fool of."

"You made a fool of yourself just like you're doing right now. You're the one who can't accept that we're not a couple."

If I couldn't beat this ho senseless with my fists, the next best thing was to beat her over the head with my words, I decided.

"You were nothing more to me than a pity fuck," I informed her, while stepping closer.

"Is that right?"

"Real talk; I usually only fuck dime pieces. I usually only let five-star bitches put my dick in their mouth, while keeping slow hoes like yourself sitting on the sidelines wishing you could fuck with a nigga like me, wishing you could drink my cum like a nice cold Gatorade on a hot summer day."

Zaria seethed in silence. I could tell I was getting to her.

"You're a third rate ho," I kept on. "With third rate pussy and third rate head. I knew that the first time I saw you," I smiled, seeing that I was getting under her armor.

Zaria's eyes narrowed.

"But hey," I said. "I'm a fair nigga. I think every bitch deserves a chance to suck my dick at least once. Even a broke down ho like you, Zaria." I stepped closer to her and peered into her face. I wanted her to know that I meant every word.

Zaria's frame began to tremble, though she tried to mask her hurt feelings.

"I lowered my standards and gave you your chance in the spotlight," I told her. "You couldn't cut it. A bitch like you aint got what it takes. But don't feel bad, sweetheart. Some bitches just can't handle the pressure. They were born to sit the bench."

Each word chipped and chiseled painfully away at Zaria. Her eyes reddened. Tears began to fall. "I can't believe you're married. And I can't believe you're saying these things to me."

"Yes. So now what?" I asked, stepping back from her

and spreading my arms. Knowing that I was getting to her was
sending a silent excitement through me. "You're mad because I
won't give you another chance to get down on your ashy ass
knees and choke on my dick again?" I asked. "That's what it
is?"

No answer.

"Yeah," I said, sucking my teeth cockily. "That's what it
is."

Zaria shook her head sadly, wrapped her arms around
her self, and continued to let her tears fall.

"You miss the taste of it, don't you?" I asked, showing
no mercy for deflating her self-esteem. She shouldn't have tried
to stomp with a big dog. "Your mouth is watering for my dick
right now, aint it?" I asked, placing a hand over my crotch and
squeezing.

Still, no answer, only more tears. Then suddenly she
began to talk to herself. Almost like a chant; Smiley Face, smiley face, can you see my smiley face? Wrinkles formed across
the top of my head. *What the fuck?* I thought. Then she began
again. Smiley face, smiley face, can anyone see my smiley
face? Suddenly, Zaria wiped the tears from her eyes, turned
around and headed for the door.

"What's the matter, Zaria?" I asked sarcastically. "You
don't want to play the game anymore?"

Zaria chuckled. She slid her hands into the back pockets
of her jeans, and turned to me with a smile when she reached
the door. "Oh, I still want to play," she assured me. "In fact, I
quit my job today just so I can devote myself to playing this
game."

I didn't like the way that sounded at all. My cell phone
rung. I knew it was Dana from the ring tone.

Zaria now smiled as if she hadn't just been broken down
like a fraction a moment ago. "Cute ring tone," she complimented. "If that's Dana, tell her I said hello."

How the hell did she know my wife's name, I wondered.

Zaria winked an eye at me and walked out the door.

I answered my cell phone and was immediately attacked by more yelling and more curse words than I'd ever heard come out of Dana's mouth. She was screaming on and on about my cheating ways, her now truly being tempted to divorce me, and a bunch of other shit. I had no idea where all of it was coming from. What the fuck? Are all these bitches on their damn period today?

"Dana, what the hell are you talking about?" I asked with my mouth wide open.

"You know exactly what I'm talking about, Hardy!" she screamed.

"No, I don't," I said.

"Then maybe you should ask your pregnant girlfriend!"

"What girlfriend?" My mouth dropped.

"Yeah, Hardy," Dana said. The bitch came by the house this morning!"

15··· *Zaria*

The next day, I hauled myself into Dr. Seethers' office like someone would kill me if I didn't go inside. She was the infamous psychiatrist my Aunt Lisa had recommended I see a long time ago. But after the way Hardy had dissed me, and after my 24 hour crying spree, I figured it was best I get help. My thoughts had been getting increasingly dangerous with every hour that passed so Dr. Seethers was desperately needed at the moment. As soon as I knocked on the door a feeling of uneasiness spread all over me. It had been over two years since I'd last seen a psychiatrist and the memories of what happened weren't that great.

When I heard her sweet voice say, "Come in," all I could think about was some uppity bitch with the intent on making me out to be some nut and then taking my money. I'd rather her just say bend over, Zaria, I wanna fuck you with no Vaseline. That's what my life had become…people always wanting to get over on me. Simply saying fuck me! It seemed nobody wanted me to succeed in life.

"Zaria Hopkins, I presume?" she asked peering over her skinny rimmed frames.

I shot her a fake grin, thinking those glasses are way too

small for her chubby face. "Yeah, that's me." I stood folding my arms tightly across my chest letting her know I wasn't interested in gaining a new friend. I had stopped by just to keep from murdering a muthufucka.

"Have a seat," she told me standing behind her big, mahogany desk.

I decided to wait. I wanted to check her spot out a bit more before she started getting all up in my business. Besides, why didn't she have a receptionist? I wondered. And why did she look so young? She couldn't have spent years training for this because her skin told me she was in her twenties. My eyes quickly did a virtual tour of her spacious office, noticing how neat it was, except for the pile of papers stacked high on a round table to the right of her desk. Plastered across the walls were one degree after another framed in what looked like rich, imported wood. This bitch had money, I told myself. I should've known from the expensive looking pant-suit she wore. At that point I decided to sit in the over-sized brown, leather chaise behind me. It sat facing Dr. Seethers' desk where she could see me clearly, and monitor my moves closely.

"Get comfortable Ms. Hopkins," she instructed while grabbing a long, yellow legal pad from the right side of the desk. "I want us to get to know each other a bit."

"Ummmph," I grunted under my breath. Quickly, I sat then leaned back instantly feeling like a patient.

She sat in her plush seat and stared at me like a new, imported piece of china. "So, your Aunt has told me a little bit about you and your history, but I'll want to hear from you about a few things shortly." She paused. "But first, are you aware of my fees?"

"No," I said in the most unfriendly tone I could muster. "My aunt didn't tell me that. I thought she was paying since she wanted me to come so bad."

She smiled then proceeded slowly. My guess, she was attempting to figure out the best way to handle a pistol like me. I sorta wanted to play nice since she was smart, young and a full-figured woman. She wasn't intimidating like so many others I'd met during my mental illness battle. Besides, we shared the same bronze complexion, so I was willing to work with her. She wasn't one of those high yellow bitches that I hated so much.

"Well, I charge $250 per hour. Is that alright with you?"

My shoulders shrugged. "I guess." Of course, my initial thought was, *two-hundred and fifty fucking dollars to talk to you! What the fuck*! But I just chilled. Money had never been a big issue for me. It was nothing I craved. Call me plain, but I'd learned to make ends meet on my measly teacher's salary. But the fact was that I would be coming into a nice piece of change on my thirtieth birthday, a little over a month away. I smiled at the thought.

The one thing that my mother was able to do for me was finally going to come to fruition. It wasn't a fortune, but it would help my lifestyle a bit. The two hundred and fifty thousand dollar trust fund she'd left me before she killed herself would become available on my 30th birthday. It was money passed down from her father's father and money that could only get passed on if you abided by certain rules. The only regulation I was aware of was graduating from college, and maintaining a job. I had done both so I was good.

"You're not getting that money, bitch!" that crazy voice inside my head blurted.

Shock spread across my face. Now wasn't the time. And certainly not the place. I wanted to portray a decent image to Dr. Seethers on my first visit. Now, she would definitely think I was crazy if the voices continued.

"Are you okay, Zaria? she asked with wrinkles forming at the top of her forehead.

"I'm good. Let's get started."

"You're not good, bitch!" Tell her everything you've done. And tell her how you gave up the ass on the first date then got dumped! Go ahead. Tell her!"

I twitched in my seat, gritting my teeth like a hungry lion. Dr. Seethers just grinned real plastic-like again. By now I knew every one of her teeth personally. She was too cheerful for me.

"Tell'er, Zaria," the voice taunted.

"Shut up!" I yelled out.

The docs eyes bulged. And her next question stopped me cold. "Are you hearing voices?"

Color flushed my face. How did she know? I was so embarrassed. Surely, she would think differently of me now. "No," I lied with a straight face.

She hit me with a long oooooooooookay, as if she didn't believe me. "So, let's talk," she added. "When was the last time you saw a doctor dealing with mental health?"

At first my shoulders shrugged. I wasn't really sure. "About a year ago. I stopped shortly after February."

"Why?"

"The guy got on my nerves," I blasted. "Plus, I don't think he liked me much."

Finally, her pen took a break giving her time to gaze up at me. "So, you think that was a good enough reason to stop going to him? It was for your benefit."

Definitely. "Do I look stupid to you?"

"Ahhhh, no. Of course not," Dr. Seethers added calmly. " It's just that since your aunt told me your were diagnosed with psychosis, I figured you knew the seriousness of it. Plus, she said you'd been crying constantly over the last 24 hours. I would call that serious." Her voice slowed. "Don't you think so?"

I gave her another nonchalant look then started scratching my arms again. The fact that Dr. Seethers' office appeared to be plush, but was loaded with bugs was starting to anger me. "Yes, I know the seriousness, but I'm better now. I'm just here because my Aunt was worried about me."

"So, you haven't been having a break down, unable to

stop crying?"

"Yes. But because my dog died," I lied.

"Ummmmm, I understand." Her eyes widened. "But the fact of the matter is…once you have a mental disease, quite honestly you never just say I'm better and think it's over. Constant care is needed. Are you still on any meds?"

"No way!" I spat. "That crap made me feel terrible so I haven't taken any in over a year."

"Really?"

"Ahhh. Yeah, really," I said sarcastically, wondering why she was looking at me so crazily. I was starting to feel like the doc had something personal against me. But little did she know her dirty looks wouldn't be tolerated.

"Do you remember what you were on?" she asked while picking up the pace of her writing.

"Thorazine."

"Ummmm," she mumbled.

"What's that supposed to mean?"

"Nothing really. Just not a good choice for your condition from what I can see so far."

I jumped up at the thought of more medicine. "I hated the way it made me feel. I felt drugged and it gave me rashes on my skin…just another reason to have people talking about me even more." My voice trembled. It was clear I didn't want any more drama.

Dr. Seethers paused before speaking. She rested her pen slowly. "Zaria, I want you to realize that psychosis is a severe mental disorder in which reality is highly distorted. Think of it as an abnormal condition of the mind. So while you think someone is always talking about you, or plotting against you, they're really not."

"You don't know these people doc. I mean it's cool for you to sit behind that desk with all your fancy degrees talking from the textbook, but I know! People out there are hating on me. They want to be me," I added. "They want my men, they want my job, and they want my looks. And they definitely want this shape," I added, sliding my hands down my hips."

"Well, yes Zaria, you're a beautiful woman, but one of the symptoms of your disease is always thinking people are plotting against you. Do you think you have unrealistic ideas about life sometimes? 'Cause that's another sign."

"Who me?" I pointed at myself. "No, not at all."

"So no voices, or feeling like things are there that aren't?"

"Nope." I quickly thought about the bugs I thought I saw in her office.

She shot me another shady look which was now starting to piss me off. Then spent another fifteen minutes talking about my childhood, my teenage years, and when I first starting seeing psychiatrists and mental specialists. She started getting deep, asking for names and phone numbers of previous doctors.

Finally, I'd had enough. "Look, doc I've got some business to take care of. Can we wrap this up?"

"We sure can. But cut me some slack." She grinned. "I did agree to see you today even though tomorrow is a holiday. Now, I just want to quickly talk about your father."

Thinking about him made my stomach ache. Why'd she have to bring him up? Was it necessary? I began asking myself that question over and over again, hitting myself in the head. Then the voices started. This time I tried to remain calm, blocking each word out. Out of the blue, I rose up letting Dr. Seethers know our little session was about to end. For a moment, I caught a glimpse of my beaten up tennis shoes, then caught a smirk slip from the side of her mouth.

"Are you laughing at me?" I asked her boldly.

"I'm not laughing at you," she stated firmly. "But I do need to ask you just a few more important questions."

"Shoot." I folded my arms but refused to lean back on the chair. I was done with this bitch for the day. And she'd have to pay me to come back."

"I believe your father suffers from psychosis, too. Is that correct?"

"Why don't you ask him?"

"Zaria, you're not making this easy. I'm here to help you."

"Oh, don't play mind games with me!" I shouted. "I'm smart. That's how I passed that hard ass teacher's exam. So, don't sit here saying you're helping me. I'm good. All I need is a good man in my life!" I began to cry as Dr. Seethers surveyed me like a twisted science project. "A good man, that's it!" Tears flowed like the Nile in Egypt.

"Zaria, sweetie. I want to do two things. First, I want to schedule you for another appointment with me on Monday. At that time, we'll talk more and it'll give you a chance to get to know me better. But just know that I'll never laugh at you. I'll never think less of you." She smiled that warm smile again. "As a matter of fact, I think you're beautiful."

My insides brightened, and I wiped the tears with the back of my hand. Did she really think I was beautiful? I hadn't heard those words since I was a little girl. Quickly, I opened my purse and whipped out a small mirror that Milan had given me for Christmas. I began scrutinizing my skin looking for blemishes, or anything that would make someone disagree with Dr. Seethers.

"Zaria, sweetie. I need you to pay attention to me for a few moments. This is important," she added, tearing a small sheet from her prescription note pad. "I want you to get this prescription filled as soon as possible. "All of a sudden her voice was soothing like that of a mother. "It's important." She waved the paper above her head still summonsing me with her eyes to stay focused on her lips. "It's called, Risperdal."

"I will," I told her, still thinking about how beautiful she said I looked.

"Understand that your situation only gets worse over time if left untreated; especially when you feel rejected or unwanted. You need to take the medication as prescribed and make sure you show up at your next appointment. If you do this, the voices will go away."

"I told you I don't hear voices."

"I know you did, beautiful. That's all for today," she said rising from her chair.

I was all of a sudden starting to like this woman. Her spirit reminded me of Oprah, just a much younger version. She was someone I could really spill my guts to all of a sudden. "Doc, one last thing," I turned to say.

She walked around her desk and placed her hand on my shoulder. "What is it?"

"Have you ever been in love?"

She began to choke, followed by a strange laugh. "Well, I may not be the best to give love advice. I'm divorced," she admitted. "But I can listen."

"Well, there's this guy, Hardy. I love him so much, but he betrayed me." My voice weakened even thinking about Hardy. "I know he made a mistake… and the truth is….I still want him." I paused to see if I could catch one of her expressions. "I just want to be loved," I added.

"How long have you guys been together?"

I could feel myself getting choked up just thinking about the way he touched me. Then I thought about his magic stick. Hardy had a beast living within his pants. Damn, I thought, I love that nigga. "Not long. A few weeks," I finally answered, but just before the tears welled up in my eyes again. "I love him so much, doc."

Dr. Seethers' eyes grew with worry. "And did he ever say he loved you, too?"

"No. But I know he does. We had sex the first night we met and it was explosive. We knew right then we were meant to be together. We're like salt and pepper," I joked. "Like peanut butter and jelly; you know the perfect match."

When she didn't joke back I got serious again. "Then he

just started acting crazy like someone was trying to turn him against me. I think it's this lonely teacher at my school, Wanda," I said making sure to roll my eyes to the top of my head.

"Zaria, make sure we discuss Mr. Hardy on our next visit," she said pushing me toward the door. "I've got another appointment to prepare for. For now, I would say just relax and take your medication. I'll see you on Monday."

I insisted on getting my point across as she opened the door ready to throw me out. "But, he loves me, Dr. Seethers. We had great sex. And he said I was the best he'd ever had."

Dr. Seethers stopped dead in her tracks and sighed as I stood outside her door. She held onto the edge of the door frame as she told me a bold-faced lie.

"Zaria, what you had was a one-night stand, baby. Yes, the sex may have been good. But nine times out of ten all he wanted was one night. My suggestion is to let it go. There are other men out there who would love to date you. Just keep your options open."

"Doc, you need to sit on your own couch," I told her jetting away from the door. "Hardy wants more than one night. He wants to be with me forever. Watch. You'll see." *The door slammed and reality hit me in the back. Dr. Seethers wanted Hardy.*

16 ··· *Zaria*

A frigid breeze and slight drizzle from the graying sky made me tighten the collar of my coat as I headed up the walkway to my Aunt Lisa's house, the house in my nightmare. As I walked up the steps and onto the porch, just like in my nightmares voices could be heard. The only difference is these voices were recognizable. I knew exactly who they belonged to. They brought a smile to my face as I knocked.

"Who is it!" someone shouted. But without giving me a chance to answer, Aunt Lisa's pudgy face appeared from behind the door's curtained window. "My baby," she said, smiling at me.

That smile always warmed me. It always got me through. It was as welcoming to me as a lighthouse in an ocean of overwhelming darkness. The locks flew off the door one by one quickly and it swung open.

"Hey, Zaria, baby," Aunt Lisa greeted me.

"Hey, Auntie," I returned.

The two of us hugged. Tightly.

My Aunt Lisa was the spitting image of my mother. Her long hair, brown eyes, clear brown complexion, and even her short height matched perfectly with every detail I could remember of my mother's appearance. Time had aged her but not terribly. The only difference between her and her sister was Aunt Lisa's weight. She was every bit of 275 pounds. She'd been that way for as long as I could remember. Most of it undoubtedly came from good eating.

As a child I could always remember there being a pleasant and heavy aroma of soul food coming from my aunt's house. It stayed clouded over the entire neighborhood; fried chicken, pork chops, chitterlings, pig's feet, collard greens, chocolate cake, apple pie, etc, etc. The aroma was so hypnotizing that nearly all the neighborhood kids were constantly asking my aunt if they could eat there, not even wanting to eat from their own stove at home. Aunt Lisa always obliged them. Seeing a child go hungry was never her thing.

My aunt was pretty much the only family I had on my mother's side, besides her own two children. My grandmother died when I was only three years old. And from what I heard my grandfather was an abusive, womanizing drunk. Someone stabbed him to death during a card game shortly before aunt Lisa was born. My aunt often said that even after his death, despite how abusive and womanizing he was my grandmother never even looked at another man.

I'd always loved hearing my Aunt tell old stories, especially of childhood memories she'd shared growing up with my mother. After she petitioned for custody of me from my father and won, mainly because I'd told the judge I would slit my throat from ear to ear if they made me go back to that bastard, she would sit up with me night after night and tell me the countless exploits of she and my mother. I never grew tired of them. I still haven't.

"Girl, come on in here," my Aunt said, closing the door as I stepped inside the warmth of the home that taught me what family really meant. "How was the appointment?"

"It was okay," I said dryly, not really wanting to talk about it. "I did it for you."

"Baby, I know you don't want to, but it really is best for you to start going back on a regular basis.

I gave her a look of surprise. "I'm not crazy, Aunt Lisa."

"I know," she said quickly, and lovingly placing her hands on my shoulders. "I'm just saying that you should at least think about it. It can't hurt anything."

After she took my coat, I walked into the living room to see both my cousins Kenneth and Sonia sitting on the couch eating and laughing at an episode of Jersey Shore. Kenneth was 20 and Sonia was 22. Both had jobs and their own apartments but they would always pleasantly remain in my memory as the two hardheaded little brats that I used to baby-sit when I moved in. The thought made me chuckle.

"What's good, Z?" Kenneth said, noticing me immediately.

He got up and gave me a hug, still holding his plate of food. Hugging him was always like hugging the little brother I never had.

"Same ole, same ole," I told him, trying to be hip like him. "Just trying to make it like everyone else."

"Yeah. I see you still wearing them same ole clothes, too. Girl, you got that fly body, why don't you get a make-over or somethin'? He grinned like the shit was amusing. "I know plenty niggas who'd love to rock you on their arm if you fix yo'self up."

"Not interested," I told him as my cousin Sonia approached me.

"Girl, I haven't seen you in a long time." She paused to snicker. "Not since you were here last and wanted to fight Ms. Lula down the block. You remember that shit?" she asked her brother.

Smiley Face… Smiley Face…Can anyone see my smiley face? I made sure to chant quickly. I wasn't about to let Sonia, who I could still remember being knock-kneed with pigtails, play me.

Kenneth began laughing. "Yeah, Z," he said sitting back on the couch. "You know you been doing, crazy, wild shit all your life, right? You crazy as a mufucka," he added while ripping into a piece of pig feet.

"Zaria, come here," Aunt Lisa said, saving me.

I followed her into the kitchen.

"You hungry?" she asked.

"No, I'm good, Auntie."

"You sure? There's plenty."

"I'm good, Aunt Lisa," I assured her. "Why are you always trying to make me eat when I come over here?" She'd always been one of those types of Aunts from the old school who felt that if you stepped foot in her house, you couldn't leave without getting a hot meal inside you. She said my grandmother was from Alabama so southern hospitality was inherited. I sure didn't have the shit.

"Because don't no man want no skinny woman," she said, answering my question.

"I'm not skinny, Auntie. I'm what the men these days call, 'thick'". I placed my hands on my hips and swung my ass to the right.

Aunt Lisa laughed. "Child, I don't know what I'm gonna do with you."

The two of us sat at the kitchen table. My aunt slowly let a serious look come across her face. She looked directly across the table at me. "I don't mean to pry in your business," she said. "But have you decided what you're going to do with the money?"

When auntie said she didn't mean to pry, I knew she was going to do more than pry. Honestly, the thought hadn't crossed my mind since I'd been told about the money years ago by the judge who'd given my aunt custody of me. "I haven't really given it any thought," I answered, shrugging it off.

"Zaria, December nineteenth, *your* thirtieth birthday is less than a month away. Don't you think you should start giving some thought to it?"

"Not really," I finally said, "maybe pay a few bills."

"Baby, I care about you. And $250,000 is a lot of money. People are going to be coming at you right and left for a piece. Even that Hardy guy may decide to come into your life, and try to sweet talk you if he finds out."

Hearing Hardy's name lit a match inside of me.

"How he played you like that with that other woman and embarrassed you in front of the whole school wasn't right," she said as if each word was paining her terribly to speak. "Sweetheart, he made you lose your job, he made you look bad, and I hate him for that."

With tears in my eyes I thought back to what he'd done to me. Her words were meant to console me, instead they were now, silently reigniting my rage. Hardy *had* broken my heart, and he *had* made me look stupid in front of the entire school. But I'd be damned if he was going to get away with it. In my heart I couldn't stop believing that our night in his truck could blossom into so much more. I knew it could. And in time he would see it. But first I had to have my revenge. Going to his wife about us was simply not enough. I needed complete satisfaction.

"Zaria, I'm just not sure where your head is right now," Aunt Lisa went on. "If you want, when your money comes, I can watch over it temporarily."

My thoughts had tuned my aunt's words out completely. With what I knew was a blank stare my eyes only glared at the kitchen table. Voices began to chatter in my head again. My anger with Hardy had begun to cause a domino effect, beginning with Milan. Her threat still rang as loud as a church bell inside my head. It still had me highly pissed off.

"Child, I worry about you," Auntie was still talking. Still not hearing a word she said my body began to tremble. Jamal's face and broken promises began to flood my mind. I could feel my pressure rising quickly. An immense hatred for that lying ass muthafucka swept over me.

"I just be so scared that someone may try to take advantage of you," Aunt Lisa continued. "People develop ulterior motives when it comes to money. You never know who you can trust."

From Milan to Jamal, my thoughts of revenge swung back and forth like a pendulum. Visions of slowly slicing Milan's pretty face wide open and plunging a knife into her repeatedly flashed quickly. I could see myself cutting and carving on that bitch like a Thanksgiving turkey until all her beauty was gone. Her screams were like a song urging me to keep cutting and maiming her. Jamal's agony filled screams intertwined. Destroying his car wasn't enough. It was nowhere near enough. I wanted his balls…literally. I'd always wondered how agonizing a man would sound while having his prized possessions removed.

"Zaria," Aunt Lisa said, noticing that I'd zoned out.

Hardy hadn't gone forgotten neither. I had something more special than words could describe for him. As a matter of fact, not just him…Dana and Terrell also.

"Zaria!" Aunt Lisa called again.

For a second I'd forgotten I was even at her home. Vengeful thoughts had consumed me just that much.

"See, that's what I'm talking about, Zaria," she said with a worried look on her face. "It's like you're not even a part of this world sometimes. Your face goes blank and you look like you're out in outer space at times, girl."

"I was just thinking about some things," I said, growing agitated. I loved my aunt to death. But damn, hadn't the psychiatrist probed me enough for one day?

"Baby, I called you four times. What thought could detach you from reality like that?"

Oh God, I wish she would just let it go. I'd heard a word or two here and there while she was rambling, but I wasn't that far gone, I didn't think.

"That's not normal," she said. "It really isn't. Do you know that your landlord called me and told me that you've been sleepwalking in your building late at night?"

"No, that's not true. And why would he call you?"

"Did you forget that your apartment is in my name?"

"Still, not true," I blasted.

"And the last time you were here, I had money missing." Her eyes seemed to feel sorry for me. "But I know it wasn't you, baby. It was your other personality. Just like when you tried to slit your wrist over here, then pretended that you did-n't."

"Lies! All lies! "I shouted. I tried to calm myself. But between my aunt's psychotherapy shit mixed with my frustration with Milan, Jamal, and Hardy, I was zoning out.

"Don't lie to me, child," she said, reaching across the table and softly placing a hand against the side of my face. "You're a threat to yourself and don't even know it. I need you to start being honest with me about your sickness."

I couldn't take it anymore. "Why are you trying to make me out to be crazy?" I shouted, standing up and slamming my hands on the table.

"I'm not, sweetheart."

"Yes, you are! I never tried to slit my wrist in front of you. And you're diagnosing me like a fuckin nutcase when there's nothing wrong with me!"

"I'm not diagnosing you," she said, raising her voice and growing serious. I'm just trying to get you to understand that there *is* something wrong. That's the whole point of going to see Dr. Seethers."

I shook my head in disagreement. The voices began to chatter again. "That's not normal," Auntie's words played over and over again like a broken record. She'd never told me anything wrong in my entire life. This time though she was definitely wrong.

Aunt Lisa stood from the table and walked around it,

stopping directly in front of me. "You need to accept the fact that you're not like other people," she said. "I think in your heart that's why you agreed to go to see Dr. Seethers."

"Wrong. I went to Dr. Seethers because you've been asking me to. It had nothing to do with me doubting my sanity."

"Zaria, you've got…I love…The money should…"

I squinted my eyes, trying to get clarity on her words. Too much was going on inside my head.

"I know what's best…Your father…Birthday…

It grew worse and worse.

"Just…All…Money…"

My aunt's words were too overwhelming. I could no longer hear Aunt Lisa at all. I could only see her lips moving. Was she right after all? Was I really losing my mind? My hands gripped both sides of my head like a vice grip. As Aunt Lisa placed a hand on my arm and looked at me closely my eyes shut tightly, nearing my breaking point. Then suddenly…silence.

"Baby," Auntie whispered, both hands now holding my arms.

My eyes opened slowly, as if fearing they'd possibly catch sight of something horrifying. I looked at my aunt, not knowing what to say.

"Child, it's okay," she gently assured me, while slowly taking my hands from the sides of my head. "It's okay."

As my aunt tried to pull me into her arms, I pulled away, suddenly realizing that I needed to make two phone calls. I reached into the pocket of my jeans with trembling hands, pulled out my cell phone, and began to dial.

"Zaria, what's wrong?" Auntie asked, looking puzzled. "Who are you calling?"

After several rings, as usual these days I only got Milan's voicemail. The memory of her threat towards me played like a bullhorn in my ears, setting me off. "Why won't you answer your fucking phone, you scary bitch!" I screamed into the phone angrily after the voicemail permitted me to leave a message and beeped. "Your boyfriend got what the fuck his ass deserved!"

Aunt Lisa's eyes grew wider than all outside.

I hung up and called Hardy, not noticing that I was now pacing the floor. But just like Milan all I got was his voicemail. "Fuck!" I screamed to the ceiling.

Kenneth charged into the kitchen. "What's going on, Z? Need a Valium, huh?" He laughed wildly.

The kitchen had grown too small for me and was growing smaller by the second. I needed to go. I had shit to do. People to take down. Within what seemed like only a second, I grabbed my coat from the foyer's closet and charged out the front door.

"Zaria!" Aunt Lisa called from the porch.

My feet were moving as fast as they could carry me.

"Zaria!" she called again.

I stopped just before reaching the sidewalk in front of the house and turned.

Aunt Lisa was already making her way down the walkway. As soon as she reached me she took me into her arms and squeezed me tightly. "Do you know that I love you?" she whispered in my ear.

"Yes, Auntie," I answered. "I do."

She let me go, placed a hand underneath my chin, and looked into my eyes. "Are you sure?" she asked.

I nodded, knowing without a shadow of a doubt that it was true. She was my heart.

She kissed me on the cheek and headed back to the porch. "And make sure you stop by for dinner tomorrow," she said over her shoulder. "You hear me?"

"I got you, Aunt Lisa," I answered, thinking about my next move.

17 · · · *Hardy*

The kitchen counter near the refrigerator now filled with trays of deserts, and my favorite sweet potato pie couldn't even get me excited. I waltzed around the kitchen with my phone glued to my ear hoping Mario would answer. I'd been calling him for three days now, but still no answer. Didn't that nigga get my messages? I was in a state of emergency and had been relying on Kyle's advice.

Finally, he answered, giving me some lame excuse as to why he hadn't called. It took nearly five minutes to tell him what Zaria had done on Monday at the school and how it all went down. He remained silent for the most part until he gave me one of his one liners that often sounded like a sermon.

"I told you that it was stupid to fool with a woman in the workplace," Mario lectured. "I told you it was gonna be nothing but problems."

"Nigga, would you quit with all the damn 'I told you so's," I said. "You were right, I was wrong, okay?" I paced the newly renovated hardwood floors.

"I know," he said. "But when you play with fire, you get burned. I've always told you that."

I began to give Mario blow by blow about how Zaria

147

visited my house when I wasn't home. I gave details on everything she told Dana about us. I told him every lie she spat and every attempt she made at splitting us apart. But when I told Mario that Zaria was claiming to be pregnant, he went off.

I sighed, irritated. "Mario, I don't need sermons. I need advice," I said. "Can you stop gloating and give me that?"

"Alright," he said, with contempt in his voice. The situation was probably frustrating to him because it reminded him of the white girl. He couldn't believe that I'd found one who could even come close to being loonier than her.

"Mario, I really want to kill the bitch," I said, almost meaning it, as I leaned back against another counter top, unable to enjoy the delicious aroma of turkey, macaroni and cheese, collard greens, mashed potatoes, and so much more. "The fact that she had the nerve to come see Dana, sit on my couch, and tell her that ridiculous lie got me wanting to commit a crime. Then, as if she hadn't made shit bad enough, what she did to Dana's mini-van last night got me wanting to choke her until her eyes shut for good." I paused to catch a breath. "I'm gonna get that bitch!" I blurted.

"Whoa!" Mario shouted. "Calm that down, Hardy! I'm an attorney. Client attorney privilege doesn't cover death threats. You know that if she really came up dead somewhere, I'd be required to share my knowledge of that statement with the police. Come on, man."

He was right, I realized. "You know I didn't mean it," I assured him. "The bitch has just got me at wits end right now. I don't know what to do about her." My insides shook from nervousness.

"Did you actually see her let the air out of Dana's tires last night? Did you see her car pull off or anything?"

"No," I said frustratingly, taking a sip of beer. Neither Dana nor I had noticed all four of her mini-van's tires had been slashed until she stepped outside this morning to go to the store and get a few finishing touches for the Thanksgiving Dinner today.

"The neighbors didn't see anything either?"

"No, but I know for a fact the bitch did it. Who else would? The police should be locking her crazy ass up right now. This is fucked up, Mario."

"You're preaching to the choir here," he said. "I understand. But knowing she did it isn't enough. She can't be arrested, never mind convicted. Either you or a witness would have had to actually see her commit the crime or there is nothing the police can do."

"Well, what about the threat she left on the mirror at the school?" I asked. "Can't I get her for making terrorist threats or something?" Whatever could be done short of killing that ho, I wanted it done. All options whatsoever had to be explored.

"No one actually witnessed her leave the message, not even you," Mario said. "She'd simply deny it; probably say it was one of the other teachers or parents you were banging."

"But, Mario..."

"Hardy," he said, cutting me off. "Knowing isn't enough. It's not what you know. It's what you can prove. That's the way the law works."

"Shit," I said angrily.

"The best thing you can do is get up first thing tomorrow morning and file a temporary restraining order against her. Her abundance of texts, voice messages, and the written statements of teachers who'd witnessed her go off on you in the hallway that day would be enough to obtain one."

"A piece of paper?" I asked. "That's it? She's trying to ruin my life."

"Look, Hardy," he said. "Putting paperwork on her ass is the best thing you can do right now. That way, from this point forward if she comes near you, calls you, or even texts you, you can have her locked up."

I closed my eyes and pinched the bridge of my nose between my thumb and forefinger. Another headache was coming on. What a Thanksgiving this was going to turn out to be. I just wanted Dana and I to have one day this week without an argument.

"Did you make a report with the police about the van?" Mario asked.

"Yeah," I said. A lot of good it'll do though, I thought.

"That's good. It'll come in handy later on down the line in court. Trust me on that. How's Dana dealing with the situation?"

"Not good. She keeps repeating all the lies Zaria told her. She even threatened to tell Terrell that I fucked Ms. Hopkins and that her son will be his new brother." I stopped to sigh then hit my fist against the wall. "And when she saw the tires on her van this morning, she simply came back in the house, tossed her keys on my lap while I was sleeping on the couch, and said I needed to be gone by Sunday. Mario, this bitch is wrecking my life."

"You think she's really pregnant."

"I don't know, mannnnnnnnn," I wailed like a bitch. "I did fuck her raw." I mean this is all bullshit," I continued. "I mean, she's really trying to ruin my marriage. Shit, I'll pay for the abortion if she is."

"Hardy, I love you like a brother," Mario said. "I'm always going to have your back, no matter what. You know that don't you?"

"I know."

Then I have to be real with you. Your marriage was wrecked all along. If you're being honest with yourself, you already know that. Zaria just added to it."

"But it gets worse, man."

"What?"

"I think Dana is cheating on me. Somebody keeps calling her cell from an unknown number then hangs up when I answer. And she keeps sneaking off to talk when she's on the phone."

"Hardy, you've got to ask yourself if being married is what you really want. Cause all of this is making you crazy."

I knew he was right. Facing it was difficult. But it was still true. I'd been avoiding the thought and the question for entirely too long. I had an appetite for women that Dana couldn't compete with.

For seconds, Mario made all these crazy sounds then spoke like I was a client. "If what Zaria told Dana is true," he continued. "It's going to complicate things between you and Dana tremendously. It's going to complicate things in a way you could never imagine. And unless you're willing to fight for your marriage just as strongly as Dana has, what the two of you have is not going to survive."

Mario's words hit home. For the first time in a long time I felt Dana's pain. I now found myself asking what would I have done if she'd left my bed? What would I have done if I had constantly found condoms and phone numbers stuffed underneath the driver's seat of her car.? What would I have done if I had discovered that she had fucked a few of my friends behind my back? But most importantly, what would I have done if a man she'd fucked rang my doorbell, sat on my couch, and told me that he'd gotten my wife pregnant? What would I do?

I shook my head, disappointed in myself. I'd been playing the only woman in the world who'd ever held my back, besides my mother, and it now felt horrible. Now I understood her tears. Now I understood her attempts at loving a man who didn't deserve her love. I understood it all now.

Dana pranced into the kitchen and opened the oven, not even looking in my direction. There had been a lot of that going on over the past couple of days. Usually the atmosphere around our household on Thanksgiving was of happiness. But now it was of growing resentment. And I was the cause.

"I've gotta go, Mario," I said, hanging up without giving him time to answer.

Dana took the turkey from the oven and sat it on the

table. Knowing she wasn't having it, I reached to touch her anyway. I had to. And just as I expected, she stepped away from me.

"Dana," I pleaded. "Can we talk?"

"Terrell!" she called, ignoring me. "Come help set the table!"

Terrell had been downstairs in the basement playing video games since he'd gotten out of bed this morning.

"Sweetheart," I attempted again.

Dana ignored me as she shut off the stove, and began to take numerous pots and pans of food to the dining room table. Our families would be arriving soon. They would soon all know our business and that shit was gonna spread like a wild fire through the family tree.

"Dana, we've got to talk about this," I reasoned, while carrying food to the dining room behind her. "I know I fucked up."

Dana continued to ignore me. She remained stone faced and silent throughout our several trips back and forth from the kitchen.

"Terrell!" she called again on about our fifth trip. "Turn that game off and come up stairs! Your grandmother called. She'll be here soon!"

I couldn't take being ignored by her anymore. "Talk to me, Dana," I ordered, grabbing her by the arm.

Dana snatched away immediately. "Let me go!" she shouted.

"We have to talk about this, Dana. Ignoring it isn't going to make it go away."

"I don't want to talk to you right now, Hardy," she said, her broken heart and pain of my betrayal reflecting in her eyes. Although her mascara was covering the swelling around her eyes from crying so much since Zaria's visit, it was still there if you knew what you were looking for.

"I can't stand the sight of you right now," she roared.

"You're a liar!"

"Dana, listen…"

"I hate you, Hardy!" she screamed. "I hate you!"

My mouth had no response for that one. I'd never imagined I would one day hear those words come from her mouth no matter how much of a dog I'd been to her. It hurt.

"I felt like a fucking idiot when that woman knocked on my door Monday, sat on my couch crying, and said she was pregnant with your child!" she shouted. "And you fucked her in our home!"

I couldn't speak. I'd pushed her to speak and now my guilt wouldn't allow me to say a word in return. Those were lies but I was still guilty.

"I hate you for that, Hardy! You've made me look stupid for the last time!"

My head dropped, afraid of what she meant by the last time. I thought she wanted me to leave just for a few days until things blew over, but now this seemed more permanent.

Dana exhaled and placed her hands against the sides of her head. This one had truly gotten to her. My other fuck ups couldn't have held a candle to this one. They weren't even in the same league. This one was the Super Bowl of all fuck ups. "I don't think she's really pregnant, Dana. And if she is, we'll get a blood test." My head lowered.

"What did I ever do to you other than be a good mother to our son?" she asked somberly, trying not to cry. "What did I ever do to you other than give you my mind, body, and soul?"

There was no answer. What could I say? She had given me all of her and I had given her nothing but headaches and betrayal.

"What did I do to make you want to hurt me this badly, Hardy?"

The doorbell rung.

"Tell your son that it's time to come upstairs," she said, storming out of the kitchen, hating me and the fact that she would have to hide her pain this evening in front of our family.

It took a moment for me to finally move. Like they say, 'the truth hurts.' Damn it hurts. Her daggers had hit their mark and pierced all the way through with no mercy and were now infesting every inch of my own heart with sadness. As I made my way across the kitchen to the basement door and opened it, memories of our wedding day bombarded me. The memory of seeing her hold Terrell so lovingly in her arms shortly after bringing him into this world followed. The memories were coming quickly from everywhere as I headed down the stairs feeling ashamed.

Damn, Id truly fucked things up this time, I thought to myself. She was never going to forgive me for this one. I wouldn't blame her if she was intending to file for a divorce. I deserved it. The problem was NOW I realized that losing her would destroy me. I wouldn't be able to bear the thought of her being with someone else. And I DEFINITELY couldn't bare another man coming into Terrell's life. Being a 'Baby Daddy' wasn't what I wanted. But realizing I'd possibly destroyed my family had now probably come a little too late.

"Terrell!" I called, halfway down the stairs. My head was still lowered. Raising it was too difficult. Even facing my own son was hard. I was honestly dreading looking him in his eyes, knowing that I had possibly made him another statistic; the child of divorced parents.

Terrell didn't answer.

"Lil Man!" I called when I reached the bottom of the stairs. I finally raised my head but immediately froze in one spot, overcome with my worst fear. My blood ran completely cold. This can't be. This can't be. My entire world was crashing and burning at the sight of what was in front of me.

Zaria smiled as she stood beside Terrell with one arm snuggly wrapped around his neck, with her hand over his mouth, while using the other to point a gun at his temple. "What's the fuckin' procedure when you got a gun to your head?" she asked me through gritted teeth.

At that moment I knew she was crazy. She was quoting the famous line from the movie, *Set It Off*, and holding a .32 caliber like she'd done this before. It was crazy 'cause her gun was old, a greenish color, and made we wonder where she'd gotten it. My chest heaved up and down while my breathing nearly stopped.

"I told you, Hardy," she said. "I've devoted myself to this game."

My heart pounded so loud I wondered if she could hear it from where she stood. And my son, my baby boy was terrified. "Zaria, what are you doing!"

"What does it look like, Hardy? I'm forcing you to face your love for me."

Her eyes appeared to be demented; a demon in gray sweats. "Zaria, my son has nothing to do with this. Let him go, pleaseeeee."

"He has everything to do with this. Without him we can't be a family." Quickly, she turned the gun in my direction.

The fear in my son's eyes was killing me. His body shook uncontrollably as his body leaned into Zaria from her strong grip around his neck. I stepped towards him.

Zaria cocked the gun. "Stay where the fuck you are!" she ordered.

I raised my hands. "Okay, Zaria. I won't come any closer. Just please don't hurt him." Tears began to blur my vision. Terrell was my heart. The fact that my selfishness had gotten him involved in this was getting too difficult to take. I'd never forgive myself if something happened to him. Without him I wouldn't be able to function.

"You made it this way, Hardy!" she shouted. "You did this!"

"Oh God," I whispered. "This can't be happening."

"All you had to do was love me."

"Okay, Zaria. I'm willing to try to work it out with you,"

I lied, knowing I had to say whatever it would take to get her to release Terrell. "I realize you're the only woman for me."

"You think I'm stupid, don't you?"

"No, I don't."

"Yes, you do."

"Zaria, I really don't. Let Terrell go."

She smiled. "A third rate ho. Isn't that what you called me? She grinned wickedly."

"I'm sorry, Zaria. I didn't mean that. I swear I didn't."

"Yes you did! Stop lying to me!"

My body tensed.

"You hurt me so badly with that. You really did. But I've got a way we can fix it."

"Okay," I said quickly. "Anything, I'll do anything. Just tell me what you want me to do."

"We have to be a family, Hardy. Me, you, and Terrell. There's no other way."

"Okay," I falsely agreed.

Zaria's face brightened with excitement. "Do you mean it, Hardy?"

"Yes."

"Can we go away from here and get married?"

"Yes, Zaria,' I said, trying my hardest to sound sincere. "We can do whatever you want."

"Are you really serious, Hardy?" she asked excitedly. "Do you really mean it?" She dropped the gun to her side. I mean I expected you to drop Dana without question and tell her that you wanna be with me. I mean didn't you see, *Harlem Nights*?" She paused and blew me a kiss. "Don't you remember when the fat guy called his wife and told her he was never coming home again?"

I nodded.

"That's because he wanted to be with Sunshine," she told me softly, while batting her eyes. "Don't you want to be with me like that, Hardy?"

"Yes," I said, taking a step forward. "I'll buy you the most beautiful dress in the store and the brightest diamond ring in the showcase."

"See, Hardy. I knew you loved me. I knew all I had to do was make you see it."

"You were right all along," I said, smiling and taking another step forward.

"But what are you going to do about Dana?"

"Don't worry about her. I'll take care of her."

Suddenly Zaria pointed the gun at me again.

"I quickly raised my hands in front of me. "What are you doing, Zaria?"

Her face turned serious again. "I have to be sure,' she said.

"What do you mean?"

"Terrell has to come with me."

"No, Zaria," I said straight forwardly. That was not an option.

"It's the only way."

She began to back toward the door that led to the outside staircase that led to and from the basement. My son's face showed his fear as tear after tear dropped to the ground. Time meant everything. I wasn't sure whether to scream for help, or dive on her ass. It was clear that once he left my sight there wasn't anything that said I'd ever see him again.

I followed. "I can't let you take him, Zaria," I told her.

"I told you, Hardy. It's the only way. Now stay where you are." She yanked Terrell even harder.

"Zaria, I can't…"

She placed the gun to Terrell's head. "I said stay where you are, Hardy!"

I froze, knowing that if I tried to charge her, I'd be too late. The gun would kill all that I've ever loved more than myself. From the top of the stairs, Dana's voice could be heard. She kept calling for us both, asking what was going on.

Zaria reached behind her and opened the door.

"Zaria," I begged, "pleaseeeee, no."

"It' the only way to prove you love me and that you truly want us to be a family. It has to be like this. And get rid of Dana for good," she added, waving the gun in my direction. "If you follow me, I swear I'll kill him. I swear I will."

Butterflies filled my gut. I knew there was nothing I could do. I was helpless. More tears began to fall from my eyes at this moment than the day Terrell was born, as I was forced to look my son in his terror filled eyes and say what I hoped and prayed he would understand was not a betrayal...

"I'll get rid of Dana. I promise."

Next thing I knew, Zaria threw up her fingers, showing me deuces and was out.

18 ··· *Zaria*

My father stumbled backwards so hard he fell to the floor as I shoved his door open and stormed into his apartment, passing him, dragging Terrell behind me by the collar of his bright orange polo shirt.

"Zaria, what's going on?" my father asked me, unable to get up.

Not answering him, I grabbed a chair from the kitchen, headed straight for the bedroom, and ordered Terrell to sit down. He was still wailing like a three year-old and had been ever since we sped away from his home over an hour ago.

"Ms. Hopkins," Terrell pleaded. "I wanna go home. I want my mommy."

"So, what! People in hell want water!" I snatched the .32 from underneath my belt and pointed it at his forehead. "What did I tell you in the car on the way here? What did I tell you? Huh?"

Through a stream of falling tears he answered, "You're my mommy now. And you're gonna marry my daddy."

I grabbed his jaws and squeezed them together, noticing how he looked exactly like his father; same eyes, same nose, same facial features. "That's right," I said. "So from now on I

159

don't want to hear anything about your old home or your old mommy. They're dead to you. Do you understand?"

Terrell was too scared to answer. The gun was bigger than his face. Before I knew it, the crotch of his pants were wet, and I could've sworn I saw him making faces at me.

"Do you fucking hear me?" I shouted, now squeezing his jaws together so tight that if I didn't have such a bad habit of biting my nails, they'd probably be poking sharply through his skin right now. "And now that I'm your mommy, understand that pissing on yourself will not be tolerated. Now sit there and learn from that nasty mistake you just made."

Terrell nodded as his body began to shake.

"And don't be hardheaded," I told him. "You heard what your father said. We're going to be a family."

"Zaria, what the hell is going on?" my father asked, limping into the bedroom wondering what this was all about. "Who is this?" His eyes filled with worry "And that's my gun you're holding."

"You never talk, so why now?"

"Who is it?" he asked again.

Voices began to chatter inside my head.

"One of my students," I lied, my heart hammering against my chest. "He's been misbehaving."

"What do you need a gun for? Where are his parents?" he badgered while looking at me like I had two heads. "And, misbehaving on Thanksgiving? Why would he be with you and not them?"

"I need some duct tape," I told him, ignoring his question.

"Something's not right, Zaria. Why is he here?"

The voices in my head grew louder.

"Duct tape!" I screamed to his face. "Quit being so nosey and bring me some fuckin' duct tape! This boy has been misbehaving," I told him, running my fingers through Terrell's curly head.

"Zaria, I've done enough in my life. I don't want any parts of this. That gun…," he tried to say.

I placed the gun underneath his chin hard enough to slightly raise his head to the ceiling. "I don't give a fuck about all that damn self righteous ass bullshit you're trying to run on me right now. I don't have time for it."

"Pull the trigger!" that voice that I hated so much screamed out of nowhere, drowning out the others. "Pull the trigger, Zaria."

"You didn't seem to have a conscience when you were letting those perverted bastards molest your own daughter," I said angrily, jamming the gun even harder underneath his chin. The memories of what he had put me through as a child running rampant in my mind among the voices, the hatred for him just as fresh as always.

"Pull the trigger!" the dominant voice in my head continued to scream at me like a sick chant or war cry.

"You don't even know this little muthafucka," I said. "But you've got a conscience all of a sudden? You actually care more about what happens to him than you did me?"

"Zaria," my father pleaded, the fear of the gun possibly going off and splattering his brains all over the bedroom wall showing in his face. "You need help, Princess."

"Don't call me that! Don't ever fucking call me that! Ever!"

Tears escaped his eyes. "What have I done to my baby? Oh God, what have I done to her?"

"Kill him now!" the voice shouted.

"If I was your princess, you wouldn't have hurt me!" I screamed. My head began to pound. "If I was your princess, you wouldn't have pimped me out like I was whore. Do you know how that made me feel? Do you know how badly it hurt?"

"Zaria, I wish I could erase the past," he pleaded sincerely. "I wish I could've been the father you deserved. Not a

161

day passes by without me wishing I could change it all."

"You don't mean that. Aunt Lisa told me you would try to brainwash me with those types of lies just to make yourself feel better about what you did to me. She told me you hadn't changed. She told me that you would never care about anyone but yourself."

"Baby, I really do mean it. It's your Aunt Lisa who you really have to watch right now. She's not what you think she is. She has an agenda."

"Don't you dare speak about her like that! She loves me. She's the only person who's had my back since you betrayed me."

"Zaria, you don't understand. Her love has deceit hidden behind it. There are things you don't know about her. And she's taking advantage of that."

"Stop it." Hearing him talk about the only other woman on this planet who ever cared about me besides my mother like she was just as evil as him made me want to smack him. She had always praised me. She had always treated me like I was special. And she had always been there when I needed her. She would never do anything to hurt me. He had no right to make her out to be a snake. He was just jealous that she had the balls to be a parent when he abused the job.

"Baby, I know that I'm the last person you should ever believe about anything. I know you'll never trust me again. I don't deserve your trust. But, I swear I'm telling you the truth about your Aunt Lisa. She's hiding something from you. You've got to believe me."

"You're lying!"

"Baby, I'm not."

"Stop talking about her like that or I'll kill you right now!"

"I'm telling you what you need to hear, Zaria. I really am."

I grabbed my head and grimaced at the pain. The pounding was splitting now, aching behind my eyes. I dropped the gun to my side.

"Zaria, it's too late for me," he continued. "But it's not too late for you. Let's take this boy back to his parents." He backed away from me and turned to walk to Terrell.

"Get away from him!" I ordered my father, raising the gun to his back. "I'm his parent now," I told him.

"No, you're not, Princess," he said, turning to me. "The disease is telling you that you are. Don't let it win. Don't let it make you go out this way. Don't let it do to you what it did to me."

"Fuck you!" I spewed. "You don't know what you're talking about!"

My father's body tensed even more, fearing the gun would definitely go off on his ass very soon.

"I'm his mommy now and forever," I said. "And there's nothing you or anyone else can say about it."

"Zaria, please don't." His head bobbed from side to side.

"Shut the fuck up! This is my life!"

"You're destroying your life, Zaria. And not only yours, his also. Baby, you don't have that right."

"Aint that a bitch! You didn't have the right to destroy mine but you did it anyway! Where was all this caring when I needed it from you, huh?"

"Zaria, I was sick just like you."

"I'm not sick. So stop saying that."

"Baby, you've got to break the cycle. If you don't take this boy back to his parents, that'll make you no better than me. I don't want that for you. I swear, I don't. You've still got a chance to live a normal life."

My finger stiffened around the trigger. I hated my father now more than ever. Why did he wait so long to show me the love I needed? Why?

"Zaria, this sickness is consuming you," he said, taking a step towards me.

Instantly, I jammed the gun to his forehead.

"Kill him!" the voice in my head screamed. "Kill him now, Zaria!"

"Baby, I don't care what happens to me anymore," my father said. "I know I'm going to burn in hell for hurting you. But I don't want to see you burn with me. That gun has been cursed, Princess. It's the…"

Hearing his voice annoyed me now too much to take anymore. I smacked him across the mouth with the gun so hard he fell to the floor with blood running from his mouth. This time, positive he wouldn't be able to get up. Swiftly, I ran to the kitchen, knocking over the old bowl of grits on the counter. I scurried through the drawers until I found a roll of grey duct tape. I rushed back to the bedroom and attempted to tape Terrell's ankles and wrists to the chair. But he jumped from the chair and darted past me out of the room so fast that as I tried to grab him I missed. I could only catch the thin air, missing his shirt, then falling to the floor. I hopped up like Jason, unable to be beaten, and chased him to the front door, vowing to beat the blood from his little body.

"Someone help me please!" he screamed. "Help!"

I quickly placed my hand around his mouth, clutching his body with mine. That is until he bit. Hard. Breaking the skin. "Oww!" I screamed.

"Help me!" he yelled again, while kicking and screaming muffled sounds into my other hand.

Out of pure reflex the back of my hand swatted him across the face so hard he fell to the floor. I dragged him roughly, like old carpet, crying and dazed back to the bedroom. Like a ragdoll, I slammed him back in the seat. "You made me do that, Terrell," I told him as I taped his ankles and wrists to the chair. "I'm trying to be nice." I placed a strip over his mouth. "I gave you life Terrell!"

"Zaria, don't do this," my father continued pleading from the floor, crawling like a toddler. "You're throwing your life away."

Ignoring him I began to pace the floor in front of Terrell with the gun at my side. "I'm sorry I had to do this," I told Terrell. "But it was the only way." Immediately, fictitious visions of me on the delivery table giving birth to Terrell invaded my mind. His father was there, by my side, holding my hand and watching my contractions on the monitor. Each time Hardy smiled at me, it gave me the ability to push harder. Sweat filled my face that ironically was lighter; light like Milan's. I pushed and pushed. Then some more. Then, it happened. My beautiful baby boy was born.

Terrell's whimpering interrupted my thoughts. My head was still aching tremendously. I needed to lie down. "Terrell, this was the only way to get your father to see that I'm the woman he was meant to be with forever," I continued, still pacing. "It was the only way to get him to see that I should be his wife and the mother of his son."

"Oh God," my father whimpered.

"Everything is going to be alright though," I said, suddenly cheering up a little. The possibility of what *could be* began to make me smile. "Just watch and see, Terrell," I promised. "Your father's going to come around. I know he is. Then we're going to be a family. Just watch. We're going to move away from here and start all over. You'll get new friends and everything."

Smiley Face, Smiley Face, Can anyone see my Smiley Face... I chanted.

Terrell could only stare.

"I'm going to be a great mother, you'll see. I'm not going to hurt you like my father did to me." I shot my father my cold set of eyes. "I'm never going to subject you to that. I'm going to love you. Watch and see. I'm going to throw you birthday parties every year. I'm going to put more Christmas presents underneath the tree for you than you can count; more than Dana ever did. And I'm going to spoil youuuuuuu," I sang, grabbing hold of one of his cheeks. "Your OLD mother is no match for the type of mom I'm going to be. I'm going to make you so happy." I kissed him on his forehead. "I promise, Terrell."

My headache became unbearable.

"Get up!" I ordered my father, who was now curled up in the corner critiquing me like I was the star in a scary movie.

He slowly got to his feet.

I ran and grabbed another chair from the kitchen as my father struggled to land on his feet. After I managed to get him in the chair, I taped his wrists, ankles, and mouth just like Terrell's. As I closed the bedroom door he mumbled something underneath the tape. Ignoring him, I shut the door and pulled my cell phone from my pocket. I dialed Milan's number and got her answering service again.

After hanging up, I dialed again.

And again.

Still, no answer.

My hand gripped the phone in its palm like a vice grip. A strong anger swept over me so heavy that I wanted to sling the phone against the wall as hard as I could. Why the fuck won't she answer? I'd called her four times today. "You bitch!" I shouted, like she was standing directly in front of me. My shouting made my head pound like a drum, forcing me to lie on the living room couch. The pleasant thought of a bright future with Hardy and Terrell began to comfort me. But within moments I was asleep and those pleasant thoughts were quickly replaced with that nightmare I dreaded so much.

Once again I found myself all alone on that dark street in the pouring rain holding my bags. Once again the sight of a dark figure appearing at the corner sent terror through me. I ran to a nearby familiar house, the stranger's splashing footsteps approaching from behind quickly. My fists pound on the door but no one answers. The stranger is rapidly getting closer. I keep pounding on the door, knowing someone's there, someone who loves me. I can hear their voices. But this time, differently than the original nightmare, I realize that the voices inside belong to my father and my aunt Lisa. I can't make out what they're saying. Why won't they come to the door and help me? The stranger is getting ever so close. I place my ear to the door in time to hear my aunt Lisa say, "We've got ourselves a deal." The stranger grabs my shoulder. Fearing turning to face him, I force myself to awaken.

My shirt was soaked with sweat and I was still clutching the .45 when I opened my eyes. Immediately, I began to wonder why my nightmare had new changes. That nightmare had plagued me for years. But never once did anything in it ever change. This was the very first time. And what did Aunt Lisa mean by 'We've got ourselves a deal'?

Out of the blue, a loud sound came from the bedroom.

Suddenly remembering that Terrell and my father were taped up in that room, I sprung from the couch, ran for the bedroom, and opened the door in time to see my father free from his chair and holding a cell phone to his ear. *When the fuck did he get a cell phone? And who was he calling?*

19 ··· Hardy

"What's the procedure when you've got a gun to your head? What's the FUCKIN procedure when you've got a gun to your head?" I repeated to myself thinking about Zaria's words.

I never imagined in a million years that like Vivica, in *Set It Off* I'd one day be faced with a situation so similar. But in my case the dilemma was more like, what's the fuckin procedure when the one person you love more than the air you breathe has a gun to their head? What do you do when it's your son? The questioned haunted me.

Second by second, and minute by minute, that nightmarish moment had been played over and over again inside my head for the past sixteen hours. I keep searching for the moment when I could've grabbed the gun from Zaria. But I couldn't find one. I couldn't see it anywhere. But it had to be there. It had to be. God, how could I have let her take him? I failed my son. My head fell into my lap as I sat on the couch getting drilled by the lead detective.

"Do you know any of her friends or family?" Detective Santiago, a tall, thirty something year old Hispanic, dressed in a navy blue dress suit asked me. "Anybody she hangs out with?"

It was now Friday morning. The house was filled with

cops and family. At least ten other people walked in and out of the living room making their own conversations about what could've happened, what should've happened, and why. They all had their take on the situation, especially the other detective, a black gruesome looking male who seemed to hate me from the start.

"I said, do you know anybody that she hangs out with?" Santiago repeated.

"No," I answered standing, then pacing the floor, still wearing the same clothes from yesterday. I was exhausted and my eyes were red from shedding tears and getting no sleep.

"Any addresses where she hung out?" the other detective asked.

"No," I answered with frustration.

Dana was sitting on the couch holding herself and slowly rocking back and forth, her eyes swollen from crying all night. Her mother sat beside her, rubbing her back and holding a box of Kleenex in her hand. Every chance her mother got, she rolled her big, bubbly eyes at me, like I was the only person responsible for all of this.

"Are you sure?" the detective asked, looking up from his notepad. "Anyone she…"

"No," I answered again, agitated. "I already told you. We only dated once."

"Dated?" Detective Santiago interrupted. Her eyes grew more puzzled. She gave the other detective a sign letting him know she would take over from there. I'd already explained to her that Zaria and I had fucked in my Tahoe. It embarrassed me to not only admit it in front of Dana during a situation like this one, but also her family. What happened in our marriage was supposed to stay between us, no matter how trifling I had been. But here I was having to admit it in front of our families, especially hers, that I was nothing more than a dog. It was the most shameful feeling.

"Mr. Hardy," Detective Santiago said sympathetically. "I

understand your aggravation. But we have to be sure we know everything. Nothing can be left out or forgotten. Your son's life may depend on it."

"She said something about having a roommate." My adrenaline pumped at the thought. "I don't know her name though."

"We know about that. Her name is Milan. We found that out from the landlord when we went to her apartment. Does the name sound familiar to either of you?"

I shook my head. Dana stared off into space.

"Mrs. Hardy?" the detective asked, while flickering with her fingernails. "Is there anything else you know?"

"No," Dana answered, wiping tears from her eyes. "Have you found the roommate? Maybe she knows something."

"We haven't been able to locate her yet. But we're looking."

"You're looking?" Dana asked angrily and jumping to her feet. "You're looking?"

"Dana," her mother called, standing and trying to console her. "They're doing their best."

"I'm tired of hearing, you're looking! she screamed. "Find my son! He's all I have!"

Her mother placed her arms around her daughter and held her tightly, sitting her back down on the couch as Dana cried uncontrollably. Snot trickled from her nose, and tears flooded her cheeks. Dana held onto her stomach as if she needed to throw up. Her heart was broken, along with her spirit. From the emotion seen in her eyes, I knew Dana would never be the same until we found Terrell.

The sight broke my heart in pieces. I wanted to comfort Dana myself like a husband was supposed to in a situation like this but she wouldn't allow me to. She'd screamed that she hated me just moments ago and that she never wanted me to touch her again when I tried to hug her.

My thoughts quickly rolled back to the day before.

"How could you let her take him!" she screamed, beating her fists against my chest when I rushed upstairs from the basement yesterday with tears in my eyes and told her Zaria had taken Terrell.

"Baby, she had a gun to his head," I tried to explain. "She said she would kill him if I tried to follow her."

"You son of a bitch!" she continued, shouting to the top of her lungs while punching and scratching mc. "How could you let her take him? How could you let that bitch take my child!"

I remembered those screams and those words over and over again, and the memory of me grabbing hold of her in my arms; the two of us finally collapsing to the floor, and her screams finally turning into whimpers muffled by my chest.

The two of us remained near the front door until the police came. Now, as I looked at her breaking down in her mother's arms, her screams of, '*how could you let her take him*' started to echo throughout my head again, killing me with guilt. I'd thought I was doing the right thing when I let Terrell go. I'd thought I was saving his life. Now I wasn't sure.

Detective Santiago walked over to Dana and knelt in front of her. "Mrs. Hardy," she said softly, placing a hand on her thigh. "I have a son also." She reached into her suits inside pocket and pulled out a picture of her son dressed in a soccer uniform, offering it to Dana.

Dana sniffed and wiped away one of countless falling tears. She accepted the picture, looking at the young boy in the photo as if he were her own.

"His name's Miguel," the detective said just above a caring whisper. "He's nine. The picture was taken a few months ago."

"He's beautiful," Dana said, wiping away another tear and focusing on the boys face with a smile.

"Thank you," the detective said. "Now I have a picture of Terrell, too. And every law enforcement agency in our area will be searching for him."

Dana nodded. She couldn't stop looking at the photo. And I couldn't stop looking at Santiago's ass. It reminded me of J. Lo's just camouflaged by her outfit. Dana was captured by the boy's innocence, his ignorance of everything bad in the world. But still an ass was an ass.

"Dana," the detective said.

Dana looked at her, silently knowing why Detective Santiago now called her by her first name. They were now more than cop and victim. They were two fellow mothers who loved the children they had brought into the world.

"If anything ever happened to Miguel," the detective continued genuinely, "I don't know how I'd be able to find the strength to make it through another day. So I understand your frustration."

Both women were looking directly into each other's eyes.

"Mother to mother," Detective Santiago said. "We're doing, and will continue doing everything we can to bring Terrell home safely. You have my word on that, okay?" She squeezed Dana's thigh.

Dana nodded.

I was still pacing nervously as the detective stood. "Mr. Hardy," she said, focusing her attention back on me. "Do you know anyone else that might have wanted to get back at you in any way?"

"No," I answered, thinking about Yvonne, Keisha, Monica, Lolita, Ebony, Leslie, and Cynthia…just to name a few.

She wrote something in her notepad.

I couldn't help feeling like my standing here answering questions wasn't enough. I could do so much more to find Terrell myself but had no idea of what. Damn, I felt so helpless.

"You told me earlier that you think she's mentally disturbed. During the short time that you've known Ms. Hopkins," she asked. When was the first time she came off to you as being

173

even the slightest bit unstable? And did you ever see her take any medication?"

"The day she went off on me in the school hallway was the first time I noticed she was a little crazy. As far as medication, I never saw her take anything."

"And you're sure that nothing else happened between the both of you sexually after the evening in the truck?"

"Yes, detective. I'm sure."

"I'm asking because she's coming off to me as more than just mentally unstable. The constant calling, threats on the mirror, explosions in the workplace, and coming by your house. She sounds like she may be a threat to society. We ran her name through our system. She has a record of countless incidents." The size of Santiago's eyes multiplied, putting fear into my heart. "Some psychotic," she added.

"Oh, God," Dana said fearfully.

"I'm going to check with some area psychiatrists and psych wards,' the detective said. "And see if she may have been a patient at any time."

The thought of me turning my son over to a basket case nearly made my knees buckle. Visions of him sitting in some dark basement being tortured brought a fear over me like no other I had ever imagined.

"In the meantime," she said with confidence, "we're staking out every bus station, train station, and airport in the city. We've got officers stationed at her apartment, just in case she shows up there."

Her words brought absolutely no comfort to me. The room seemed to be getting smaller and smaller by the second, making me claustrophobic. I needed air…could barely breathe. As soon as she'd asked her last question I went out on the porch, stuffed my hands in my pockets, and stared into the morning sun, hoping God could feel my pain, hoping he could ease it as the cold, November air battered my skin. Memories of seeing Terrell riding his bike up and down this street made tears begin to fall endlessly. My world felt shattered from the ground up without my Lil Man. I needed him. Without him I'd never be able to function again.

I'd brought the devil herself into the lives of the people I loved in the worst way imaginable. I didn't know where to turn or what to do. For the first time in my life I felt totally lost. And as the sun shone from the sky my world remained dark.

All of a sudden, my cell phone rang. I snatched it from my pocket, hoping it was Zaria. Like the police, I'd tried calling her cell but it just rang. The number coming through now on my screen was one I didn't recognize.

"Hello," I answered.

"Hi, sweetheart," blared Zaria's voice. Strangely, she talked pleasantly, as if she hadn't just kidnapped my son.

My heart raced. I tried to remain calm as I spoke with fear. "Zaria, where is Terrell?" I asked quickly, desperate to hear him.

"He's with me, silly," she said playfully. "Where else would he be?"

"Let me talk to him."

"Baby, he's okay."

"Let me talk to him, Zaria! Please!"

I needed more than anything in the world right now to hear his voice. My heart and sanity needed it in order to keep me moving forward.

"Okay, baby," she agreed. "Calm down. But only for a second."

I listened to her telling him that someone wanted to speak to him. Anxiously, I waited. Each fraction of a second felt like an hour.

"Hello," Terrell said fretfully.

My world brightened. I closed my eyes. "Lil Man?"

"Daddy!" he screamed happily.

"Are you okay?"

"Yes, but I want to come home. I'm hungry and I miss

you."

"I know, Lil Man. I know you do. And I'm going to get you home. Where are you?"

"I don't know," he sniffled.

"Are you at someone's house?" I opened my eyes.

I heard the phone get snatched away from him.

"Hardy?" Zaria said.

"Zaria, bring him home," I demanded, wanting to talk to my son a little longer, missing the brief sound of his voice already.

"Now you know I can't do that," she said. "You promised we would make a new home for him. Have you gotten rid of Dana yet?"

"Zaria, stop it! I don't want my son to hear you speak of his mother that way."

"He needs to start living the truth." Her voice grew more evil, filled with venom. "He has to find out at some point. Hardy, he'll never see her again, right?"

Anger and rage built up inside me as I took the phone away from my ear and squeezed it tightly in frustration. I wanted to kill her with my bare hands. I wanted to make her suffer like I was suffering, but I realized I had to keep my composure. That was the only way I'd get Terrell back. I put the phone back to my ear. "Zaria, I know I promised you that," I said calmly. "And I'm going to keep that promise."

"Do you mean it, Hardy?" she asked with excitement in her voice.

"Yes, Zaria." I lied. "I mean it. I have someone taking care of the Dana problem. Now tell me where you are so I can come see you guys. I miss you."

"I miss you, too, Hardy." Zaria's tone had now gone back to a happy child on Christmas morning. "This is going to work out so beautifully. You, me, and Terrell are going to make a great family. I can't wait to do the family portrait," she told me crazily. "And Terrell is already calling me mommy."

"That's good, Zaria," I said, nauseous at the thought of my baby calling her mommy.

"It's really going to work out, Hardy."

"I know. Now where are you guys? I paid a guy to rob our home, and kill Dana while I'm away from the house."

Zaria gasped. She rattled off an address and room number to a Red Roof Inn motel in Secaucus, New Jersey. I could tell she believed me. I memorized it with ease. "Okay, Zaria," I said in a panic, "I'm on my way."

"Hardy, make sure you're alone, okay?" she uttered. "No police. Nothing funny, okay?"

"Nothing funny. It's all about us."

"Promise me that from here on out it's just me, you, and Terrell."

"I promise, Zaria."

The phone went dead.

Millions of thoughts ran through my mind from the backseat as Detective Santiago drove like a bat out of hell. I felt like Obama riding deep in a motorcade with an entourage filled with police, ammunition, and one mark in mind; Zaria. I stared out of the black Crown Vic's tinted windows watching street after street. They each whizzed by in a blur. The siren wailed loudly, forcing traffic to the side as we, along with several other unmarked cars and patrol cars sped through New Jersey neighborhoods at nearly a hundred miles an hour.

I looked over at Dana, wanting to touch her. She hadn't said a word to me since we left the house. Santiago tried to keep her from coming along but she refused to stay home. I wondered what she was thinking. Were her worries identical to mine? Did she have the same fears? Would she ever be able to look at me again? Detective Santiago was now on the radio telling the New Jersey Police Department that Zaria was armed and dangerous, and that they were not to make any moves until she arrived.

I turned back to my window. The thought of my son soon being surrounded by so many guns made my heart hurt tremendously. If one accidentally went off and hit him, I'd never forgive myself. I kept wishing over and over again that I hadn't gotten him into this. My body jerked with every turn and swerve of the darting car. The closer we got, the farther away we seemed. My heart pounded rapidly. It hadn't slowed since we left the house. Silently, I prayed to God to let this turn out for the very best, to let me have a second chance to be a father and husband. I'll do it right this time, I told myself.

Several minutes later, the car pulled into the parking lot of the Red Roof Inn, and screeched to an abrupt stop. My eyes scurried the area realizing that it was highly populated with tons of people walking about. I noticed the three other hotels nearby with one being across the street, and wondered why she'd chosen the Red Roof Inn. Then out of the blue, my phone rang. I jumped, figuring it was Zaria. I'm sure by now she had looked out the window and figured out that I'd brought the police. We each quickly jumped out of the car as I held the phone to my ear with all eyes on me.

"I'm gonna have to call you later," I told Yvonne firmly. I was done with cheating and would have to let all my bitches know at a later time. With that I hung up and listened to Santiago relay instructions on our plan.

"I'm going to need you two to stay here," Santiago told me and Dana as she put on her bulletproof vest and cocked her black 9mm Glock.

"No," me and Dana argued, refusing to stay behind. "We have to go with you."

"I can't allow that," she said, signaling for another officer to follow her. "Believe me, Mr. Hardy, we know what we're doing."

"Detective!" I called as she rushed to the front of the motel. An officer slid in front of me and Dana, blocking our path. Santiago met up with several other officers at the front office, congregating and sorting out what would be done. From the right side of my peripheral vision, I could see three others dressed like SWAT already taking their positions at the top of the stairs, and noticing a sharp shooter on the roof.

I folded my hands behind my head and turned to keep from throwing up. I had no idea what to do with myself. Police cars and flashing lights were everywhere. I kept thinking about Zaria's words, "No police." I was so nervous, I didn't know what to do.

I turned around just in time to see Detective Santiago and several other officers quickly make their way up the motel's stairs to the second floor with their guns drawn. "Oh, God," I whispered as they stopped at room 24. My heart felt like it would explode. Detective Santiago identified herself and demanded entry but received no answer.

I watched from below without blinking even once. After identifying herself again and still not receiving an answer Detective Santiago nodded to another officer. He quickly positioned himself in front of the door and kicked it in, with the force of a bulldozer.

Goosebumps invaded my skin. I gasped then watched Dana place a hand over her mouth. Together, we watched as the officers rushed into the room with guns pointed. I knew it would be only a matter of minutes before we'd hear gunfire. I felt dizzy. Everything around me began spinning. The moment seemed like it would never end. The seconds dragged on like weights were tied to them. I wanted to hug Dana as the seconds ticked by. Detective Santiago finally came out of the room and holstered her gun. By the look on her face, I knew she would be the bearer of bad news as she slowly walked down the stairs and made her way toward us.

"I'm sorry," she said genuinely. "They weren't in there."

"No," Dana said angrily, refusing to believe it. "Terrell!" she called up to the room. "Terrell!"

I tried to hug her.

She quickly snatched away and slapped me. "You did this!" she screamed. "I hate you!"

Detective Santiago and another officer pulled her away as she kicked and clawed to get to me. Then my cell rang again, starling us all. It was the same number Zaria had called from before, but I refused to tell them it was her. I answered, then listened trying to keep a straight face as she shouted, making a wide range of threats. I hung up hoping a good plan would come to mind. It was clear that she'd seen us arrive with the police. I just couldn't figure out how she escaped. "Honey, let's go home," I told Dana, feeling sick once again. She snatched away from me and stared at me like I was a murderer.

"Home?" she asked in disbelief. "You no longer live with me," she told me with a vengeance. "Find someplace else to live. And I mean it," she ended while getting back into the Crown Vic, and locking the back door.

Santiago just looked at me and motioned for me to catch a ride with the other detective.

20 · · · *Zaria*

"I told you that you were nothing more than a naïve, foolish bitch", the voice in my head teased, as if taking pleasure in my misery.

I couldn't tell the voice that I really did believe Hardy would show up at the hotel alone, without Dana, without the police. Then it would never leave me alone. With the gun in my hand, my body had been rocking back and forth on the bed for hours. My hair was matted to my head and looked as if I'd been stung by a police taser gun. The pain of being betrayed felt like nails being driven into my hands. It was unbearable...difficult to even breathe. Hardy had done it this time, leaving me no choice but to hit him with the ultimate revenge. I would kill myself and our son.

Even in the darkness, which now felt like the greatest shelter on earth, I was now sitting in the back spare bedroom of Aunt Lisa's house, which still looked exactly as it did the day I moved out. Absolutely nothing had been touched or rearranged; pictures, stuffed animals, nothing. My bed was still even made the same way I'd left it.

"You can't let them get away with this," that voice reasoned. "You have to get them all back. You have to let them know by any means necessary that there is a steep price for hurting you."

Finally, the voice was right. They all needed to pay: My father, Milan, Hardy, Dana, Jamal…the list continued. They all needed to finally know that I was the wrong bitch to fuck with. They all needed to know what pain truly felt like. Hardy would feel it for sure.

I stopped thinking for a moment to check the floor for Terrell. Like a trained boy he was still in place, with his hands tied behind his back and his curly hair completely shaven. I'd done it moments ago in retaliation for how much he reminded me of Hardy. Terrell never shouted, he simply cried, and looked at me strangely through the darkness as if I were some sadistic murderer. His heart was completely broken in half and it showed clearly. I wanted his father to hurt the same way.

The fact that he'd played me for a fool had me hyped, ready to kill. He must not have known that I knew how to play the game. He really thought I'd given him the correct hotel and room number? *Fool*, I said to myself out loud. Thankfully, I'd checked into the Howard Johnson's directly across the street from the Red Roof Inn, under another name, using cash. I told the clerk that my abusive boyfriend, Terrell's father was after us. Luckily, he gave me a room facing the street, the same street that I watched the militia roll in on, with Hardy leading the pack. It hurt so badly to lie to him, but something told me he couldn't be trusted. His deceit made me sick to my stomach.

My mind flashed back to seeing about eight police cars with flashing lights pulling into the Red Roof Inn parking lot like something out of a movie I'd seen. My heart began to race as I told Terrell to get his coat on. I stood in the window from the 8th floor, with the perfect view watching, Hardy and Dana emerge from the Crown Vic; surveying it all in disappointment, rage, and disbelief. Each fought inside my heart for the dominant spot. Dana needed to be disposed of.

I remembered screaming, "You lying son of a bitch! You

promised!"

I snatched Terrell by his hand, bolted out the room into the hallway, and out the backdoor, setting off the fire alarm. The two of us dashed up the alley to the next street where I'd parked the blue Ford Taurus I had rented before we left New York, and quickly sped off. As we rode away, Terrell placed both his knees into his seat and stared out the back window, desperately watching for his daddy. Desperately hoping someone would save him.

"Terrell, you'll never see your daddy again," I told him coming back to reality. Quickly, I leaned toward the floor, checking to make sure my old jump rope was still tied tightly around his wrist. "But don't worry, a father means you no good anyway."

Terrell began to cry once again.

"Just think about it. I should've killed my father," I told him, getting back onto the bed and rocking back and forth much faster. I began zoning out again. "He betrayed me too." I thought about how my father had managed to get out of the tape when I had Terrell at his place, and cut himself loose with a switchblade that he'd obviously had in his pocket.

When I caught him on his cell phone attempting to call the police, I should've blown his fucking heart to the back of his chest. I should've murdered that miserable son of a bitch. He had the 911 operator on the line claiming that he was doing it for me.

I thought about how I'd jammed the gun into his eye. "Hang it up!" I demanded.

He slowly took the phone away from his ear and flipped it closed. "Baby, I'm sorry," he pleaded.

With a backhand so brutal, slapped him across the face with the gun, sending him to the floor. "You son of a bitch!" I screamed, grabbing the lamp from the nightstand and crashing it over his back. Visions of all those sick, child-molesting bastards forcing themselves inside me over and over again filled my head, causing me to angrily let loose on my father with two kicks to the ribs.

"Ahhhhh," he screamed in pain.

His screams of agony nearly made my pussy wet. I quickly took aim and kicked him in his mouth, sending blood and teeth spewing everywhere. "How does it feel?" I remembered asking.

He held a hand over his bleeding mouth, groaning in pain. Then I kicked his legs open, took aim at his balls, and kicked them into his stomach as hard as I could. He grabbed his crotch and slammed his legs shut immediately, rolling onto his side, gasping for air.

"Going somewhere, Daddy?" I asked, kicking him in his back.

He screamed as he grabbed his back and arched it inward. But there was only one way to top it all off. "Turn over on your fucking back!" I ordered. He was now tucked into another fetal position, moaning like a wounded animal. "Turn over on your back so I can see your face!" I screamed. He slowly obliged, a battered, bleeding, and beaten mess with no fight in him. It was payback time. I stood over my father, cocked the gun, and aimed at his face.

"Do it, Zaria," he begged, coughing up blood. "Lord knows you deserve it."

I stared down into his eyes expecting them to be as cold and heartless as they were during the times when he would watch those men treat me like I was less than dirt. But they weren't. Instead, they were filled with sadness, sadness that I knew was real. And a desperate need to be put out of his misery.

"I won't be mad at you, baby,' he whispered. "I owe you my last breath."

My trigger finger loosened.

I couldn't. I dropped the gun to my side.

"That's my Princess," my father whispered lovingly, even through his pain.

I couldn't look at him anymore. That's when I quickly freed Terrell, left my father alone in his own blood, and fled to the Howard Johnson's in New Jersey.

Suddenly, a knock came at the door, abruptly snatching me back from another flashback. Panic rushed through me. Had the police discovered where we were? My heart thumped through my dirty sweatshirt. And Terrell's eyes ballooned. He wouldn't dare say a word, or call for help for fear that I'd slice his mother from the top of her tits down to her pussy. I had told Terrell step by step what I would do to her if he even screamed, made a wrong move, or pretended that I wasn't his mother.

The doorknob rattled.

I stood from the bed, tucked the gun in my jeans, and rushed over to Terrell, who was still bawled up in the corner on the floor. I grabbed him by the neck. "What did I tell you to say if anyone asks you who you are?" I asked quickly in a loud whisper, looking back and forth from Terrell to the door.

"Zaria!" someone called from behind the door, still attempting to twist and turn the knob repeatedly.

Relieved that it was my aunt, I drilled my hostage some more. "What do you say?" I asked, removing the rope from his hands and throwing it underneath the bed.

"That I'm one of your students," Terrell answered in a moping tone, running his tiny hand across his bald head.

"That's right," I said. "And don't say anything else. I'll do all the talking. Do you understand me?" My eyes were locked on his.

"Yes, Mommy," he answered.

"Yes WHAT, damn it?"

"Yes, Mommy Dearest," he corrected himself.

That was our new rule, enacted when we fled the hotel. Mommy Dearest, yes, I loved the sound of it. I pulled my shirt up enough for him to see the gun tucked underneath my belt. "Don't get cute," I warned.

"Zaria!" Aunt Lisa called again. "What are you doing in

there? Who's in there with you, girl?"

I walked across the room, turned the light on, and unlocked the door. "Hey, Aunt Lisa," I said, now smiling as I
opened the door.

"Is everything okay?" she asked, looking at me
strangely.

"Of course."

"Who is that?" she asked, looking over my shoulder at
Terrell who was now standing in the corner.

"One of my students," I said quickly, not even giving
Terrell a chance to open his mouth and spoil everything.

"Well, baby, why do you have him here?" she asked
skeptically. "Shouldn't he be at home with his parents? And
what's up with you?"

The questions were getting on my nerves. "He's a foster
child. And the school has started a new program that allows
teachers to take them home one night out the week so they can
see what it's like to be in a stable environment."

Aunt Lisa looked even more skeptical. "So why here,
and not your place?'

Why was she asking so many questions? Had the police
been here already, I wondered. Was she trying to set me up,
too? The current moment and old memories of her proving that
she would never hurt me clashed. I watched her carefully.

"With all these folks abusing children these days," Aunt
Lisa commented, "they actually let you take the kids home?"

It was obvious she was seeing through my story.

"Zaria, that don't sound right," she said straight forwardly. "What's really going on here? And who is this little
boy?"

"Look, Aunt Lisa," I said. "I need a place to stay for a
few days."

"Why? What's wrong with your place?"

"Nothing. I just really need to crash here for a little
while."

A look of worry spread across her face. "Oh my God, Zaria," she said, her eyes traveling back and forth from me to Terrell. "Are you in trouble? What did you do?"

The questions were beginning to make my head ache. "I didn't do anything, Aunt Lisa," I said, placing my hand to my head and narrowing my eyes to relieve the pounding behind them.

"Zaria, you don't look good. You should go see Dr. Seethers again. Should I call her now?"

"No, I'm fine."

"You don't look fine."

The pounding grew so bad I winced in pain. "I'll go Monday," I lied, trying to get her to ease off. I knew by Monday I would be in Heaven.

"That's it," she said. "You're going to see her today. I'll watch your student." She headed towards Terrell.

"No!" I screamed, fed up. "Noooooooo!"

My aunt stopped and stepped back fearfully.

"I don't want to go!" I shouted. "And I'm not going! Do you hear me? I'm not going!"

Everything suddenly grew silent. Neither of us spoke for several moments.

I felt bad for screaming on her. I walked past her and positioned myself in front of Terrell. "I know you mean well, but I'm grown," I said understandingly.

"I just want to help you."

I nodded. "You can help by letting me stay here for a few days while my apartment is being bombed. I got roaches," I sighed.

"No problem. You got anything planned for your birthday?" she asked, smiling softly.

"No," I answered.

"Good. I want to do something special for you. Would that be okay?"

"That would be alright," I told her.

One NIGHT Stand

The two of us hugged. It felt so good to be in the arms of someone I could trust. It felt like her arms belonged to my mother.

"I love you," she whispered in my ear. "But you've got to get yourself together."

"I know. I'll see Dr. Seethers soon," I lied.

The doorbell rang, scaring me so badly I snatched away from my aunt's arms immediately and backed myself completely in front of Terrell. My heart started pounding again and my body began to tremble. I wanted to snatch Terrell and run. It was the police, I thought. It had to be.

My father's warnings began to fill my head. Was he right after all? Was she setting me up? Was her love really genuine? I wanted to reach underneath my shirt and grab the gun but something wouldn't allow me to. I didn't know what to do. Could I trust her? Could I?

"Zaria, what's wrong?" she asked, looking at me with that exact same strange look she had when I first opened the door.

I only stared, searching for a sign of betrayal or deceit. Had she deceived me, I wondered. Could she do what everyone else in my life had done?

"Baby, calm down," she said, taking my hand. "I don't know what you need to stay here for. But you're safe here." Her words were just as warm and caring as they had always been. "Now come on," she said, slowly pulling me to the stairs.

At first I fought back like a little kid being dragged by an attacker then reluctantly I followed. Her words had calmed me but not completely. My hand was still itching to grab the .45 and bust a cap if need be.

"You too," she called out to Terrell. "I got somebody I want ya'll to meet."

Terrell stood from the floor and followed us downstairs looking like he'd gotten the balls to do something slick. When my Aunt let go of my hand and headed to the door, I stood behind Terrell and placed my hands on his shoulders. Although my heart rate and adrenaline had slowed, there was still a slight urge to run.

Aunt Lisa opened the door. "Hi, Devin," she said happily, greeting the man at the door.

"Hey, Ms. Harris," he returned with a smile.

"Come on in out the cold," she said, grabbing his hand and pulling him inside. "This is Zaria," she introduced, closing the door. "She's the niece I've been telling you about."

"Hello, Zaria," he said, extending his hand. "I'm Devin," sounding like Barry White.

"Nice to meet you," I said, accepting his hand but feeling a little awkward. What did she mean by, 'the niece I was telling you about?'

"Your son?" he asked, pointing to Terrell.

"One of my students," I answered.

"Yeah, your aunt told me you were a teacher."

"Did she?" I asked, looking at my aunt and wondering why she had volunteered my information with some man I didn't even know.

Aunt Lisa was smiling. "Isn't he just as fine as he can be?" she asked me.

"Excuse me," I told Devin. I grabbed my aunt by the arm and led her to a corner where I could still watch Terrell. "What's that all about?" I asked her.

"What?" she asked, dumbfounded.

"That over there," I said, pointing. "Why are you discussing my personal business with a total stranger?"

"He's not a stranger," she said. "He's a football trainer in the off season, and has been training your cousin lately. I see him all the time. And I wasn't discussing your personal business. I just gave him a few tidbits to get him interested in you."

"Aunt Lisa, this really isn't a good time for me to be trying to hook up with someone."

"Zaria, there's never a bad time to find a good man.

Plus, he got money, girl. He can be a good provider to you. Especially when you have kids."

"Aunt Lisa," I moaned.

I glanced over at Devin who was holding a one-sided conversation with Terrell. He was cute, I had to admit, even a little cuter than Hardy. I'd noticed, his foreign-looking skin tone, sharp cheek bones, thick pink lips, and those sort of Asian-like slanted eyes that Tyreese has. He was about 6'1" and muscular weighing about 230 if I had to guess. His hair was neatly divided into two thick corn rolls that went down the back of his head and past his shoulders. I also noticed a nasty scar on the right side of his neck.

"Come on," Aunt Lisa said, grabbing my arm and dragging me back over to where Terrell and Devin were now talking.

My eyes widened with paranoia. What were they talking about? Had Terrell told him he'd been kidnapped. I rushed by my aunt, snatched Terrell by the wrist, and dragged him to the kitchen. "What did you tell him?" I asked angrily in a loud whisper.

"Nothing," Terrell said quickly, eyes popping from his head.

I searched his eyes, unsure if he was telling the truth.

"I swear I didn't say anything," Terrell said. "He asked what I like to do and I told him I like to play basketball."

I grabbed him by both shoulders and jerked him towards me. "Are you sure?"

"Yes, Mommy Dearest," he answered. "I didn't say anything else. I swear I didn't."

Reluctantly I let him go, still not convinced he wasn't lying but I couldn't prove it.

"Is everything okay?" Aunt Lisa asked, walking into the kitchen.

"Yeah," I said, forcing a smile.

"Then come on. Don't keep this man out here waiting,

Zaria."

The three of us headed back out into the living room.
Devin had taken his coat off and was now sitting on the couch.
Before he or anyone else could say a word, still skeptical about
what he and Terrell were talking about I said, "Look, Devin. I
don't know what my Aunt told you about me. But what are your
intentions? I don't have time for games."

He stood and raised his hands in front of himself in defense. "I'm sorry, Zaria," he said genuinely. "I thought your
Aunt had told you I was coming. I didn't mean any harm or disrespect."

"You're not causing any," Aunt Lisa assured him.

"Are you sure?" he asked, looking as if leaving might be
best.

"Yes," she said.

"Zaria," he said, stepping toward me. "Your Aunt has
been telling me wonderful things about you for the past several
months. She made you sound like a very intelligent, beautiful
black woman. And from what I see right now she was right. I
just wanted to meet you, that's all. I meant no harm or games."

After a moment of staring at him, not quite knowing
what to make of him I sighed in defeat. I wasn't absolutely sure
if he was the real deal, and obviously I was still hurting over
Hardy, but suddenly, I remembered what Dr. Seethers had said
in our last session. "Move on. Forget about Gerald Hardy and
find new love."

"Can we start again," Devin asked innocently.

I nodded.

"He smiled and extended his hand. "Hi, I'm Devin."

I accepted his hand and returned his grin. "I'm Zaria."

"Pleasure to meet you, Zaria."

We both laughed.

I let down my defenses and let him in. For nearly an
hour we talked and I found myself taken in by his conversation
and swagger. But most importantly, the fact that he was taking

my mind off of Hardy and my current situation. He was truly coming off like a sweetheart and I had to admit it was working. He appeared to be the man I'd been waiting for.

By the end of the night he had asked me out and I accepted. It felt good to say yes, and to have someone interested in me again. It felt amazing to find a hint of sunshine in a situation as dark as the one I was now going through. The only problem; how could I go out while being wanted for kidnapping? I thought about calling Hardy to make amends, and return Terrell. Then it hit me. The police were now involved and they'd go for jail time. I wasn't about to go to jail while I had this man all over me. He loved me. I could tell. So Terrell had to go.

After seeing Devin out the door, and talking a few moments with Aunt Lisa, Terrell and I retreated back to the seclusion of my bedroom, its loneliness reminding me of my current problems. It wasn't long before my cell rang. I let it go straight to voicemail. When I played it back, it sent chills up my spine. It was a detective wanting to question me in Brent's murder. Immediately, I got scared. How much did he know? Did someone see me coming out of Brent's apartment after all? Did they find my fingerprints? Did Milan run and tell him lies about me? All I had was questions, no answers.

Then suddenly my cell rang again. This time it was Milan. I answered quickly, panting as if I'd walked ten flights of stairs. "Milan, I answered wildly. "I've been calling you."

"I know. I had a meltdown. I'm sorry. Can we meet in an hour? I want to apologize and share some important information with you."

"Information?"

"Yeah. It's for your own good."

Damn, I wanted to cry like Thelma and Louise after one of their major arguments, and when their friendship got back on track. Milan was my girl for life. I figured she wanted to tell me the police had probably called her about me.

21 · · · *Zaria*

The trash bag filled with Terrell's body felt lighter than I expected as I took it from the trunk of my cousin, Kenneth's car, which I'd stolen hours ago. He'd given me the keys to run to the store. But instead, both Terrell and I drove to this desolate industrial area forty miles outside of New York. I thought back to how I'd been rushing like crazy, trying to plan Terrell's death and make it back to the city to meet Milan for lunch. I told Terrell his dad had a surprise for him, which put a half-a-smile on his face.

Ironically neither of us actually saw the murder, neither me nor Terrell. His back was to me and my eyes were shut. The both of us only heard the explosion from the gun. Half a second later, I heard his young lifeless body fall limply to the cold earth. I didn't have the heart to face him as I took his life away. That was why I made him get on his knees, refusing to allow him to look me in the eye. In my heart, I felt that was the most merciful way to do it. The voices told me differently, but I'm no fool. Having him see his death would've been too cruel. It had to be done that way; especially since it was his father's fault.

Hardy had shown through his selfish actions that he didn't want me, nor did he respect me as a woman. When he

193

brought the police to that motel despite promising me that he would come alone, that was more than enough to prove he couldn't be trusted. Ever. Moving on had become the next option. I now wanted to start focusing on what me and Devin would build together. To do that, I could no longer be a mother.

More guilty thoughts flooded my mind, the more I dragged my son's body. A light snow began to fall as I carried him through the early afternoon's darkness to the nearby flowing river. The frigid temperature made my breath cloud in front of me. When we reached the river, I couldn't help wondering just how cold it might be beneath its waves. Before this moment dispensing of the child's body was something, although I didn't look forward to, I knew I *had* to do. But now standing at the edge with the sound of a passing train somewhere off in the distance, the act felt heartless.

Despite my reservations though, I stepped closer to the river with my heart pounding. My mind switched to Milan. I knew she'd be waiting to see me. She'd told me it was urgent. Then I glanced at the trash bag, thinking about Hardy and what he'd done. Hopefully, this would send the message to all men, loud and clear. *Cheaters never win.*

Closing my eyes, I took a deep breath and heaved the bag from my arms, hearing it splash loudly only a second later. I took a deep breath, realizing I needed water. Bad. Instantly, I became nauseous again, for the third time in two days. Something inside me, made me want to throw up. I wasn't sure if my lies had caught up with me, and I was really pregnant carrying Hardy's baby, or maybe I'd developed a conscious.

Two hours later, I was back to normal. As usual Times Square was loud, bustling with people. Traffic flowed through the streets busily in every direction. The sidewalks were packed like sardines with people making their way quickly to various destinations. The towering buildings, soaring street lamps, and bright lights shone down on the chaos, illuminating it gloriously.

As I stared out the restaurant's window while sipping Vodka, my mind reviewed all the past events. It placed me in a daze. Had I made all the correct decisions? I asked myself over and over again. Had I? Were all my actions past, present, and future justified? The answer to each question was 'yes'. When someone hurts you, you have the God given right to get revenge, no matter how vicious you choose to pay the person back. For minutes, I reasoned with myself.

It was time for a fresh start. The thought of starting over sent a soft smile across my face. Devin's face appeared in my thoughts. I wasn't going to make the same mistakes with him that I'd made far too many times before. I was going to be the greatest woman walking God's green earth to him. I was going to fulfill all of his fantasies, and become the most important part of his reality.

Milan slipped into the booth quietly, sitting across from me. Feeling her presence, I turned to her from the window. My eyes lit up. "Thank you for coming," I said happily. "After our last time seeing each other I didn't think you'd want to see me again."

"I really didn't either," she snapped.

"Why did you call me here if you're gonna act nasty?"

"Zaria, you're in trouble," Milan said, placing her hand on mine. She then moved away from the table quickly.

The crowded restaurant began to grow even more crowded. Every second seemed to be met with a new couple coming in out of the cold, placing their coats over the back of their chairs, and having a seat.

"Milan, I know you're mad at me," I said wanting her hand back on mine. "And I know I haven't always been the best roommate. I know all of that, but I want to work things out." I paused. "I appreciate you trying to warn me. I know the police called you, just like they called me. That's why you wanted to meet, right."

Milan chose her words carefully as she spoke closely, looking around the bustling restaurant. "Yes, they did call. I assured them that you were not all the things they said you were. For God's sake, I told them you were a teacher."

"Thanks for defending me, Milan. You've always been like a sister to me."

Milan only shifted slightly in her seat, her eyes directly on me, unblinking. "So if we're like sisters then you should tell me the truth. I'll help you," she begged. "I just don't think you should be evading the police." She paused to shuffle around in her seat again. "If you did kill Brent, we need to get you a lawyer," she told me sincerely.

"I don't want to do all of that Milan," I said as if my new glow should've been obvious to anyone looking at me. "I'm a new person." My words were now filled to the brim with tremendous excitement. "I've put the past behind me. I don't want to argue with anyone, not you, the police, lawyers, doctors, no one." I grinned then tried to grab her hand again. "My sights are set on the future."

Milan glanced at a passing couple, but immediately focused back on me. "I hear you. But if we're really sisters like you say, I would really like to know if you had anything to do with Brent's murder.'

"Nope," I said matter of factly, and began my next sentence. "I've even got a new boyfriend," I said proudly. "His name is Devin. Wait until you meet him. I swear you're going to love him. He's everything I ever wanted in a man."

"Excuse me, Ladies," the waiter said politely, stopping at our table. "Would you like anything?" he asked Milan.

"A Corona would be nice," she said, her face was still emotionless.

"Okay," he answered with a smile. "And you?" he asked me.

"I'm good for now. Just surviving off of love for the moment," I told him.

As he walked away, Milan took off her coat and draped it over the back of her chair. She leaned forward, placing her elbows on the table. "So, I see you're *finally* happy," she said, a chink in her armor finally revealing itself.

"Oh, Milan," I responded, joyously. "I am. I really am."

Milan gave a warm smile and nodded approvingly. "I'm happy for you."

"Thanks, Milan. And like I said, I can't wait for you to meet Devin. He's just so cute."

"How'd you meet him?"

"Through Aunt Lisa. And I'm so glad she hooked me up with him. I honestly think he may be the one, Milan."

Milan nodded again.

I leaned back into my seat and placed my hands into the pockets of the baggy hooded sweatshirt, the one I'd stolen from Sonia. Although I'd been stopping at the ATM once a day for the past few days, I had to be easy on my spending. Going on a shopping spree for new clothes right now wasn't a good idea. I would have to make good with only the clothes on my back until my name was cleared with Terrell and Brent.

Milan chuckled. "Where'd you get that sweatshirt? It's swallowing you."

The sweatshirt did look ridiculously large on me. Pretty much all the clothes I'd stolen from my pregnant cousin were big on me.

"From my cousin, Sonia," I answered.

"Where's *your* coat?" she asked.

My expression grew somber. "I haven't been able to go back to the apartment lately."

"Why not?"

Visions of police cars and myself tossed into the back of

one handcuffed filled my head. "Because you're not there," I lied, looking her in the eyes, hoping to truly connect with her.

Milan looked away.

My eyes dropped to the table. "I'm going to move out," I said sadly. "Without you there, it's not the same. It's not fun anymore. It's just not fun at all without my sister."

"Your sister, huh?" Milan asked, now looking at me again. "Are we really sisters, Zaria?"

"Of course," I said quickly, as if she should've known better. "I know you and I have said some bad things in the past out of anger. But that happens between sisters."

Milan placed her purse on the table and reached inside. She pulled the stacks of mail, missing checks, and photos of her mom and dad, I'd stolen and hid underneath my bed. "Sisters, huh?" she asked sarcastically, looking directly at me.

I was speechless.

"Is this how sisters do each other, Zaria?" she asked, folding her arms.

My mouth couldn't form a syllable, let alone an entire word. I could only stare at the envelopes.

"I know about you erasing important messages from Brent and the modeling agency," Milan said, with spite covering every word. "Because of you, I missed out on dozens of high paying jobs that could've skyrocketed my career!" Her voice grew angrier as she continued with all her foolish accusations.

My eyes finally looked into hers. Milan reached into her purse again and pulled out my secret black book; my diary of lost loves; my pain in written word. From Roberto to Hardy my love for each of them was expressed in the pages of that diary.

I jumped to snatch my property from her while snarling like a lion ready for attack. "Give me my fuckin book, Milan!"

"You actually believed all these men fell in love with you after mere one night stands?" Milan asked, as if the thought was preposterous.

I saw complete red. She had no business going through the pages of that book. "Give me my book!" I ordered again.

"Fuck you, Zaria," Milan said defiantly.

My breasts began to heave back and forth heavily beneath my sweatshirt. I eyed Milan with hate, wanting to leap across the table and rip her fucking face off.

"I know the *real* reason you haven't been back to the apartment," she said, leaning toward me. Her demeanor had completely changed for the worse. "Oh yes, I know."

Visions of slicing that pretty little face of hers to shreds bombarded my brain.

"I also know you killed Brent, you miserable bitch," she sneered. "Admit it."

My fists clenched.

"Admit it, Bitch!" Milan screamed, standing from the table and quieting the entire restaurant.

I couldn't take it anymore. I soared to my feet and snatched a hold of her blouse so hard my grip ripped two buttons from her shirt. It was going to feel so good to finally tear her ass apart; I salivated until my eyes caught a glimpse of what was underneath her shirt…A fucking wire!

The pounding of my heart was in my ears now, drowning out all sounds around me. The restaurant began to spin as I quickly started to look around, expecting the police to come rushing in. My eyes surveyed every patron, all suddenly looking suspicious. Were any of them detectives? I couldn't tell. Paranoia now had *everyone* looking like muthafucking undercovers. All eyes were now on me for snatching Milan's boney-ass up like a rag doll. Without a second thought, I let go of her blouse and ran like hell. I had to get out of there.

"That's your ass, Zaria!" Milan screamed. "Running is only a waste of time. They're everywhere!"

"Move!" I shouted, shoving people out of the way to the floor and dashing through the kitchen's swinging double doors. I knew that if I had attempted going out the front door, the police would undoubtedly be waiting. The restaurant's employees stared at me as if I'd lost my mind as I quickly ran over them, searching for the back door. The small kitchen seemed like a maze. When I finally found the door, I busted through it out into the gloomy alley. Snow had begun to fall heavily.

I looked at both ends of the alley. Which way? Which way! Without deciding, I just ran, sirens now filling my ears. They were not too far of a distance, but growing closer with each passing second. As I neared the upcoming street a tinted Crown Vic screeched to a stop, its siren nearly deafening me, and its spinning light forcing my eyes to squint. I stopped immediately, my heart coming through my chest.

"Freeze!" a tall female detective shouted, jumping out of the passenger side of the car with her gun drawn and pointed as more squad cars loudly screeched to a stop behind her, turning the entire end of the alley into a pool of red and blue lights.

I turned and immediately headed for the opposite end of the alley as fast as I could. Before I could reach it, several squad cars screeched to a stop and blocked it off completely. Officers immediately jumped out of each and took aim at me, forcing me to stop dead in my tracks. I was trapped!

Fear urged me to reach for the gun underneath my sweatshirt but I knew that the police would kill me before I could pull it out. It would be useless. Damn it! Something stronger than fear flowed through me. My head jerked from end to end of the alley. I didn't want to go to jail and I didn't want to die. In fact, I *refused* to do either. There had to be a way out.

"Zaria!" the female detective shouted from her end of the alley. "You're trapped! Just give up!"

Ignoring her, my eyes surveyed the entire alley. There had to be a way out. There *had* to be! Suddenly the back door to the restaurant behind me opened. Luckily, an employee stepped outside with a garbage bag in his hand. I rushed past him, fast like lighting, and darted inside his place of business. Just maybe I would make it out alive.

22···Hardy

Keisha was doing a terrible job at keeping my mind off Terrell as I sped down Atlantic Avenue in Brooklyn, weaving in and out of traffic. My cell was pressed against my ear, yet I barely listened. I was headed to Dana's, my old place of residence. It saddened me to think about even going there, knowing she wouldn't let me stay. But I had to. Dana would have the information before I did. Detective Santiago had called me over an hour ago, and left a message saying it was urgent. She said she was headed to Dana's. But when I called back, I kept getting sent to voice mail. I was hoping like hell they'd gotten my son back, and now had Zaria caged like the animal she was. I hoped they had her in a cell by now with big, gruesome women who'd rape her 'til she was raw.

All of a sudden, Keisha stopped rambling. I heard her say, she didn't think we should see each other anymore. "So, how you gonna say that at a time like this," I asked with tears in my eyes. I wasn't teary-eyed because of her words. My heart was broken because this cat and mouse shit with Zaria had gone on too long.

"It's cool, Keisha," I replied casually, while running the light, and turning onto Grey street. "I'm giving up my playa

201

card anyway."

"Ummm huh," she mumbled.

"No really. There comes a time in a man's life when he has to grow up." I paused to listen to her smirks and mumbles under her breath. "I mean… I know you think I'm saying all this because my son is missing, but it's more to it than that."

"Gerald, I got another call," she told me abruptly, not wanting to hear my shit anymore.

I gladly hung up as I turned onto my street, realizing my truck was nearly on two wheels. The tires screeched as I pulled up, noticing Santiago's Crown Vic parked out front. I hopped out, pulled my warm, Hugo Boss hoodie over my head and ran to my front door. Within seconds, I had my keys out, trying each of the seven, wondering why none of them no longer worked.

"This is bullshit, Dana!" I shouted, while banging on the door. "Open it, man. It's me, your husband. You fuckin' changed the locks? Damn, girl!"

Nothing.

Silence.

It was that get back type of silence.

I banged again. This time harder, wondering what the hell her and the detective were doing. I kicked at the door a few times feeling my adrenaline pumping. Then it finally opened. Santiago stepped back slowly as she opened the door widely with a set of gloomy eyes that she hadn't shown before.

My first thought, they were up to something. But then over Santiago's shoulder, I spotted Dana, *my wife*, being consoled by Mario, *my boy*. Her eyes were a deep red, proving she'd been crying. But why was he in my home, consoling her without me knowing? Uncertainty filled my body as I recapped how many days I'd been calling Mario, but had gotten no return calls. I thought about the few times we talked prior to that and how he kept defending Dana. Then I thought about the way he was holding her, as they stood together near the staircase that

I'd polished just a month ago. Before I could even conjure up another fact to prove that something was fishy, he cupped her by the chin, kissed her lightly on the lips, and told her he'd be there for her through everything.

I blacked out, and charged them both, but only to be stopped by Santiago, with one hand pushed against my chest, and the other hovering over her holster.

"So, this is who the fuck you been cheating on me with?" I screeched, summonsing them both with my wildly moving hands. "Yo, that's foul."

"Now is not the time, Gerald," Dana said to me between sniffles and tears.

Before I could even respond, detective Santiago told me that I needed to sit down. "I'm afraid that I have bad news," she told me in a somber tone.

My heart rate rose, and suddenly Dana and Mario were no longer important. My head began to spin, preparing myself for what was next. I looked into the detective's eyes knowing what she was about to say. Almost like a drunk, I stumbled to make it to my couch as Santiago gave the news. Her lips moved for what seemed like hours, but I could only hear one sentence. *A boy's body was found after someone reported seeing Zaria in her cousin's stolen car*. I felt sick to my stomach as my mind traveled back to the day Terrell was first born. First, I got choked up, still trying to be a man. Then, my eyes reddened and I let it all out.

"Oh, my God, this can't be, Lord!" I clutched the sides of my head. Hard. Hoping to crush my own skull so I could land in Heaven with Terrell. *They say Jesus looks out for babies and fools. I was definitely a fool.*

I stood up, pacing the space in front of the couch, crying and weeping in pain like someone had just taken a saw and severed my legs with no anesthesia. "Ohhhhh…noooooooooo…it can't be!" I continued. "Somebody tell me noooo. It isn't sooooo!"

I thought about my Lil Man and how he had big dreams. I thought about his smile as bile rose up in my stomach. Suddenly another thought registered; it was all my fault. I'd brought this wrath into my home. I brought trouble to my family by not being able to control my dick. Out of the blue, I threw up all over the carpet. The carpet that Dana loved so much. All my undigested shrimp parmesan had the house smelling like a landfill. I barely wiped my mouth good before I turned in Dana and Mario's direction.

"Dana, c'mon, baby," I cried. I had my hands high in the air as a sign of surrender. "We gotta get through this together honey," I continued, sobbing in between my words. I kept sauntering toward her like a mummy in the *Thriller* video. I was broke down, could barely walk, and simply wanted me and my wife to comfort each other. No sooner than I was just two feet away from them, Dana dove her head into Mario's chest like he was her savior.

"You love this nigga, Dana," I barked, ready to hear her say no. *She couldn't have loved him*, I reasoned for seconds.

Mario's eyes showed guilt as he looked in my direction. I wanted to ask him, how could he? I wanted to know if he'd actually fucked my wife? I had all sorts of questions for this nigga, but needed to get Dana back first.

"Dana, pleaseeeeeee forgive me, baby," I pleaded with my mouth and facial expression filled with sorrow. "I love you honey. Do you hear me? And I need you. We lost our son. Our son. Our son," I kept repeating, and crying all at the same time.

Santiago moved in our direction but was on her cell talking official business. It had something to do with Terrell's case, but at this point, I didn't care. My Lil man was gone and I was all fucked up.

"C'mon, Dana," I attempted in yet another plea.

"Hell no!" she finally spat, taking two bold steps for the first time away from Mario. "You've been cheating on me since the day we got married! And I kept giving you chances. Forgiving you! Praying I wouldn't catch a disease, my worst night-mare." She kept going on and on shouting with high pitch screams. "But this is way more than I expected, Gerald Hardy. You killed our sonnnnnnnnnnnn!" she hissed like a snake, and fell into Santiago's arms, full of more tears.

Mario turned to me slowly ready to give me a lecture. "I hope you're satisfied."

"Me, too," Dana added.

Oh, so now they were tag teaming me as a couple? Anger filled my bones faster than the space shuttle's take off. I kept breathing hard, chest heaving up and down, almost hyper-ventilating like some mental patient ready for lock down. Santiago watched me closely thinking she could control me, while still holding onto Dana. Before she could even blink, I'd hauled off and punched Mario forcefully in the jaw. He staggered back-wards. I rushed him like a linebacker. It took only seconds for me to pin Mario to the wall. I could hear Dana screaming from behind us, acting as if she were going into cardiac arrest while Santiago played into that shit. I knew the game. She wanted to save her man; my best friend.

I saw Mario's face tighten, but he was no match for me. I had way more strength. And way more fury to go such a longer way. I punched Mario again, throwing a hard haymaker to his other jaw. This time, he threw one back. Fortunately, his swing was dodged. My arms draped his entire upper body as I swaddled him to the floor, punching and kicking him along the way. Like two men in a wrestling match, we fought harshly, mostly with me on top of him. I finally had had enough so I hopped up, and without warning, snatched Santiago's gun from her holster.

"You don't want to do this, Gerald," Santiago reasoned in her calmest tone.

"Yes, the fuck I do!"

"No, you don't."

Santiago stared at me like she'd now become a police

negotiator. I could tell she was thinking hard. Then suddenly her cell began to ring. Even still, nobody in the room took their eyes off me, or the glock shaking between my trembling hands. Me, on the other hand, I couldn't help but staring at Mario, wondering, why him?

Fumbling around on the floor, Mario tried to get up, holding his hands in front of him; fearing for his life. "Mannnn, it don't have to come to this."

"You fucked my woman?" I taunted, wanting to hear him say it.

"Stop it!" Dana shouted. "Put the gun down."

"Didn't you?" I badgered Mario.

"You don't want to do this," the detective reasoned again.

"Tell me, nigga. Go ahead and tell me. I can handle it!" I kicked Mario in his side with the tips of my Timberlands like a stranger in the street, using all the force I had. All our years of hanging and trusting one another was over. And Mario would get from me what he deserved.

Just as I was about to pull the trigger a knock at the door startled us all. In a dash, Santiago had stepped in between me and Mario, making sure I couldn't blast him down on the floor, without hitting her first. Her eyes softened me as they connected with my soul, the way her words did with Dana on her first visit to the house.

"Put it down, Gerald," she ordered softly. "That's another detective with good news at the door.

I handed off the gun and jetted to the door, with new hope in my heart. I opened, asking, "He's alive?"

Santiago was already one step behind me with her hand now on my back telling me that the detective had gotten a search warrant for Zaria's apartment, and now they were waiting for another to her aunt's. "We're going to find the person who did this. Trust me."

I turned in defeat, realizing my nightmare was indeed a

reality. "Detective, call me when you get something concrete on Zaria. I can't sit here and wait for you to get the call about an approved search warrant."

"I will. It shouldn't be long," she told me.

"And Dana. You call me when you ready to work on our marriage. I still love you. Remember that."

Mario had somehow managed to get back on his feet, while Dana broke her neck to get to him. I was almost out the front door when Mario made a comment that stung.

"Hardy, put Dana on your *no fly list*."

23 ··· Zaria

"You killed my son! And destroyed my life," Hardy said, his voice cracking terribly as it blared through my cell phone. His words were filled with pain and sadness as I listened to it hover over the music in his car. He sounded far different from the cocky, arrogant, confident playboy who'd told me that I was nothing more than a mercy fuck and a third rate hoe. Now he was nothing more than a broken man, his own life now consumed boarder to boarder by thick darkness.

"Welcome to my world, Hardy. Welcome to my world."

"You destroyed my entire universe," he said, putting emphasis on his last word.

"No, Hardy," I corrected him as I pulled Kenneth's car to the curb and turned it off. I paused briefly to see if I saw Devin's BMW anywhere in sight. I was late and hoped he was too. "*You* destroyed your own universe," I told Hardy. "*You* destroyed everything. It was you who cheated on your wife. It was you who only thought about yourself. And it was you who brought the police to that motel when you promised you wouldn't. *You. And* no one else."

"I swear to God I'm going to kill you, Zaria," he promised, his voice rising with each word. "I swear, you black bitch!

I'm going to kill you!"

"Well, do it soon, playboy, 'cause I'm getting married soon. Besides, I'm not done with you yet. I've called at least three of your women who never knew you were married. I posted pictures of my pussy all across the walls of your class-room last night, and I just left your jungle monkey's house, named Yvonne. Hopes she's still breathing," I added real slick-like.

"What the fuck! You crazy ass bitch!"

"No, I'm not crazy, Hardy. I told you I knew how to play the game. The problem is you don't anymore. See, you been playing checkers. Now let's play chess muthufucka!" I said nonchalantly and flipped my cell phone shut. I had no time for bullshit or useless threats right now. I was already running late to meet my man. The situation in Times Square held me up un-expectedly.

I hopped out of the car checking to see if I could park behind the posted sign without getting a ticket. I started think-ing about Milan, that fucking bitch. There I was trying to bury the hatchet with that hoe, and she tried to set my ass up. I'd al-ways known light skinned bitches couldn't be trusted. So I have no idea what made me try to believe any different today. Well, you live and you learn, I guess.

The goofy bitch actually thought they had me though. They *all* did. That all changed when I saw that Mexican come out the back door of that restaurant. He gave me my escape. As soon as he came out, I charged inside his small carry-out like a damn maniac, rushing through the kitchen, and burst through the front door that led to the crowded main street.

After checking into a motel in Harlem and making a quick call to Devin, I took a shower and got myself cleaned up. Plans had already been made for this evening and I wasn't going to let what had just happened spoil them. I was dead seri-ous about making a new start. Absolutely *dead* serious.

Now here I was walking toward Moe's Cavern, looking

fabulous. No, fuck fabulous. Absolutely breath taking was more like it. I was dressed in a body hugging, black skirt, black hose, and black, knee high pleather boots. To top it all off, I was rocking a black fedora pulled slightly down over my face, hoping no one would notice me. I'd bought the outfit in a Fashion Bug located in a strip mall on my way to meet Milan earlier. Now, I realize that the hat came in handy.

Sexily, I strutted across the street like a Luke dancer, my ass swinging side to side like I was being paid to do so. Lil Wayne's 'Lolli Pop' greeted my ears as I stepped up the two steps and opened the door to the lounge.

"Damn, Sweetheart," a thug looking nigga said admiringly, while leaning against the hood of a white 745 BMW on chrome. "You're thick as hell. You on your way inside to see your man or something?"

"As a matter of fact, I am," I said, never slowing my stride. My man had been forced to wait long enough for my presence tonight. The lounge wasn't packed yet, but I knew it would be as the night progressed. Devin had already warned me that it wasn't a typical lounge. He said there'd be drinking at the bar, and dancing in tight spots. So far, I like the dimly lit lights, and smooth atmosphere. My cell phone rang as Lil Wayne's voice started sending chills down my spine. I loved that song. I placed my cell on vibrate as male eyes turned to me from everywhere, admiring my beauty and wishing they could take me home for the night. Their attention only urged me to stunt harder and tease their asses with no fucking mercy whatsoever. I was Devin's and only Devin's.

Devin was sitting at the bar with his back to me when I approached. Damn, his hair was now in dreads that were gathered into a pony tail and hanging down his back. My pussy grew wet at the sight of them. I've always loved dreads. They'd always been sexy to me.

"You here with somebody?" I asked over his shoulder, leaning into his ear.

"Zaria," he said in his deep, baritone voice, turning to me with a smile. He stood and hugged me.

The feel of his body against mine sent tremors throughout my entire body.

"Damn, Lil Momma," he said, letting me go and taking a step back to check me out. "You look amazing."

"Thanks," I said with a smile of my own and admiring *his* body. He was dressed in a tight fitting long-sleeved shirt that showed off his chest and muscles beautifully. His Rock and Republic jeans sagged slightly, just the way I like them. I'd never liked a man who wore his pants damn near to his chest. They were draped perfectly over his white Air Force Ones. In his ears were two diamond earrings that sparkled brightly even in the dimly lit club.

He politely took my coat and pulled out a stool.

"Thank you," I said, sitting down.

"What do you want to drink?" he asked, sitting next to me. "You can have anything you want."

A man who's not scared to spend money. That's always a plus, I thought to myself.

"A Corona would be nice," I said.

He signaled for the bartender and ordered my drink. I placed my cell phone on the bar and glanced around the club. I noticed some yellow bitch eyeing Devin from a distance. She quickly looked somewhere else after noticing that I'd caught her. The temptation to go check her ass crossed my mind but I ignored it.

"So which one of these ladies in here tried to talk to you while you were waiting for me?" I asked, turning to Devin. My facial expression was on swole.

"None of them," he assured me. "And even if they had, I would've told them that I was waiting on you."

Great answer! Excellent answer!

I smiled. "Sorry I was so late getting here," I told him. "It won't happen again."

"Don't worry about it. What happened?"

"There was some kind of accident or something in Times Square. It had traffic all the way backed up."

"Yeah, that's why I avoid going that way if I don't have to. Well just as long as you're here, that's all that matters."

My phone vibrated. I quickly flipped it open and pressed the ignore button, not even glancing at the number as the bartender sat my drink in front of me.

"Sure you don't want to answer that?" Devin asked with a smile. "It might be your man."

"I'm with my man," I corrected him.

He nodded approvingly and took a sip of his drink.

"So, when are you going to let me see your apartment?" I asked.

"When do you want to see it?"

"Tonight would be nice."

"Are you sure about that? Because I might not let you go home."

"Maybe I don't want to go home," I said, eyeing him sexily. "Maybe I want to stay with you forever."

Devin chuckled, thinking what I'd said was merely cute, but not serious.

"I'm serious, Devin," I assured him. "I moved out of my aunt's house a few days ago. I've been staying at a motel since. I could use a place to stay."

Devin looked a little uneasy.

"Look, sweetheart," I said quickly. "I know it's sudden but think about the fun we could have." I placed my hand on his thigh, only a few inches away from what I bet was a huge package in his jeans. "Think about the sex we could have."

Devin looked me in the eyes. "Zaria," he said. "I'm really feeling you but…"

"I'm feeling you too, Devin. So, what do you say?" I grinned wide and held it for like ten seconds.

"I know but moving in together is a big step."

"I know. I'm ready for it."

"But I'm not, Zaria."

I took a deep breath, pulled my hat down just above my eyelids to sulk. My heart was broken though I tried not to show it.

"Zaria," Devin said softly, seeing the change in my demeanor. He placed his hand over mine. "There's going to be plenty of time for all of that, okay?"

I nodded halfheartedly.

Unconvinced, he placed a hand softly underneath my chin and looked me directly in my eyes. "Okay, baby?" he asked.

I couldn't help giving him a smile. "Okay," I answered.

"That's my baby."

For the next few hours we laughed and talked over drink after drink. His conversation intoxicated me more than the Coronas. Every word swept me off of my feet and every touch of his hand made me feel like the Princess of Whales. But the most exciting moment of the night for me was when he asked me if I would come with him to his mother's house on Wednesday to meet her. I couldn't believe it. It was Monday so I would count the days. The word 'yes' tumbled out of my mouth *super* quickly. By the end of the night giving his fine ass some of my pussy a no brainer. I was going to fuck his damn lights out and then some.

It was almost two in the morning when Devin put my coat on me. The two of us decided we'd go to his apartment for the night. I was so looking forward to it when for what had to be the hundredth time my phone vibrated. I'd gotten tired of watching it vibrate across the top of the bar a long time ago, so I placed it in my coat pocket. Now I took it out, flipped it open, and looked at the screen. Recognizing my father's number, I answered reluctantly. My ears were greeted with what sounded like wheezing.

"Hello."

No answer. Just my father coughing, attempting to catch his breath.

"Hello," I said again.

"Z-a-r-r-r-r-i-a," my father managed to say, still wheezing and sounding out of breath. "I-I-I-I-I-I…"

"What do you want?"

Devin looked at me curiously.

"It's okay," I mouthed to him silently.

"Z-a-r-r-r-r-i-a," my father said again, this time sounding worse than before.

"What?"

"Princess…I…I…I…think I o-o-o-o-o-o-v-e-r-d-o-o-o-o-s-e-d," he managed to say. "I'm d-y-y-y-y-i-n-g."

Suddenly with those words, as if fucking Devin's brains out wasn't enough to brighten my universe, what my father had just said brightened it times ten. A smile crossed my face as I hung up on him in midsentence.

"Is everything okay?" Devin asked.

"Couldn't be better," I told him. "But I'm going to have to take a rain check tonight. I'll spend tomorrow night with you."

"What's wrong?" he asked, disappointed.

I stepped to his face and kissed him deeply, my tongue nearly brushing against his tonsils and tasting everything he'd drank tonight. When I let him go, my eyes admired his beauty. Turning his dick down tonight made me shake my head. *Damn*, I thought. "I've got to go," I said, still shaking my head at the thought of missing out..

"Where are you going?"

"To watch my father die,' I told him. "I wouldn't miss that for the world.'

Devin was speechless. He could only stare at me, wondering if I was actually serious.

"I'll call you later," I said and headed for the door. Light snow had started falling from the night sky again as I stepped outside and headed for my ride. My eyes happened to catch a glimpse of something that stopped me in midstride…my face.

In a newspaper dispenser in front of Moe's my face graced the front page of the newspaper with the word WANTED written boldly over it. I stepped closer and read the article underneath. It described Brent's brutal murder and named myself as the prime suspect, offering a reward for any information leading to my capture.

I looked around quickly at everyone exiting the place, hoping no one else had seen the newspaper's cover. Not sure if they had, I pulled seventy five cents from my coat pocket, placed it in the dispenser, and grabbed all the papers inside. Tucking them underneath my arm I dashed across the street to my car, headed to my father's.

24 ··· *Hardy*

I couldn't believe it was two a.m. and I was in my car headed to meet detective Santiago. She'd called me in a panic, saying that she'd gotten three search warrants signed by the judge and was headed to the south side of the Bronx. I had no idea what was there, but threw on some sweats and a bomber jacket, and now rode the Triborough Bridge with my music blasting.

Oddly, the song, *I Hope She Cheat On You Wit' a Basketball Player*, blared from the radio. It made me ill. It seemed that every song that played had something to do with cheating, and infidelity. And all of it made me think about losing my wife to Mario. Quickly, I hit the button for Hot 97. I shook my head hearing Jasmine Sullivan's, *"Bust Your Windows."*

Of course I thought of Zaria. At that moment, I decided to go old school, and switch to the XM station, The Groove. They could always be trusted. Those sounds were for a more mature audience, a brotha like me. When the lyrics to, *"Me and Ms. Jones"* began, I hit the power off button, and rode the next ten minutes in silence.

Everything seemed to bother me; the amount of time it took the street lights to change, the way people drove slowly

217

through the night, and even the way the yellow cabs rode too closely up on my ride. My mind kept fuckin' with me. It kept tossing back and forth ideas on the way I'd live my life from here on out. Although I'd learned a huge lesson, nothing mattered anymore. My wife was out of my life, and I had no one to carry on the Hardy name. One part of me said, make a change for the better, teach other men the true meaning of monogamy, and advocate for good, long-lasting marriages. The other half of me said fuck that shit! I had already lost everything, so the sky was the limit. I would eat, drink, and submerge myself in pussy.

Pussy for breakfast.

Pussy for dinner.

Pussy on a platter.

Pussy, pussy, pussy.

While trying to make sense of my life, I hadn't realized that my navigation system was repeating, 'I was now at my destination'. Quickly, I began scanning the neighborhood wondering if I had input the address correctly. Suddenly, two knocks bang against my window. A little alarmed, I rolled it down telling Santiago, "This better be good."

"It will," she replied as I stepped from the Tahoe into the cold.

The frigid, night air swept across the bare skin of my head so fast, I whipped out my skull cap then leaned against the truck with a slight attitude. "I'm just wondering why we're here?" I asked looking up at the ten story office building.

"It's where Zaria came for a psychiatric appointment a week ago."

"And? Why would you want to search her doctor's office because of that? You think she knows where Zaria is?"

"Probably not. But any clue is a good clue; especially if she has any other addresses on file for Zaria that we don't know about." Santiago had a hard expression as if she really meant business. "Just so you know, Mr. Hardy, our team has been working around the clock trying to track every move she's made within the last month, down to the place where she's bought her last meal. We'll get justice for you."

"Umph." I had become pretty numb over the last 24 hours when it came to Zaria. If it wasn't seeing her fry in the electric chair, I wasn't really interested anymore. I made a funny face asking the question, is any of this really helpful, as I watched two other police cruisers pull up to the curb.

"Damn, we need back up for a psychiatrist?"

"You never know when it comes to Ms. Hopkins," Santiago told me as we all moved inside, and caught the elevator up to the third floor.

I felt like a part of a S.W.A.T team as we exited onto the floor, walking in pairs, me and Santiago bringing up the rear. There were about twelve office doors that lined the hallway, each having a letter, and bronze plate identifying the business. Finally, the officer leading the pack stopped in front of the plate that read- Dr. Seethers. The thought of Zaria going to a doctor had me mystified. If her crazy ass had been seeing a doctor, she needed a refund 'cause it wasn't working.

Before I knew it, the heaviest officer in our six people crew kicked the door in, until it tumbled down, flying across the room like paper. Gangsta, I thought, looking at the size of his monstrous neck. No calling a locksmith, or figuring out another way. That's NYPD, I said under my breath.

Santiago must've been a mind reader because our eyes locked. I couldn't believe it. The entire office, empty. The feeling in my gut told me something suspicious was going on. I just wasn't sure what. With the exception of a few papers spread across the floor, and wires here and there, it was clear someone had moved out in a hurry. Like clockwork, Santiago rushed back downstairs with me quickly following, ready for the next spot.

"So what do you think all of this means?" I asked, walking fast, attempting to keep up with her.

"Not sure. But something's not right. What psychiatrist

just closes abruptly and cleans out their office? Maybe we'll find out something from her aunt," Santiago commented when we reached the street level. "You ride with me," she ordered, then turned to the other detective and officers.

"You guys lead."

I really wasn't down for doing police work at 3 o'clock in the morning, but maybe I'd find Zaria and get to retaliate for my son, so I obliged, and hopped in the Crown Vic. As soon as we took off, speeding through the city streets, Santiago started her many phone calls. It was one call after another, all police talk, and updates on what the other detectives had found out. I just leaned back in the seats thinking about the plans for Terrell's funeral. The autopsy had already come back proving that the body found in the upper area of the Hudson River was indeed Terrell's. Since I couldn't get Dana to answer my calls, I'd asked my family to start helping me with the arrangements. If she wanted to play dirty, I could get dirty. And Mario's ass damn sho' wouldn't be allowed at the service.

As I thought about the details, Santiago talked more and more on the phone like the pieces of the puzzle were being put together. I heard her speak to two different detectives, and now a lawyer. Why weren't these people sleep? Suddenly, she hung up and told me things were definitely fishy with Zaria, her aunt, and Dr. Seethers. I was shocked when she revealed that Zaria's trust attorney said that Zaria's aunt was awarded power of attorney over all her money and affairs because of reports filed on behalf of her psychiatric doctor, Dr. Seethers.

"Trust fund?" I asked slowly with crinkled eyebrows. "And now the doctor's gone?"

"Yep. 250 k probably gone, too."

"Damn. So I was messing with a real lunatic, who got money, huh?"

"Yep, and the reports also say, she's having your baby, just so you know."

"Nah, that's just her talking. Don't believe anything

Zaria says or tells anyone," I warned.

Santiago just kept shaking her head. I could tell she really wanted to crack the case, filling in all the missing pieces of why she did it, and who else was involved. I just wanted Zaria locked down. And now I wanted some of Santiago's pussy.

The entire time this ordeal had been going on, I'd never been attracted to her. But there was something about the way she put pieces of information together that turned me on. I liked smart, witty women; women who knew how to figure shit out. Plus, after three a.m everything began to look better and better to me. Just when my dick started jumping around in my pants we pulled up on a short block, and a house that I assumed belonged to Zaria's aunt Lisa.

Santiago hopped out while I stayed in the car trying to get my meat to calm down. I told her to go ahead and I'd be shortly behind. It shocked me to see one of the officers knock on the door after what they'd done to the doctor's office earlier. They waited seconds, then a minute after banging furiously on the door. After no response, they got gangsta again, and were inside roaming the place by the time I made it to the unstable front door.

The house was small, nothing spectacular. Nothing that screamed money. I eased inside slowly watching Santiago and the other officers rummage through mail, and papers spread across the living room table. Nothing really stood out for me other than the messiness of the place. Somebody needed to come back home to clean-up. Suddenly, we heard an officer yelling from a back bedroom. We all rushed back hoping nobody was found dead. By the time I made it to the back, I caught the tail end of the conversation. The officer had reported that the closets had been cleaned out, and clothes sprawled about. Then he produced a note to Santiago, followed by a not so good expression.

Defeated, she told me the note was to Lisa's son, telling him that she was leaving town and would be in touch with him soon. It was that jab coming my way again; the same jab that had been fucking me up every since I first said hello to Zaria. I'd had enough and just wanted to go back to my place to hear the rest of Santiago's report, with her lips wrapped around my dick. The facts were clear. The doctor was gone, Zaria's aunt was gone. And we weren't able to find Zaria, which told me she was gone too. I placed my hand on Santiago's back as the officers told her they needed to call it a night.

"It's cool," she responded. "Something will pop up."

They left, but we didn't while Santiago searched every inch of the house, hoping to find a connection to Zaria's whereabouts. Soon, an hour rolled around too quickly, and before we knew it, we'd found ourselves at a breakfast spot on Fordham road, next to the lawyer's office that Santiago wanted to question next.

Despite the fact that I wanted Zaria caught too, I was tired. With my eyes blood shot red, staying awake had become a problem. I wasn't even sure why Santiago wanted me so involved. I mean…I wasn't a cop. Then it hit me. She liked my swag.

With a devilish look, I quickly slipped my hand on her thigh beneath the table, caressing it like her body needed it…wanted it…just like the air we breathe. I was ready to get shit popping until she grabbed a hold of my hand and squeezed it so tightly I thought all circulation had been lost.

"Don't try it, Mr. Hardy," she warned. "That's not why we're here. Control yourself."

I stared at her giving her a blank look.

"Isn't that what got you and your family in this situation in the first place?"

I hit her with the silent treatment and pulled out my cell. Just about the same time, hers rang too. It seemed the lawyer had called her back and agreed to giving her the information she needed over the phone. At that moment, I contemplated trying to get in touch with Kyle again. It was clear he'd been ducking my calls. Instead, I sat and listened to Santiago speak a mile a minute. While she talked to the lawyer, I noticed an old piece of pussy strut through the door. She reminded me of a stripper although I knew she wasn't; weave down to her ass, and draped in a long faux fur.

"Hey, Jaquan," I called to her, stepping in her direction.

"What's up, Hardy," she returned.

"Long time, no see. What's good?"

"You honey. You look good as always," she flirted, signaling for her girls to follow her to the table near the window.

I got happy, rubbing my hands together like I was in for a treat. I didn't have my ride, but was ready to dip on Santiago. Jaquan would be my new ride. "So look. It's so good to see you. I've been missing you," I told her with a smile. "Damn, you look good," I added like I couldn't help but notice her beauty.

She laughed. "I see you still got game, boy."

"Game. Man, come on. Let's get outta here and go someplace to talk."

"Talk huh?"

"Yeah. I been calling you for months. You never returned the call."

Jaquan fell out laughing, rearing back in her seat. "Not tonight, Hardy," she said in a more serious tone. "You know you haven't called me in months, and now you think you gonna get some ass. Not," she added, followed by throwing the palm of her hand in my face.

"I mean…does time really matter?" I commented with an expression that was meant to make her look stupid. "Shit, as many orgasms as I blessed you with, I should be grandfathered in with that pussy."

"Fuck you, Hardy," she blasted, bringing attention to us both.

Within seconds, just like a hound dog, Santiago was all over us, sniffing like Deputy Dog himself. With a quick movement of the finger she told me we needed to talk.

I walked back over to where Santiago stood as she told me we might as well call it a night. "I finally got the info I needed," she told me in sadness. "Zaria's aunt and head doctor were in cahoots together to take Zaria's trust fund money. They succeeded by showing the trust attorney false reports saying Zaria was mentally incapable of handling her own affairs. Because the aunt was her power of attorney she was able to do that legally."

I couldn't understand why Santiago was so upset, and so worried about trust funds. I didn't care about Zaria's money, or her aunt for that matter. I wanted her found to face the music for what she'd done to Terrell. "So tell me, why do we care?" My shoulders shrugged with a touch of sarcasm.

"Because I'm trying to crack a murder case, and I need to prove that Zaria is the murderer."

"Sounds like even if we catch her she could get off on insanity, right?"

Santiago's cell rang again. I huffed loudly. I wanted to get to my car. Within seconds she perked up again. "The trail just got warm again, Mr. Hardy. Let's head to Zaria's father's house. Somebody just spotted the stolen car she's been driving."

25 ··· *Zaria*

I huffed when I saw the door to my father's apartment cracked open slightly. Hoping I hadn't missed all the action and gory details, I quickly pushed it open completely and walked inside. If he wasn't dead yet, I was sure as hell going to assist his ass, making his final moments as miserable as possible. Then I was going to get on back to Devin. My love. My man. That dick was calling me.

He'd called me moments before saying he couldn't go to sleep without me tonight and was coming to get me. I'd rattled off my father's address, but told him not to come inside. I would handle my business then come right out.

"Dad!" I called.

No answer.

The apartment was dark and the television was on, but turned down low. I could see a pot cooking on the stove, telling me he'd probably been making his favorite meal. My first thought was to turn the stove off so the house wouldn't burn down, then I said fuck it. Hopefully, he'd die, then the apartment would burn down, and there'd be no funeral. I took a few steps forward and heard the door slam shut behind me. When I turned around my father was standing there with fire in his eyes. Before I could react or even say a word he punched me in the face so hard my purse flew off my shoulder, and my body swung hard, into the kitchen sink. I dropped to the floor; my jaw feeling like it was nearly broken.

My father quickly knelt beside me and stuck a long, needle in my arm. The punch had dazed the hell out of me but whatever he'd just shot me up with had dazed me even more. The feeling of numbness slowly began to take over my nervous system, affecting various parts of my body in different ways. He lifted me by my armpits and began to drag me towards the bedroom. My head was in complete dizziness. I could barely lift my chin from my chest. My brain told my fists and feet to fight back, defend yourself! They weren't reacting. I felt totally weak from my head to my toes. What had he done to me?

When we reached the bedroom, my father placed me in the same chair I'd had him strapped into several days earlier and began to duct tape my wrists to the chair's arms. Then he spent extra time taping my ankles to the legs of the chair, working laboriously, making sure I was secure. When he finished, he went to the kitchen, grabbed my purse, and came back to the bedroom, turning on the light. His hand rummaged through my purse and took out my cell phone and the gun. Tossing my purse to the floor and my phone to the bed he looked at me with the gun at his side.

"Zaria," he said. "This is all for the best."

I couldn't speak. My eyes were heavy. My head was cloudy.

"This gun is cursed, Princess," he said pausing between each word, and now looking at the gun with contempt. "It's the same gun that took your mother away from us."

Still, my mouth could only remain silent, my jaw still throbbing.

"This is the gun that destroyed our family."

I could feel saliva seeping from the corners of my mouth while I listened to him continue with pain in his voice.

My father stepped towards me. "Zaria," he said.

I couldn't answer. Then my cell rang. I couldn't see who was calling from where I sat, could only hear it.

He knelt down in front of me. "Zaria," he said again.

My head felt like it was being held down by a ton of bricks but I forced myself to raise it. My eyelids felt just as heavy, but I forced them open, at least halfway and looked my father into his face.

"Baby," he said. "This is the gun your aunt used to kill your mother."

I hadn't heard him right. I know I hadn't. Whatever he shot me up with must have clouded my hearing. "What…what are you talking about?" I mumbled. I was sure it was difficult for him to understand my slurred speak. I strained heavily to keep my wobbling head from dropping back into my lap.

"It's true, Zaria," he said. "Your Aunt Lisa killed your mother, and she used *this* gun to do it with."

No matter how damned woozy and high this bastard had gotten me, believing that my Aunt Lisa killed my mother was impossible. The accusation was fucking blasphemy. His tongue should have been cut out for speaking those words. I should have killed his ass when I had the chance.

"You're…lying," I managed to say.

"No, I'm not, Princess," he said. "I swear it's the truth."

Hatred and spite boiled inside my gut like acid. His words nauseated me. God, I just wanted him to die. How fucking dare he tell a lie so terrible? Why didn't I kill him when I had the chance? Why?

"Baby, your aunt killed your mother," he said.

I shook my head, wishing with all my heart I could free my wrist from the tape and cover my ears. His words were like poison seeping into my eardrums.

"She killed her over me."

"Mom…Mom killed…herself," I muttered, listening to my phone ring again in the background.

"No, she didn't. We just made it look that way."

We? Hearing his lies was torture.

"It was a homicide," he said.

"No," I told him in a whisper.

"I hate to tell you this, Princess," he said painfully. "But I'd molested your cousin Sonia at a very young age."

Oh God, no! My mind had to be playing tricks on me. What was he saying?

"Your aunt found out and came over to confront me but I wasn't home. She told your mother instead. Your mother refused to believe it. But it was true."

My eyes welled up with tears.

"The two of them were arguing when I got there," he said, shaking his head regretfully at the horrible memory. "They began to tussle as soon as I got through the door, and your mom had the gun in her hand ready to threaten your aunt because of her accusation. It only took seconds for Lisa and her heavy weight to take the gun from your mom. Before I could do anything, the gun went off."

A teardrop ran down my cheek.

"She was going to tell the police what I'd done to Sonia if I told on her. So I had to stay quiet. I had to."

"You're a liar," I spewed. It was crazy how I'd somehow gotten enough energy to lift my head. "Muthafuckin' liar."

"Zaria, your…"

"Aunt Lisa would never do that."

"She's not what you think," he said. "It's all an act. She only took you in for a chance to get the trust fund money."

I shook my head. His lies were giving me a headache.

"It's true," he said. "When she found out what I'd been doing to you, she threatened to tell on me. I told her about the money to shut her up. I told her that I would let you come live with her and we could split the money on your thirtieth birthday if she stayed quiet. That was our deal."

'Deal'…that word brought back the slightly changed

version of the nightmare I'd had on my father's couch. "You got a deal," I remembered my aunt's voice saying.

"Your aunt came up with the plan to hire that fake psychiatrist fresh out of college. She doesn't even have a license to practice yet. The three of us were to work together to aggravate your sickness and to site instances to prove you're mentally unstable and unable to make sane decisions."

"You got a deal," my aunt's words repeated themselves in my head. "You got a deal."

"As long as everything worked out," he continued. "The psychiatrist's faulty evaluation would be enough to make you seem mentally unstable. That would be more than enough for a judge to grant power of attorney over your trust fund to your aunt."

I couldn't believe it. How could she do that to me? After all the horrible things I'd been through how could *she,* of all people to turn around and betray me. Her love had all been only an act, I forced myself to realize.

The conversation at her house the day I'd went back to see Dr. Seethers came back to me. Although I'd been in a revenge filled daze for most of it, I could now remember her mentioning my money and suggesting that I put her in charge of it. How could I have been so stupid? As badly as I hated to admit it, my father was right.

"Baby, I'm sorry," my father whispered softly.

The effects of the needle were beginning to wear off but out of sadness my head still drooped. Finding the strength to hold it up right now just didn't seem worth it anymore. My heart was shattered and my will to fight was gone. I felt totally alone.

"Zaria," my father whispered.

My eyes were now closed. I didn't want to see the world or anyone in it.

"You and I have hurt too many people," he said. "I know you killed that little boy and your roommate's boyfriend. It has to stop."

I couldn't speak. I could only cry.

"We're demons, Zaria. We *have* to kill ourselves," he said.

Milan, Hardy, Jamal, Dana, Terrell, Aunt Lisa, and so many other faces flashed through my mind. Memories both pleasurable and painful filled my head.

My father reached into his pocket, took out a switch-blade, and sliced open the duct tape around my wrists. He placed the gun in my lap and stepped back. "It has to be done, Zaria," he said, "we have to kill off our demons now."

I opened my eyes and looked at the gun in my lap. Taking my own life had now become a temptation. There was nothing to live for. I had no friends and no family; only Devin. The police were looking for me and chances were that if they found me, I'd spend the rest of my life in prison. Being caged in like an animal wasn't an option.

"It has to be done," my father urged me.

My hand slowly wrapped around the gun's handle. The sight of it and the newfound knowledge of its blood stained history now brought back memories of my mother, her beauty, her smile, her love for me. If I did this, would I get to see her in heaven, I wondered. Would she be there waiting for me?

"Do it, Zaria," my father continued urging me on.

Would my mother still love me after all I'd done?

"Do it, baby."

My mind was twisted and filled with uncertainty. Then that voice came back. It hadn't been around since I'd found happiness with Devin.

"Yeah, do it, Zaria," the voice pushed.

"This is the only way, Princess."

'Princess'…That name suddenly stirred something inside me. 'Princess'. I saw Sonia's face in my head. My stomach turned at my father's admission to what he'd done to her. I hated him for it. What he'd done to her bled over to my mother's life. It unfairly shaped her destiny. It took her away from me.

I raised my eyes to my father along with the gun pointed to my head. My mother deserved to see me again. And my father and Aunt Lisa had to pay with their own lives. But, *I* had to be the executioner. Fuck letting my father kill himself by his own hand. What right did he have to say how he died? Neither he nor Aunt Lisa deserved a choice in the matter. They would die by *my* hand, I thought as the gun turned, and was now pointed at his forehead.

"Zaria, don't do this," my father said, taking two tiny steps backwards.

My finger locked around the trigger. I wanted so badly to get up but my feet were still strapped to the chair.

"Baby, no," he pleaded.

Ignoring his pleas, I squeezed the trigger, wanting so badly to send him to hell. My ears were welcoming the gun's roar but surprisingly were greeted only by the click of the trigger. The gun was empty.

Both our eyes locked on each other's across the room.

Then he dashed out of the room, disappearing into thin air. Without hesitation I wiggled around, my adrenaline pumping wildly, trying to free myself. Then my cell rang gain. It had to be Devin, I thought sorrowfully. Next thing I knew, my father was back in the room, holding a smoking hot pot of grits in his hand.

"You're going to kill yourself tonight, or get tortured," he told me, then slung the full pot of grits into my face.

I screamed horrifically as I grabbed my face. The unbearable pain was the worst I'd ever felt in my life. It burned worse than fire, making me have a panic attack. It felt like it would never stop burning. Through my screams my ears heard a familiar sound, the cocking of a gun. Despite my suffering I forced myself to open my eyes to see my father standing over me. He'd reloaded the gun and was staring at me with it in one hand and a needle in the other. Tears began to roll down his cheeks.

"We had a beautiful family," he said softly. "And I destroyed it."

I only stared at him, face burning, hoping he wouldn't destroy what I really did think was growing in my stomach. I hadn't mentioned my dizzy spells to anyone, but between that and the missed period, I was pretty sure I was pregnant.

"I don't want to be this way anymore, Princess," he said. "The cycle has to stop."

He tossed the gun behind him and with a lifetime of regret for everything he'd done in his eyes he jabbed the needle into the side of his neck and dropped to his knees. His eyes rolled completely into his head as he fell to the floor and began to go into violent convulsions, his mouth foaming. His legs kicked hard but began to slow second after second until they stopped completely.

For what seemed like eternity I could only sit in the chair and stare at my father's lifeless body in silence, numb to reality. My body couldn't move. I'd hated him for so long but I'd also loved him. Both emotions were now battling inside me. The silence was broken by the ringing of my cell phone again. I knew it was Devin. It had to be. I wiggled my way over to my dad's body, and leaned over in the chair to pull the switch blade from his pocket, freeing my legs. The phone rang, again, but at the same time there was a loud banging sound on the door. I grabbed the phone from the bed, flipped it open and answered. "Devin, baby," I said, my voice cracking with sadness. I wanted so badly to cry in his arms and hear him tell me everything would be okay.

"Devin," I said again, my eyes closed, needing to hear his voice.

"This isn't Devin, bitch," a female's voice said. "This is Devin's wife. Stay the fuck away from my husband."

Then the front door opened.

I chanted…Smiley Face. Smiley Face. Can anyone see my Smiley Face?

Stay tuned for the sequel
Another…One Night Stand- August 2011

CHECK OUT THESE LCB SEQUELS

 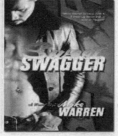

PO Box 423
Brandywine, MD 20613
301-362-6508

FAX TO:
301-579-9913

ORDER FORM

Ship to:	
Address:	
City & State:	Zip:

Date: Phone:

Email:

Make all money orders and cashiers checks payable to: **Life Changing Books**

Qty.	ISBN	Title	Release Date	Price
	0-9741394-2-4	Bruised by Azarel	Jul-05	$ 15.00
	0-9741394-7-5	Bruised 2: The Ultimate Revenge by Azarel	Oct-06	$ 15.00
	0-9741394-3-2	Secrets of a Housewife by J. Tremble	Feb-06	$ 15.00
	0-9741394-6-7	The Millionaire Mistress by Tiphani	Nov-06	$ 15.00
	1-934230-99-5	More Secrets More Lies by J. Tremble	Feb-07	$ 15.00
	1-934230-98-7	Young Assassin by Mike G.	Mar-07	$ 15.00
	1-934230-95-2	A Private Affair by Mike Warren	May-07	$ 15.00
	1-934230-94-4	All That Glitters by Ericka M. Williams	Jul-07	$ 15.00
	1-934230-93-6	Deep by Danette Majette	Jul-07	$ 15.00
	1-934230-96-0	Flexin & Sexin Volume 1	Jun-07	$ 15.00
	1-934230-92-8	Talk of the Town by Tonya Ridley	Jul-07	$ 15.00
	1-934230-89-8	Still a Mistress by Tiphani	Nov-07	$ 15.00
	1-934230-91-X	Daddy's House by Azarel	Nov-07	$ 15.00
	1-934230-88-X	Naughty Little Angel by J. Tremble	Feb-08	$ 15.00
	1-934230847	In Those Jeans by Chantel Jolie	Jun-08	$ 15.00
	1-934230855	Marked by Capone	Jul-08	$ 15.00
	1-934230820	Rich Girls by Kendall Banks	Oct-08	$ 15.00
	1-934230839	Expensive Taste by Tiphani (SOLD OUT)	Nov-08	$ 15.00
	1-934230782	Brooklyn Brothel by C. Stecko	Jan-09	$ 15.00
	1-934230669	Good Girl Gone bad by Danette Majette	Mar-09	$ 15.00
	1-934230804	From Hood to Hollywood by Sasha Raye	Mar-09	$ 15.00
	1-934230707	Sweet Swagger by Mike Warren	Jun-09	$ 15.00
	1-934230677	Carbon Copy by Azarel	Jul-09	$ 15.00
	1-934230723	Millionaire Mistress 3 by Tiphani	Nov-09	$ 15.00
	1-934230715	A Woman Scorned by Ericka Williams	Nov-09	$ 15.00
	1-934230685	My Man Her Son by J. Tremble	Feb-10	$ 15.00
	1-924230731	Love Heist by Jackie D.	Mar-10	$ 15.00
	1-934230812	Flexin & Sexin Volume 2	Apr-10	$ 15.00
	1-934230748	The Dirty Divorce by Miss KP	May-10	$ 15.00
	1-934230758	Chedda Boyz by CJ Hudson	Jul-10	$ 15.00
	1-934230766	Snitch by VegasClarke	Oct-10	$ 15.00
	1-934230693	Money Maker by Tonya Ridley	Oct-10	$ 15.00
	1-934230774	The Dirty Divorce Part 2 by Miss KP	Nov-10	$ 15.00
	1-934230170	The Available Wife by Carla Pennington	Jan-11	$ 15.00
	1-934230774	One Night Stand by Kendall Banks	Feb-11	$ 15.00
	1-934230278	Bitter by Danette Majette	Feb-11	$ 15.00
			Total for Books	$
			Shipping Charges (add $4.95 for 1-4 books*)	$
			Total Enclosed (add lines)	$

* Prison Orders- Please allow up to three (3) weeks for delivery.

Please Note: We are not held responsible for returned prison orders. Make sure the facility will receive books before ordering.

*Shipping and Handling of 5-10 books is $6.95, please contact us if your order is more than 10 books. (301)362-6508